HOPSCOT(

D0841473

"*Hopscotch Life* is an utterly charming contemporary fairy tale for adults. If you've ever faced the homely monster of self-doubt, you'll gladly worry about and cheer for good-natured protagonist Plum Tardy on her quirky quest for self-belief."

— Beate Sigriddaughter, author of *Dancing in Santa Fe and other poems*

"In *Hopscotch Life*, Kris Neri skillfully brings her hapless protagonist, Plum Tardy, to life like a good ol' country song as Plum loses her man, loses her job, and loses her home. With a bevy of fun secondary characters, enough sparkling dialogue to fill a dozen champagne flutes, and just enough charming humor to keep Plum's plight from breaking our hearts entirely, Neri finally walks her heroine through the execution of a plot twist worthy of Danny Ocean...oh, yes, utterly satisfying. *Hopscotch Life* is fun, charming, and rich in emotion."

— Sally J. Smith, *USA Today* Bestselling Author

"When a rotten guy turns your life upside down, maybe it's time to find a new life. Wonderful writing, a captivating protagonist, and one humorous complication after another add up to another winner for Kris Neri."

— Bonnie Hearn Hill, author of *The River Below*

"This is truly an entertaining story filled with humor, heart-felt family drama, crime, a hint of romance, and a thoroughly refreshing and realistic heroine. Highly recommended!"

— Denise A. Agnew, multi-published author and screenplay writer

"Filled with moments of humor, *Hopscotch Life* is a great read for anytime of the year and any place, be it sofa, bed or beach. *Hopscotch Life* by Kris Neri gets both thumbs-up from me."

— Susan Wingate, #1 Amazon bestseller and award-winner of *Storm Season*

HOPSCOTCH LIFE

KRIS NERI

Cherokee McGhee
Abingdon, Virginia

Copyright © 2020 by Kris Neri

ISBN 978-1-937556-12-9

First Edition 2020

Cover Design by Braxton McGhee

Published by:
Cherokee McGhee, L.L.C.
Abingdon, Virginia

Find us on the World Wide Web at:
www.CherokeeMcGhee.com

Printed in the United States of America

Dedication

To Joe, as we move forward on our next great adventure.

HOPSCOTCH LIFE

If you're lost, how do you find your way to where you need to be?

It troubled Plum Tardy that she couldn't answer that question. Her mom, Crystal's, life depended on it. Plum scooted her chair closer to her mother's bedside.

"Come on, Crystal," she said, the sound of tears clenched in her throat. "Follow my voice back to us."

Crystal was stretched out, as always, with her closed eyes facing the ceiling. If it weren't for the apparatus keeping her heart pumping and making air whoosh through her lungs, she looked as she might have in a coffin.

"Listen to my voice. I'll lead you."

Crystal's doctors insisted she never would return, describing her condition as a vegetative state. But Plum considered doctors such alarmists. She thought of it more like a coma. People came back from comas all the time. She clung to that belief with all the tenacity of someone gripping a life preserver in a flood.

Still, the hand Plum clasped felt unnatural. Oh, it was warm enough, alive. The machines made sure oxygenated blood flowed through all of her vessels. What the hand lacked was energy—the boisterous, pulsing, shouting-from-the-rooftops energy that had always defined Crystal.

"We're all here for you. You need us." *And we need* you. *I do anyway.* "Wake up. I'm begging you, Crystal."

Plum struggled to remember a computer-related term she'd learned. She wasn't really computer-literate; she was actually more of a digital disaster. But there was a concept she'd discovered from computer work that pointed to an amazing way to solve most of life's problems: rebooting. With a reboot, everything simply resets to the original place, like the mistake or tangent never happened.

"Reboot, Crystal. We need a reboot."

We? Wasn't this all about Crystal?

After an unspoken silence, Plum admitted that maybe it wasn't. *Well, sure it's also about me,* she admitted to herself. *Everyone needs a mom.* The admission, and how lost it made her feel, stunned Plum.

It couldn't be about her now. Crystal was the one trapped somewhere. Even if Crystal had never been enough of a mother for her, a rare admission from Plum, somehow Plum had to be all the daughter Crystal needed now.

But when you're lost, how *do* you find your way to where you need to be?

Plum wasn't sure anymore which of them she was asking for.

CHAPTER ONE

The rain bucketed down in drops as big as quarters, thousands and thousands of them. A rarity in sunny Southern California, where traffic now snarled in every direction.

Plum stared through a rain-soaked windshield, which the wipers couldn't begin to clear, at a line of cars jammed up before her. "Move, dammit!" she cried. Nobody budged. Within the sultry confines of Plum's aging Jeep Wrangler, she sighed, not a sound of frustration, but of confusion and loss.

"It never rains unless it stalls," Plum muttered aloud. That was one of the many proverbs Crystal often quoted. Crystal had an adage for every occasion, although others never seemed to find the wisdom in them that Plum did.

Is that what's wrong with me? Is my life just stalled?

It had been two days since Plum had tried in vain to awaken Crystal. Two days in which she'd remained brittle, seemingly without cause.

Plum knew her reaction to today's conditions was excessive. Rain wasn't an everyday occurrence in Southern California, but when Pacific storms did hit, they were usually heavy. And traffic was always ever-present. This wasn't much worse than usual.

But she'd faced some tough truths during her time with Crystal. She hadn't uttered a word since about her needs and Crystal's inadequacy, but she feared those revelations still cried out inside of her, in some emotional language she didn't want to translate.

Plum suddenly gave her head a shake, as though snapping out of it. Why was she making so much of this? Finding meaning where there was none. She was just overworked and under-appreciated. Plum had a great life. She did! Well, she would if she could wrestle Crystal's house into shape. And fix the problems at work. And maybe squirrel away some time alone with her fiancé, Noah.

Besides, Plum almost never became angry. If anything, she was the type to take it on the chin and say nothing about it.

Only…Plum wasn't sure she was willing to keep silent anymore.

Grasping for something that would boost her sinking morale, she reached into the bulky tote bag filling the passenger seat for her cell phone. She skipped using the earpiece in her glove box, and just put it on speaker, resting the phone on her thigh. She punched in her fiancé's office number. It went straight to voicemail.

"You've reached Noah Rowle, of Westside Homes and Offices," his voice proclaimed in a tone of boundless enthusiasm. "If you're calling to sell land that will allow you to become part of Budget-Mart's most aggressive expansion in decades, press one. If you're an existing client…"

"How about if I'm a fiancée, in need of a verbal hug?" Plum muttered, while the menu rattled on. Finally, after the beep, she said in a too-bright tone, "It's me. I hope your meeting later today goes well." Actually, she hoped it would end early. That way Noah might be there when she stopped home before work. "See you tonight… Hey…I miss you," she blurted, immediately regretting that she sounded so needy. She clicked the call off before she could say anything to further humiliate herself.

At thirty-six years old, it was past time she figured out how to hold a relationship together. Still, no matter what she did to try to stop it, she knew that she and Noah were drifting apart. "You're like ships passing on the Nile," Crystal had once observed, which Plum recalled now with uneasy desperation.

The line of cars finally began inching forward. At a crowded intersection, Plum glanced to the side. The pelting rain and the low cloud cover made the small houses lining the road—the little Spanish or seaside bungalows, punctuated by the occasional modern home—appear as murky as a dream. The ocean off to the right, which should have been visible, wasn't today. Yet in her mind's-eye, Plum could see the rising charcoal waves, topped by angry whitecaps, twisting and swirling in a furious show of might. After a lifetime there, she knew the ocean's every mood. Maybe too well.

Moments later, her cell phone rang. Thinking, *It's Noah calling back*, her mood inched up. Only it wasn't Noah. Instead, her sister, Sunni's, sharp, efficient voice filled the car. "You're late, Plum. I don't know which of these boxes you expect me to take, and I can't wait much longer. Where are you?"

Plum said she was only a few blocks away. "But with this traffic, it could still take me a while. How did you make it there already?" The Century City law firm where Sunni was a rising star in the corporate department was even farther away.

"I set out early, but I used a car service so I'd be able to work during the drive. Besides, I knew I'd need the driver's help with the boxes. But he'll be returning for me soon. Time is money, you know?"

Not in Plum's life. In Plum's life, nothing was money.

"How long would you say—" Sunni began.

The call dropped. When Sunni's voice cut off, Plum not only didn't dial her sister back, she turned the phone off. Noah wasn't going to call her—he rarely did lately—so what did it matter? She'd see Sunni soon enough.

Crystal's big Venice Beach Craftsman home finally came into view. Locals called it "the sherbet house," since Crystal had it painted in bands of what she'd described as, "strawberry," "lime," and "melon." Even though Plum had worked tirelessly in that house every single day for the last month, at the sight of it, a sense of peace settled over her. That had been her grandmother's house originally. After her father's death when Plum was little, she and Crystal, and later, Sunni, would crash on friends' couches between Crystal's marriages, until the friends informed them it was time to move on. They never knew much stability until Plum's grandmother built out the attic rooms for them. Eventually, upon their grandmother's death, the house passed to Crystal.

These days weeds replaced the immaculate lawn their grandmother had cultivated around winding brick paths, and the sea air had faded Crystal's unconventional paint job. Yet it still felt more like home to Plum than anywhere else.

She jerked the Jeep onto the cracked driveway, and taking a moment to pat down the wild corkscrews the soaring humidity had made of her natural auburn curls, sprinted through the rain toward the door. As soon as she reached the wide porch, the front door flew open.

Sunni stepped outside, offering Plum a conspiratorial grin, like from when they were kids. "Hey, we're throwing out mom's stuff," Sunni said with a giggle.

We, Kimosabe? But Plum couldn't bring herself to short-circuit that rare grin with a snarky remark.

Even though they had different fathers, sometimes it was hard for Plum to believe that she and Sunni had come from the same mother. Plum was short, the shortest person in their family. Her big green eyes, with thick, dark lashes, and her rounded cheeks and little bee-stung mouth meant she'd always be described more as "adorable" or "cute." Sunni, on the other hand, was tall and model-thin, with wide lips and a beautifully sculpted oval face. The form-fitting black suit she wore today, which probably carried the name of some snooty designer Plum had never heard of, was a perfect complement to her willowy body and the straight highlighted hair that fell to her shoulders.

If Sunni weren't her younger sister, Plum had to admit that Sunni's glamorous perfection would intimidate her. Stylish women always did. Like successful people of all stripes. Plum often thought that if life were a race, complete with starting point and finish line, while other people sprinted or jogged through that racecourse—she was off somewhere playing hopscotch. Taking a jump here, another there, with no pattern that ever made sense to anyone else. Or even, sometimes, to Plum.

Hopscotch accentuated how different Plum was, and made her wish that she could be more like everyone else, and less like…her. She couldn't have said exactly what "like everyone else" meant, but just as with the Supreme Court's definition of porn, she knew it when she saw it. When she looked at someone like Sunni, and some of the women Noah worked with, she saw it in spades. When she looked in the mirror, she saw someone so out of synch with everyone else, she would always fumble through life, for reasons Plum could never quite figure out.

"You've sure gotten a lot done here," Sunni said, guilt shading her voice.

Plum saw the big room the way it must have appeared to her sister. Its seedy quality was less noticeable with the worn furniture pushed against the walls, and with the whole center of the room bulging with cartons stacked to the ceiling.

Sunni had the grace to look embarrassed for all the work Plum had put in over the prior month to bring order to the House of Debris. The medical bills had piled up since Crystal's last stroke. Now, their stepfather, Roy, needed to offer Crystal's home for rent to keep up with expenses. That Crystal never threw anything away made that impossible until they were able to clear it out. With Roy always at Crystal's bedside, he left the removal of their mother's things to her daughters. Besides, they hadn't been married long; he didn't know what Crystal would want to discard. With Sunni's favorite expression being "billable hours," that meant the chore fell to Plum. Today, Sunni had finally agreed to take some of the boxes and store them in the extra bedroom of her chic condo.

Refusing to let Sunni off the hook, Plum merely identified which among the stacks of keeper boxes would be housed at Sunni's place, which at Plum's, and then, she indicated the largest pile, which would form the basis of the mother of all yard sales.

"Is this most of it?" Sunni asked.

Plum choked. "I know you haven't stopped by here much in... well, years, but surely you've noticed Crystal has moved past packrat all the way to hoarder. This barely scratches the surface."

An uncomfortable silence settled between them.

"I used to take mom to brunch when she was mobile, more often than you know. It's just that we usually met somewhere." Sunni bit her lip, scraping off her coral lipstick. "We never had much in common, the way you did. You two were always talking about what books you'd read lately. Mom and I, we didn't have much to say."

Crystal and Plum were both readers. Still, without the books they'd read to talk about, the silence would have made a divide so awkward, it would have dwarfed the Grand Canyon. Maybe Crystal hadn't connected well with either of her daughters, she just disconnected with them differently.

"She mostly keeps my books," Plum said, making a mental reminder to raid the library before she left. "I guess you don't get to call yourself a hoarder if you aren't ruthless about stealing other people's stuff."

Plum's comment broke the tension, and the sisters shared another laugh like they did when they were kids.

That Crystal's two daughters referred to her in different ways was like a carbon dating of their mother's life. Crystal and Plum's father, the late race car driver, Ben Tardy, were only in their early twenties when Plum came along. They considered it more hip and fun for their child to call them by their first names. Sunni's father, Alan Meadows, a lawyer like his daughter, preferred the more conventional approach. Now, instead of feeling at all hip or fun, it made Plum feel like she always had to remind Crystal that she was her daughter, too.

"Can't Noah help you with this work?" Sunni asked.

Not that again. Sunni had never liked Noah. When he and Plum got engaged, Sunni had shouted at her, "You're going to *marry* him? Can't you see Noah Rowle is just an empty suit?" Why couldn't Sunni understand he was so far out of Plum's league, she was lucky to have him?

"Noah is working on such a big deal, he doesn't have a spare minute." Her own delivery sounded stiff even to Plum's ears. It got old, always defending him.

Plum led Sunni through the still over-flowing rooms, ending up in the kitchen. That room was so old-fashioned it would have looped around to retro, were it in better condition. The mother of pearl Formica table, with its metal trim, might have garnered a few bucks in some Venice antique shop, if duct tape hadn't been holding the matching chairs together. There were even two refrigerators straight out of the fifties, with rounded corners and Art Deco logos. Two—because their cooling powers were iffy, and food sometimes had to be shifted from one to the other.

Sunni didn't appear to notice any of it. She planted herself behind wherever Plum happened to be, resolutely bringing her disapproval back to Noah. "Why *did* Noah leave residential real estate sales for commercial?"

A question Plum had asked herself many times, though she'd never admit that to Sunni. "He said he was tired of selling lower-priced first homes to newlyweds, especially in a down market."

"I bet he sold more houses to those newlyweds than land to corporate executives." Sunni ended with a knowing snort.

That was true. Noah kept promising Plum that the big commissions were coming. Yet somehow most months she contributed more than half of the mortgage on the posh house in Santa Monica that he had wanted. Factor in the salary cut her boss foisted on her and what she gave Roy for Crystal's care, and Plum barely scraped by. She'd finally had to instruct her bank to switch her debit card from her checking account to her savings.

From the time of her first part-time job as a teenager, Plum had always saved some of her salary. Now, she had forty-two thousand put aside. She knew that was probably nothing to Sunni, even though Sunni was younger. Plum's forty-odd thousand in savings was probably more like petty cash to Sunni's 401K plan, what it used for fun money when it went off on wild weekends with other retirement plans. Apart from Sunni, though, in their family, that represented a fortune. And now, by using it to cover some of her expenses, Plum's savings would probably dwindle away.

Plum grabbed one of the boxes she'd made up the day before, which were stacked beside the pair of fridges. She propped it on a countertop and yanked open a cabinet door to see what might be worth keeping. Tupperware, though only lids.

Sunni still stood behind her. "What's he working on?"

Plum tried to sound optimistic when she said, "He's putting together a big Budget-Mart deal." She pulled open another couple of cabinets. Nothing to fit those lids.

"Aw, yes—Budget-Mart. They don't have an in-house real estate division like many of the big-box companies, or use prestigious national firms," Sunni said. "They pick a couple of small fries and let them duke it out. Winner take all. That's why the big firms won't work with them."

That was also how Noah described it. So why had he signed on with Westside Homes and Offices, which was surely the bottom of the heap in commercial real estate? Was that the best he could do? Javier Silva & Associates, their competition, were several rungs higher. Did he really have a chance?

He said he'd joined forces with someone more experienced at the office to work in partnership. Considering how many hours he was putting in, Plum thought it had better pay off. She wanted to support him, but at what price?

Sunni finally started to walk away, but Plum took hold of her sister's wrist and pulled her back. "You know, Sunni, Crystal isn't his mother, she's ours. Shouldn't the people who care about her be the ones to decide which of her possessions to keep?"

Sunni sagged against the cracked green tile counter. "Why keep any of it? Why not back up a Dumpster and toss it all in?"

Plum glanced uneasily at the Tupperware lids. "Are you really ready to conclude that she'll never recover and come back to us?"

Sunni lowered her head for a moment, before finally pulling a smartphone from a pocket on her sleek suit jacket. "Look, let me call my assistant and see if I can rearrange my afternoon. I'll help you finish sorting through the important papers today. And…maybe I can hire a mover to work with you. But I can't do more than that."

The favorite daughter never has to try as hard. The spontaneous mental remark stunned Plum. She'd never faced uncomfortable truths. Lately, they were coming at her like fastballs in a batting cage.

While Sunni called her office and rescheduled the car service for later, Plum went to the master bedroom. The walls of this house were all different from most people's more conventional choices. Some were pretty standard faux finishes, albeit in atypical colors, while others featured murals. The far wall in the master bedroom depicted a painting of a shoreline view that wasn't visible from this room, but which was from others. Crystal's daughters had learned to paint quite creatively early in life.

The closets were equally unexpected. The walk-in closet in the master bedroom was filled, floor to ceiling, with what Crystal considered important papers.

When she joined Plum there, Sunni had put a stylishly ruffled apron over her ritzy suit. Had she brought it with her? Plum just wore old clothes.

"Okay, let's get..." Sunni's voice trailed off when she saw that over-stuffed closet full of boxes, with some contents identified, and others not. "Is there nothing mom won't keep? Look at this—how ridiculously gigantic," she said, pointing to one sizable cardboard box, which was labeled, "Plum's birth certificate." Sunni propped her fists on her hips and hissed so furiously, it sounded like steam escaping from a pipe.

Anyway, Sunni was wrong. The box wasn't actually gigantic in the sense that a homeless person couldn't live in it, though it probably could hold three or four reams of copy paper.

"Isn't your birth certificate a single sheet like everyone else's?" Sunni asked.

Plum nodded. "And I have it. I keep it in my strongbox at home."

"Should I toss this?" Sunni gestured at that box.

"No, I'll put it with the things I'm taking home. It might make for fun reading some night when I can't sleep." Considering Crystal's typical organization, though, it was just as likely that box contained nothing that had anything to do with Plum's birth certificate. Besides, how much paperwork could there be about an ordinary birth?

They worked for an hour and barely made a dent. Lots of boxes were filled with pointless things like throwaway newspapers. But in some containers, every item was different, and they had to proceed slowly so they didn't accidentally toss out the deed to the house, or something equally critical. Plum left it to Sunni, and went up to the attic to fold clothes.

Every bit of the attic space had been transformed into an on-going closet, with rods attached to the walls and freestanding racks filling the centers of the rooms, all teeming with Crystal's expansive wardrobe. Plum envied Crystal's flashy taste in clothing, many items of which she'd designed and made herself. They were too dramatic for Plum's utilitarian lifestyle, but how she wished she had the nerve to wear such showy things. She could, too. Though she was shorter, she was also a bit wider than their frail mother. From the few times she'd borrowed Crystal's dresses, she knew they usually fit her every bit as well.

Sunni came up sometime later carrying a couple of soda cans, suggesting they take a break together.

"Did you know that there were no less than a hundred empty envelopes with a return address from someplace called Applewood, Arizona?"

Plum nodded. "428 West Pony Lane. You don't want to know how many empty envelopes I threw out yesterday." Plum noticed because the town was associated with Noah's Budget-Mart deal, but there was also something more to it than that. "Someone we knew as kids used to vacation there." Plum remembered someone describing in vivid detail a Western decor, with horses, and a beautiful lake. "Do you remember who?"

Sunni said she didn't. "My only childhood association with the word *vacation* was Crystal going off on Las Vegas jaunts with some new guy and coming home without the rent money." She gave her head a pensive tilt. "There's no name on the return address on all those envelopes. Who are they from?"

Plum shrugged. "Don't know. They were all empty, though I did find a bad copy of one letter Crystal sent to that address."

"Did it say anything of value, anything that would explain such a loyal correspondence? Especially from Mom, who couldn't even write a shopping list."

Plum pursed her lips pensively. She'd hesitated about reading it at first. Once when she was a kid, she'd found Crystal's diary. After coming across a sordid account of cyclone sex with a guy Plum had regarded as the last living, breathing Cro-Magnon man, she'd remained scarred for years. Now, though, Plum was an adult, and curiosity got the better of her. After all that wrangling, the letter proved disappointing. That really bad copy started out with a description of some novel, with which Crystal seemed enthralled, about a couple raising an orphan baby. That sounded like the kind of women's fiction Crystal had always favored. Then, after some blank space, fragments of lines appeared in faint text. Phrases like "baby always cared for" and "never want for anything," which clearly related to the book. While Crystal had been a devoted reader, writing that much about a novel to someone in another state revealed a whole new side of her.

"Nothing that made any sense to me," Plum concluded. But she'd stuffed that copy into her voluminous tote. It was probably still there.

While Plum sat on the floor and sipped, Sunni flipped through the racks of clothing. She pulled out a black dress with flowing lace skirts, under a colorful Bolero top.

"Can you imagine wearing something like this?"

Plum could do more than imagine it—she could remember it. She had borrowed that dress to wear to some function at Noah's old firm. She'd overheard some of the women snickering that she looked like a flamenco dancer. For once Plum didn't care. She'd never felt so glamorous.

"I love it, Sunni."

Sunni looked surprised, but she thrust it out to her sister. "Then take it."

"Where would I wear it?" Plum asked. Yet she decided on the spot that she would pack some of Crystal's garments and put those boxes with the ones she would bring home. Stalled? Hah! Not her.

Sunni left after the break to continue work on the contents of the master bedroom's closet. She returned again a couple of hours later to say she had sorted through everything there. She added that the rain had stopped and the car service driver was on his way.

While they waited for the driver in silence in the living room, Plum stared out absently. After a moment, Sunni broke into Plum's reverie.

"Plum, it's not just sorting through this mess that's getting to you, is it?" Sunni asked. "You seem sad. You have for months now. What's wrong?"

Tell her. Despite Plum's best efforts to hold them back, images tumbled through her mind: of blood, so much blood; pain that made her double over; cramping that signaled life draining away. And later, an emptiness that consumed her. But she wouldn't tell Sunni.

She'd never told anyone.

Finally, Plum shrugged. "You know, Sunni, if life is a bowl of jelly, mine is missing a thick layer of peanut butter. All work and no play is making Plum a dull girl."

Sunni burst out laughing. *"Jell-O. A bowl of Jell-O,* not *jelly.* You still quote proverbs like mom. Haven't you ever noticed how wrong she always got them?"

"Jell-O?" That sounded odd. "Why do you assume it's Crystal who gets sayings wrong? Why not other people?"

"Probably because she hasn't really listened to another soul more than a few times in her entire fifty-nine years. How could she hear what anyone else says?"

Harsh, Plum thought with a wince, *but true.*

"Is this...as good as it gets?" Plum asked.

Sunni gave her a fierce hug. "Little Plum." Though Plum was five years older, sometimes they both acknowledged that Sunni really did seem like the elder sister. "After the way things were for us as kids—with mom's ups-and-downs, with being homeless— how can you even ask? In this life, if you don't get what you want, you better want what you've got, because it's all there is."

No! Plum wasn't sure she could live without peanut butter.

CHAPTER TWO

Plum was normally hyper-disciplined. That was her problem—in their family, she was the go-to girl to burden with responsibility. She couldn't explain what came over her when she left Crystal's house. Maybe it was simply the fun of being with her sister, but she craved more of it. Rather than fill her car with some of the boxes from the keeper pile as she intended, she stuffed into the Jeep cartons of Crystal's clothes, shoes, and costume jewelry.

It wasn't as if she planned to wear any of them. But maybe if Noah was still at his business dinner when she came home from work tonight, she might open those boxes and marvel at their contents. That would make her feel good. Well, better.

The Jeep didn't hold all the cargo that the giant SUV the car service had sent for Sunni did. After Plum squeezed in all those clothing boxes, there was only space for that one labeled, "Plum's birth certificate." She slammed the tailgate closed, then made one last dash back to the house, raiding the floor-to-ceiling stacks of books in a room without bookshelves that Crystal had loosely referred to as "my library," for a few of her own favorite titles that their mother had kept. She threw those on the floor in front of the passenger seat.

Though it was inching past mid-afternoon now, without the rain, the traffic flowed freely enough. Before too much longer, Plum had parked the Jeep in her own driveway in Santa Monica. While it was bigger than she wanted, the house she and Noah shared was a graceful old dowager on an attractive, tree-lined street. Spanish in design, the stucco body was tastefully painted in ivory, with neat amber trim, along with the requisite red tile roof.

With no time to unpack the car now, Plum grabbed the books from the floor and raced inside. She scarcely noticed a living room every bit as refined as the exterior. It had been decorated by one of

Noah's designer friends, with butterscotch leather couches and rustic tables, and artwork that, while not exactly inexpensive now, was expected to appreciate more in value in the future. Plum regarded it as static as a magazine spread; Noah considered it his ideal space. He always insisted it made a statement about the success the man who lived there had achieved.

The master bedroom, which they rarely showed guests, looked far less grand, having been pulled together with the hodgepodge of pieces Plum had assembled when she first went out on her own. She deposited the books she carried on the walnut dresser, and then, hastily stripped in the adjoining bath, shampooing and showering in record time.

After the quickie shower, she stepped into the huge walk-in closet that the home's prior owner had customized with a selection of high and low rods and assorted shelves. Plum's things—the cook's uniforms that she wore for work and her meager personal wardrobe—took up less than a quarter of the space. Nothing like the on-going rooms where Crystal stored her clothes, but also not much like Noah's larger share of this closet. His many high-priced suits and designer casual wear all hung with precision in their assigned compartments. Plum's side housed the stack of various pieces of his tweed-and-leather Hartmann luggage set. Noah had plopped the roomy satchel on top of three different-sized roller suitcases.

After dressing, and remembering to the take the books she'd left on the bureau, Plum made a pit stop in the gourmet kitchen. With its acres of granite and cherry wood, punctuated by stainless steel, the kitchen had always been a bit showy for Plum's taste. Still, she had made good use of it for much of the time they'd lived there. Lately, though, she simply couldn't be bothered cooking. Today, she grabbed a bag of chips from the pantry. Junk made up most of her meals these days.

The room adjoining the kitchen, which Plum and Noah called their den, was her favorite spot. One side contained Plum's floor-to-ceiling bookshelves, which were only marginally neater than Crystal's arrangement. She stuffed the titles she took from her mother's house onto a partially empty shelf. Then, as she munched a handful of chips, she wandered over to Noah's part of the room.

The other half of the room contained Noah's stylish home office desk. Tacked across the wall above it were maps from numerous states, showing the towns where Budget-Mart intended to build new stores. The maps featured varying degrees of detail. Some were state maps, in which the towns that interested Budget-Mart were just dots among lots of other dots. Yet some maps detailed those towns to such a degree, spaces were broken down by their plot ID numbers. Plum studied them all. Especially the ones with the lot designations, wondering which of those people might grow richer by selling their properties, and which would become holdouts, foiling Noah's and Budget-Mart's plans.

Plum knew the maps were there merely to provide Noah with inspiration. He couldn't read a map to save his life. Whenever they took driving trips, such as their rare visits to his parents in Indiana, Plum always navigated. Other people could rely on their nav devices or cellphone directions, but whenever Plum drove somewhere new, she kept a map beside her, folded to show the next part of the journey. Ironically, she didn't need a map at that point—once Plum studied a route, she always knew precisely where to go from memory.

She'd never told Noah how often she stood here, wondering what it would be like to visit some of these places. Damn! She yearned to steal some vacation time with him. Why didn't he need it as much as she did?

One town on one of those maps caught her eye—Applewood, Arizona. Not just where Budget-Mart wanted to build a new store, but the site of the return address on all those empty envelopes in Crystal's closet. And also where someone she couldn't remember had shared talk of great getaways. *Who was that?*

Plum had stared at these maps too many times to count. Still, she'd always brought such ambivalence to it. While she wanted Noah to succeed, she wasn't certain the world needed any more individuality-crushing Budget-Mart stores.

Popping one last chip in her mouth, Plum neatly pushed Noah's chair under his desk, and left the den. She tossed the bag of chips back into the pantry, and a moment later, grabbed her big tote and rushed out the front door.

* * *

Plum made a detour to the care facility where Crystal was a patient. She hadn't been there since two days earlier, when she'd tried to awaken Crystal. Plum had to break the negative spell that time had cast on her. She breezed through the cheery lobby with its warm colors and inviting lavender scent. Visitors were supposed to sign in, but Plum came so often, a nod to the receptionist was usually enough for her.

She paused outside the door to Crystal's room to paste on her most optimistic smile, which she found harder than usual today, before pushing through it.

The pale peach walls and sleek furnishings, reminiscent of an Ikea catalog, seemed chosen to make that space look as homey as possible. But the hospital bed dominating the center and the equipment for monitoring the patient's vital signs negated that impression.

Almost everyone knew Crystal would never regain consciousness. Some, like Plum, held onto a sliver of hope. Roy, Crystal's present husband, was the only one who believed she could come home tomorrow.

"Oh, hey there, Plum," Roy said absently from his usual bedside chair, never removing his eyes from his beloved wife's face.

Roy was a portly guy, with a silver brush haircut, who wore polyester short-sleeved shirts, often with pit stains. Something Crystal would have deplored, were she able to make any judgments.

For years, Roy Casey had been their mail carrier at the Venice house. In those days, Crystal always referred to him as, "a schmo." That didn't stop her from exploiting his obvious affection for her by sending him off to perform errands, sometimes when he was supposed to be delivering mail. That would surely have gotten him canned, had his superiors discovered it. But Crystal hadn't cared.

She never even agreed to go out with him. She preferred flashy guys to schmoes. It was only after her first stroke that she agreed to date him because all the sexier men had vanished. After her second stroke, she accepted his proposal, so if the worst happened—as it did with the next stroke—there would be another person to take care of her.

Plum knew if Crystal recovered, she would prop Roy out on the curb in front of the Venice house, waiting for the trash pickup. Instead, he won the prize, purely for hanging on when the doctors insisted there was nobody home.

Plum tried to position herself in Roy's line of sight. "Roy, you wouldn't believe how much we got done today. Sunni actually worked her way through the entire papers closet." It embarrassed her that she wanted his attention, but that didn't lessen the need.

"You girls are the best," he said, though he put no punch behind the words. He didn't even glance at her.

Give it up, Plum. Roy is never going to fill that dad-sized hole in your heart.

Finally, he looked in her direction. "She made a face today. You should have seen it, Plum. She looked so cute. No question, she's getting closer to consciousness."

He said that all the time.

"My Cryssie was smiling at me, you know. I told her a joke, and she heard me. She found it funny."

It must be easy to love someone in a state like Crystal's. They can be whatever you want them to be. Real people are much harder.

The punishing thoughts kept coming.

A few moments more were all Plum could manage. She feigned looking at her watch and acted surprised at the time. "Ooh! Gotta go, Roy, or I'll be late for work."

She needn't have bothered. He didn't care.

"Uh-huh. On your way out, stop at the front desk, would you, Plum? Get them to send the doctor down here. I have to tell him about Crystal's progress."

Plum's spirits fell the instant she was through the door. How much longer could she do this?

CHAPTER THREE

Plum's often-battered self-esteem had enjoyed a high five when *Southland Weekly* magazine declared Dylan's on Montana "one of the most exciting restaurants to hit Southern California in decades." And it plummeted when the article didn't even mention her.

As always, after leaving Crystal's care facility Plum pointed the Jeep toward Dylan's, the restaurant where she *worked* as the executive chef, but was only *credited* with being a cook. When Dylan Grant, along with a silent partner she'd never met, opened the eatery that had become such a trendy hotspot, he wanted to be known as an owner-chef. Too bad he couldn't cook. Needing a good job in a hurry when her last place folded, Plum agreed to be his cooking beard. Par for the course in Plum's hopscotch life.

It wasn't too bad at first. Sure, Dylan paraded around the restaurant stealing her thunder. He also presented himself as the executive chef in all the interviews he snagged.

Plum had spent days schooling him in the dish he would prepare for the *Southland Weekly* reporter. He didn't even manage to make that work. When it started falling apart, the ever-dazzling Dylan popped the incomplete concoction into the oven, before leading the media types out to the dining room for some wine. Meanwhile, Plum took her own completed version of the meal from the oven and let a waiter serve it to the fawning reporter.

Both she and Dylan knew how to play their parts.

Still, her job made her feel as if she'd swallowed a boulder that crushed her insides more every day. At least Dylan had let Plum run the restaurant the way she wanted, at first. That made it a success. In a town that destroys new restaurants, even if nobody knew it, Plum had scored a bull's-eye.

She had been a popular executive chef at another successful Westside spot. Only the landlord of that building decided to tear it down and build a condo complex on the site, and her boss regarded that as his signal to retire. To keep the paychecks rolling in, she accepted Dylan's questionable offer.

At a stoplight, she glanced in the rearview mirror and saw those boxes of Crystal's clothes behind her. *Turn right*, Plum told herself. That would take her home for an evening of playing dress up. Left would take her to the restaurant for another evening of drudgery. *Don't I deserve some fun? When did I become a schmo?*

Naturally, she made a left. She knew she had to, though the disappointment nearly hobbled her. Now, she zeroed in on the staff parking lot, around the back of the restaurant. When she pulled into the lot, she noticed far fewer cars than there should have been.

A shiver of panic went through her. *Did they all walk out?* She wouldn't blame anyone, given Dylan's austerity kick. Yet neither could she stretch herself any thinner.

Six or so months earlier Dylan began demanding that she use cheaper ingredients and stretch them farther.

"Dylan, are you crazy," Plum had argued. "The farm-to-table ingredients are part of what lends us our panache. Even the *Southland Weekly* article raved about it."

She couldn't change his mind; if anything, the cost-cutting measures accelerated. When kitchen workers quit, Dylan insisted that they couldn't afford to replace them, requiring others to do double-duty. Plum herself did the work of multiple cooks. Most nights she could barely drag herself out the door after cleanup.

Still, thanks to Plum's creative direction and the diligence of the staff, the restaurant's star kept soaring. "Dylan, we're full every night, sometimes to the point of turning people away. How is it we can't afford more staff?" Plum would ask.

"Plum, Plum, Plum," he drawled, while staring over her head, rather than looking her in the eyes. "You cook like nobody's business, but you don't know shit about running a restaurant."

After that remark, she'd longed to hurt him, as never before. But she had bills to pay.

"If you ever own your own place, you'll understand that it takes more than the butts we put into our chairs to make a restaurant profitable," Dylan had maintained airily.

It might take more, though butts in the chairs surely had to be a big part of it.

Plum would have given anything to open her own restaurant. Once Dylan started whittling away at her salary, the dream slipped farther from her grasp.

She hadn't started out cooking. She had been putting herself through community college as an English Lit major. Unlike Sunni, she didn't have a father to pay her way through school; her dad, race car driver, Ben Tardy, had died too soon in a flaming car wreck years earlier. Plum took a job working at the library. Along the way, it occurred to her that her major wasn't that marketable. She thought about switching to Library Science, but she found libraries too regimented in their organization. *Were we ever asked to vote on the Dewey Decimal System?* If she had her way, they'd be set up entirely differently.

But she'd always been the family cook, from the time she was so small she needed to stand on a box at the stove. When she happened to drive past a culinary academy, and the sign caught her eye, she thought she'd found a path. She quit college and signed up for the cooking classes that same week. Well, she quit college and signed up for cooking school, then reconsidered that choice, and thought instead about joining the army, before finally settling back into the culinary academy where she belonged. Unlike confident people, who could nail a straight-ahead direction, she couldn't stick with decisions even when she knew they were right. Plum, the hopscotch girl.

Yet cooking was right for her. It gave her something that nothing else ever had. It brought color into her life, creativity. She remembered during her days in the culinary school, the excitement she'd felt when she mastered a new technique. She'd become positively giddy when she developed a new recipe.

She asked herself honestly now how long it had been since she'd experienced that level of excitement? When had it ceased to be her joy and just become her job? Was it because of the ridiculous conditions she had to work under, or something else?

When those awful images of blood and pain and loss threatened to return again, she shut them out. Plum always slammed the door on what she didn't want to see.

After jerking the Jeep into a parking spot, Plum hastily jumped out, desperate to get into the kitchen. She had to know what she'd be dealing with tonight. She took a few quick steps. Then something happened that brought her to a halt.

Was that *shouting* coming from inside?

Plum bolted through the backdoor—and came to a standstill. Totally stunned, her heart ceased to beat. Absolutely stopped—she felt sure it might never start again.

Everything was gone.

Julio, one of her cooks, stumbled over, making him look as shocked as she felt. "Plum, Dylan sold everything out from under us." He ended with what sounded like a sob.

That explained the empty parking lot—most of the staff had already left. It also explained what she saw here. Or rather, what she didn't see. Every piece of equipment, every dish and glass, every pot, all the counters were gone. The kitchen had been stripped to the bare walls.

Julio continued with, "What are what we going to do?"

Plum opened her mouth, but no sound came out. She couldn't speak. Couldn't breathe. Yet her thoughts raced. Suddenly, Dylan's austerity campaign made sense. He wasn't cutting corners because expenses were up, as he'd always claimed, he was skimming. Embezzling from his unknown partner. Now, with this move, he'd made off with the last of the restaurant's assets.

She shook her head at Julio.

Ahead in that barren space, a few employees seemed to be arguing with a strange man in a navy pinstripped suit that screamed of pricey and unusually formal tailoring for LA.

The unknown man moved stiffly toward her, but Plum dashed past him into the dining room to confirm what she now expected. Same situation there. Empty. Stripped of tables and chairs, the cases of wine beyond the wrought iron wine cellar gates, even the open bottles of liquor over the mahogany bar. Gone, all of it.

Plum wandered back to the kitchen in a daze.

That man waited there for her. He cleared his throat and said in a hoity-toity British accent. "I'm Gordon Rafferty. The workers tell me that you, not Dylan, ran the show here."

A kitchen staffer slowed his steps, while making his way past them, and muttered something in Spanish.

"What was that?" Gordon asked.

"He said, 'Dylan was a poser,' " Plum translated, finally finding her voice.

Gordon cleared his throat. "I see. I'm…I was his partner in this operation."

The silent investor. Not quite silent now, though judging by the occasional stammer in his speech, he felt as sandbagged as Plum. Through an open door, she saw her scarred desk and the rickety chairs had been left in her office. The only things not worth taking. Without a word, she led Gordon there.

"Office" had always been too grand a term for that place. Dylan squeezed a little space in the storage room, where she could work, and with the budget he'd given her, the only places she could shop for furnishings were thrift shops. It actually looked more like an office now, without the canned food cartons and burlap bags of rice, potatoes, and onions that once filled the space.

"It seems Dylan sold off everything here," Gordon said once they were seated. "We had a meeting scheduled this afternoon. The banked proceeds have been going down steadily. Unless there was a decline in business—"

"No decline," Plum said. She went on to tell him everything that had happened over the last six months or so, which now made sense. If Dylan planned to rip-off his partner, there was no reason to keep sinking funds into the business, and every reason to build up his stash.

While Gordon shared what he'd been able to learn about the movers who came for the restaurant's contents, Plum didn't pay much attention. Who needed the postmortem? Now that her shock was fading, she felt sick. How would she survive without her salary?

She had to seize the opportunity she found here. Though

successful men, like chic women, had always made Plum's head buzz with noise and caused her throat to close up, she summoned her courage and said, "Look, if you want the real thing, the person who made Dylan's the hit it was, that's me. We can rebuild this place."

Given how startled Gordon looked after she spoke, she suspected she might have interrupted him. He looked at her down his long, aristocratic nose. "I've taken quite a financial hit here...that is, Dylan was such a showman, I can't imagine..."

Plum got it. He preferred the poser. That was his measure of a successful executive chef, the guy who couldn't cook.

What a crappy doggy-dog world this was.

CHAPTER FOUR

Since nobody else would, Plum called every name in the reservation book. Some people expressed genuine regret that Dylan's had closed, sometimes reminiscing about the great meals they'd enjoyed there. Plum almost whimpered at that praise. Others chewed her out for wrecking their plans. *I really can't take this tonight.* Yet she did. She had never been able to stand up to the kind of prosperous people who made her cooking a hit.

She taped a hand-lettered sign on the door announcing the restaurant's closing, for any drop-ins without reservations. With that, her obligations ended. Good thing, too. She felt leached of every ounce of energy.

She drove home on autopilot, too spent to notice her route.

When her driveway came into view, she felt a stab of disappointment that Noah's silver Lexus SUV wasn't there. Did she ever need a hug tonight. Not that she expected to see his car. He'd told her that morning that he'd probably be out at a business dinner tonight. If he were around, his car would have been outside. Noah's routine was to leave it in the driveway until close to bedtime, in case he had to run an errand. Driving it into the garage was one of the last things he did before climbing into bed.

When she stepped from the Jeep, she did notice, through the small windows in the garage door, that the garage light was on. Strange. She hadn't noticed that earlier, when she came home to change.

Who cares? She felt too drained to worry about the damned light. Considering what her financial situation would be like now, the electric bill was the least of her worries.

Plum stepped through the front door, and gently placed her big tote on the floor beside it. If someone had told her yesterday that she was about to lose her job, she might have imagined herself slamming this door in anger. Instead, she felt so broken inside, she moved with care, as if stirring of too much air would hurt her internal organs.

In the kitchen she pulled a glass from a cabinet. When she opened the pantry door, she spotted the half-eaten bag of chips from earlier, and felt queasy. She hoped the chips had the good grace to stay down. She reached instead for the bottle of Jack Daniels on the top shelf, and poured a good slug. Plum considered going to the fridge for ice, but decided she didn't need any more chills today.

She carried the glass of liquor to the cushy couch in the den that faced her bookshelf corner. While seedier around the edges than the pristine furniture of their formal living room, that sofa was part of the reason why she genuinely liked that room. When she sank into the yielding cushions, she felt enveloped by their comforting softness. She propped her feet on the scarred coffee table in front of it.

She took a sip of the Jack. While its pleasant warmth spread through her like a vapor, the bite of the alcohol hurt her stomach. Plum decided her gut had better get used to it. She intended to pour a few more of those down her gullet before this awful day ended.

She should be making plans. She considered getting a pen and pad from Noah's desk, to make a list of people to contact in search of another job. She couldn't make herself do it. Tomorrow would be soon enough to do what everyone expected of her, so she could keep all their ships afloat. Tonight she was going to lick her awful wound.

While she took another sip, she thought she heard noises from elsewhere in the house. It almost sounded like voices. Had she left the TV on when she came home to change? No, she couldn't remember turning it on. Burglars? As long as they didn't bother her, she didn't care.

Plum's curiosity got the better of her. She plopped the glass on the table and followed the sounds through the house. It was only when she neared the bedroom that a bone-chilling cold spread through her, even though she hadn't used any ice in her drink.

She heard Noah's voice. "Oh, baby," he said. "That's what I mean." And he followed that with a moan.

There was only one context in which those sounds came out of him, and then, Plum had always been his naked partner.

She blocked out thought, though not movement. She stepped into the bedroom doorway. On the king-sized bed where she would have said their love had flourished, he was stretched out. And as she'd known wordlessly, he wasn't alone. Riding him was a woman from his office. Claire Something…Claire Denton, Plum remembered. His partner in the Budget-Mart project. And this Claire-creature was thin, dammit! Not rounded like Plum. Tall and blonde and willowy, and bringing Noah to a peak of the kind of ecstasy he hadn't wanted from Plum in months.

From out of nowhere, she spared a thought to the garage light left on. Like always, he drove his car into the garage before he went to bed. She'd bet anything that Noah hid his car in the garage. Driven in quickly so none of the neighbors saw anything unusual that they could unwittingly share with his doormat of a fiancée.

After a moment, something even more pressing came to occupy her. There, in the doorway of her bedroom, Plum started gagging.

CHAPTER FIVE

Apparently, someone else's dry heaves was all it took to dampen their sexual frenzy. The sound of Plum's gagging brought their lustiness to an abrupt halt.

Claire rolled off Noah. With a pained expression, Noah clutched a pillow from under his head to cover his privates.

Like we hadn't all seen his junk. Though some had seen it in action more recently than others.

"Plum, I– I–" Noah sputtered. "I didn't want you to learn it like this."

Even as stunned as she felt, she grasped what he meant. That he did want her to learn it somehow.

The knife of betrayal slashed her heart. Yet she admitted to herself what she'd always believed: that Noah had been too good for her. Even with discomfort and embarrassment splashed across his features, the lines of his face were still handsomely sculpted. His pained brown eyes tilted at a roguish angle. His teeth looked impossibly white. He'd always reminded Plum of a male model, someone born to show off spectacular clothing in an upscale catalog. Even if Sunni did regard him as empty, Plum knew he didn't belong with a goofy unemployed chef who couldn't pull off a pretense of social polish if her life depended on it.

The icy blonde rose and without a bit of self-consciousness began to pick up her classy clothing. She was as thin as Plum had thought, yet despite Plum's own deep insecurities, she honestly admitted this woman's body wasn't that attractive. She was as flat as an ironing board, on which someone had affixed two grapefruit-sized, obviously fake, breasts.

Plum sometimes wondered if everyone else had received a rulebook at birth, complete with guidelines for every eventuality, which guaranteed a successful life. She knew that she not only hadn't gotten one, she couldn't even imagine how it might read. She'd bet anything that Noah's naked buddy had it committed to memory.

While looking at Plum as she might a bug, Claire said at last, "We're going to want you to buy Noah's half of the house."

Plum choked out a short laugh. *Fat chance of that.*

Noah rose from bed, moving with remarkable agility for someone still clutching that ridiculous pillow. "Claire—no." He sighed heavily. "The truth is, Plum, we're losing the house."

"How? Every month I give you my share, usually more than my share." Hell, she'd even paid for those stupid suitcases he had to have.

Noah cleared his throat, while looking around for something. "I had some unusual expenses, and I got behind." He hastily exchanged the pillow for a pair of boxers. "I had to take out a large second mortgage, too. Now, we're totally under water."

Plum sputtered helpless. "You can't have. I own half the house. I never signed—"

With guilt twisting his features, to Plum he still looked impossibly good, the way perfect people always did, even in compromising situations. Not the way she probably appeared at that moment, alternately shivering and sweating like a stevedore.

"I...didn't want you to worry, Plum. I signed it for you."

He *forged* her name? Wouldn't that have required a notary? The answer to that objection immediately floated into her mind. There was always some woman—usually a dumpy doormat—who would risk her career for Noah. Why hadn't Plum expected that?

With her shock beginning to fade, the pain in her heart swelled. She was going to cry. The barf threat had passed, but in another moment she was going to start crying, and she wouldn't be able to stop. Her eyes would turn red, and she would choke and gasp, and snot would dribble down her face. Plum couldn't bear for either of them to see her like that. She couldn't become that much of a victim.

She turned away, hoping her legs wouldn't collapse under her.

"If you give us a few minutes, we'll go to a hotel tonight," Noah said. "Or Claire's place."

If Claire had a place, why were they here? How could he be so cruel as to use the bed he'd shared with her? "Don't do me any favors," Plum spat gruffly, the struggle to hold back the tears taking everything she had.

"Plum—"

"Let her go," Claire said with such social ease, she might have been making casual conversation at a cocktail party, instead of just having bedded someone else's fiancé.

Stumbling a few steps away from the bedroom, Plum knew she'd made a dreadful mistake. She should have accepted his offer to leave. She had nowhere to go. Sure, she could show up at Sunni's door—if she wanted to be bathed tonight in Sunni's need to be right. She couldn't go to Crystal's house, either. That was where Roy lived, and it would be awkward for him. He'd sold his condo to pay for Crystal's care. Once that house had a tenant, Roy intended to rent a room in a friend's house. Until then, she couldn't saddle him with Crystal's daughter.

She couldn't stay here, either. Not with Claire looking down on her, and especially not with Noah pitying her for being the victim of his own double-treachery. Besides, it had never been her house, not really. Now, when it wouldn't be legally, she didn't want to be surrounded by Noah's sterile choices.

She'd have to be the one paying for a hotel tonight. She, who lost her job, lost her home, and lost the man she'd loved. How was it possible that on this day she'd been screwed by everyone, in every way possible except for the one way she would have welcomed? Her going-nowhere life had truly come to an abrupt and miserable end.

Plum stumbled out to the den, trying to block out the sound of the murmuring voices still coming from the bedroom. With one brief glance at the maps tacked to the wall, she realized the one tiny advantage to this situation. She could take that vacation she needed, after all. And she could go anywhere without regard to what anyone else wanted. She didn't have to take a hotel here in town, where she might run into someone who knew Noah or Claire. She could go somewhere else, anywhere. Not for long, of course. She'd need another job, preferably sooner than later. And she still had Crystal to think about. But none of it had to be immediate.

Where could she go? She glanced at the wall over Noah's desk. A desperate longing to take something from him overcame her. *I need maps.* She began yanking Noah's maps from the wall. Anger overtook her pain. Plum scarcely heard her own breathlessness, as she crushed those unfolded maps beneath her arm. She didn't hear anything, apart from the sound of the thumbtacks hitting the hardwood floor when she ripped the maps away, sending the tacks flying.

She was about to turn away. To rush outside, clutching her map booty, when she saw it—Noah's tony Hartmann satchel. When she saw it earlier this afternoon, it had been on the top of his stack of luggage in their closet. Now, it rested on the desk chair, which was pulled a couple of feet away from the desk—not pushed in as she had left it—with the top unbuckled. When Plum glanced into it, she choked.

The satchel was *filled* with money. Fat bundles of cash. Loads of them.

Was *this* what Noah did with the money she gave him every month for their mortgage payment? Or was it the cash from the second mortgage he took on the house by forging her name?

Rage mushroomed in Plum.

How dare he?

Plum latched the top of the satchel shut and yanked it off the chair.

Heavy sucker.

Without giving it a thought, she took the satchel.

Hah! Who's screwing whom now?

After grabbing her tote bag where she'd dropped it on the floor, she sailed out the front door. And this time, she did slam it.

CHAPTER SIX

Anger's burn propelled Plum to her car. She tossed the crumpled maps onto the passenger seat, and threw the heavy satchel and her tote bag on top of them. She hurried around the other side and hurled her own body in, just as roughly. Burned some rubber when she peeled out of the driveway.

At a traffic light a few blocks away, another wave of hurt crashed into her, washing the anger away. *Oh, Noah! Why? And with a mean girl yet*. The more she thought about that awful Claire, the surer she was of it. Plum had plenty of experience with them. The other kids in school had often made fun of her because of her quirkiness, and the offbeat way Crystal had dressed them, but the mean girls were the worst.

She didn't notice the light had changed until the driver of the car behind leaned on his horn. She threw the Jeep into gear. The streets were clogged with traffic. It was only six-thirty, after all. Prime rush hour. Though her life was already in ruins, it occurred to her that, with the hour so early, she could suffer lots more blows before this day was over.

And despite her determination that she *could* go anywhere, she didn't know where she *should* go. She didn't have the energy to decide. Before she could think about that, another thought pushed it aside. Crystal. She couldn't go anywhere without telling Roy that she was taking off. She turned at the corner and headed toward the nursing home. There was no doubt that he would still be there. He was always there, until the staff made him leave anyway.

In the care facility parking lot, Plum thought about how tough it would be on Roy if she stopped coughing in money for Crystal's upkeep. But, hey, she had money. The money Noah had saved. She reached into the satchel and yanked out a packet. How much was in there? Five hundred? A thousand? *Who cares?* She threw it into her tote bag and hooked the strap over her shoulder.

When she opened the door to Crystal's room, a familiar sight sprang up before her—Roy at Crystal's bedside, holding his wife's limp hand, gazing at her with utter adoration. Pain spiked in Plum. It was his devotion that got to her. His devotion to Crystal, who had never loved him, who never even *liked* him. Who referred to him as "a schmo." Was that what Plum had been for Noah? She admitted honestly to herself that Noah had never looked at her the way Roy gazed at Crystal. Maybe he had never cared as much for her as she had for him. Was that always the way it was? Did someone always go unloved? Why couldn't she inspire devotion like Roy's? Why couldn't she have been more like Claire? Why was her life so miserably offbeat?

Roy looked up indifferently. "Back again, Plum?"

"Yeah. Listen, Roy. I have to take off for a short time. For work." What a ridiculous lie. Why would a busy local chef have to travel? Roy didn't notice. "I wanted to stop by and leave a few bucks with you. You know, in case I'm not here when you need to pay for Crystal's next month's care." She extended the block of cash to him.

That actually broke through Roy's usual blindness for anything other than Crystal. "Plum, this is a lot of money. Is it legit?"

The first whisper of doubt floated into Plum's thoughts, but she stomped it down. "Of course, it is. I saved it. I just haven't had a chance to take it to the bank." Well, someone saved it. Noah had sure socked away lots of her money. "I shouldn't be gone long, a few days, a week at most."

She couldn't be gone any longer than that. She had to start re-making her life. Find a job, a place to live. Though right now, she couldn't be here, breathing the same air as Noah and Claire.

"Roy, would you do me a favor?" He usually refused any request she made, insisting he needed to be at Crystal's side. Still, she had just paid him a substantial sum. "Can you tell Sunni I have to be away? Tell her I'm fine, and I'll contact her when I can."

Roy started to look doubtful again, but for once, he agreed. "Sure thing, Plum."

Another wave of tears threatened to strike. But Plum felt a stab of vengeance as well. She paused at the door, saying, "If you need anything while I'm gone, call Noah."

"I don't know, Plum. He always seems like such a busy guy."

She remembered how guilty he'd looked—she wasn't sure which form of cheating her pained him most, the sexual kind or the financial. "Roy, he'll make time for you."

Knowing she couldn't keep her composure going any longer, Plum rushed out with a feeble, "Bye."

Back in the Jeep, she sat absolutely still, with no idea what to do now. She wanted to be gone from there, she just didn't have the energy to go. Not to mention deciding where. Her gaze fell on the maps. One dot on the uppermost map caught her eye. Applewood, Arizona. The place that had produced about a million envelopes in Crystal's closet, as well as where Budget-Mart desperately needed to build one of their super stores or civilization would come to an end. It had sounded good when whoever she'd known had talked about it. Even if it sucked, it was as good as anywhere. She needed to be someplace where nobody knew her, where she could lick her wounds in peace.

With some direction finally in place, she pointed the Jeep toward the I-10 freeway. Before she even pulled out of the parking lot, her phone rang. She took it from her tote bag and glanced at the screen. Noah. No wonder it was illegal to use phones while driving. Plum's hand shook when she switched it off.

A few blocks later another blow hit her. She felt like an idiot. She'd flown out of that house in such a rush, she'd left without a stitch of clothing. She was still wearing her chef's whites. When she came to a stop at a traffic light, the cartons in the rear of the Jeep shifted, capturing her attention. Of course! She had loads of Crystal's outfits to wear. Maybe this was the perfect time to take on a new look. To something less schmo-like, less like someone who got cheated on. She didn't have any underwear or toiletries, either, or even a book to get lost in—she hated that she hadn't kept in the car the stack of books that she'd taken from Crystal's house. She decided she'd buy whatever she needed at the first store she spotted from the freeway.

Anywhere but a Budget-Mart.

* * *

Plum intended to find some discount mega-store, where she could buy everything she needed. She came upon a mall first, and decided that would do as well for some of it. She reached into the satchel and plucked a couple of hundred dollar bills. Hesitating a moment, she took another hundred just to be sure, and headed for the mall entrance.

The first store she came across was Victoria's Secret, the underwear chain that used in their ads, the eight-foot-tall models that couldn't have weighed over sixty pounds. Plum had never shopped there. Would they even stock something her size? With a shrug she decided she'd never know if she didn't look.

While she flipped through a rack of colorful bras, a gray-haired older woman in a linen dress, whose name-tag identified as her as Caroline, insisted on helping her. Before she knew it, Caroline had Plum in a fitting room, stripped down to her dingy work undies, feeling more than a little self-conscious, especially when she remembered that Claire was actually built like a Victoria's Secret model.

"What a darling little figure you have," Caroline said. Plum's skeptical shrug must have adequately conveyed that she regarded that as bull-pucky. "Oh, my dear, you're what they used to call a pocket Venus."

Nobody had ever called Plum that.

"Let's see," the sales woman continued. "34C…no 32C, right? And size five panties?"

As Plum tried things on, adding to her purchase stack, Caroline came and went and always said something nice about Plum's body.

"I always thought I was…you know, too rounded." Plum had always thought Noah believed that, even if he never said it.

"Oh, no. You have a perfect hourglass figure."

But men don't want hourglasses, they want ironing boards. And grapefruits.

In addition to bras and underpants, Plum decided she also needed a robe and slippers, as well as a sexy nightgown. Pointlessly sexy, of course. But she found herself enjoying this. It had been too long since she'd treated herself.

In one of her visits to Plum's fitting room, Caroline said, "What's wrong with me. I didn't notice you were engaged."

Plum instantly felt stricken. When the sales woman gestured toward the engagement ring she wore on her left hand, Plum realized she'd grown so accustomed to the four-carat, emerald cut diamond, it never occurred to her to take it off. Now she felt like a fraud. Had Noah stopped making payments on that, too? Would it be foreclosed by some brute, who'd yank it off her finger?

"He—" she started. She couldn't tell this encouraging stranger her fiancé had dumped her for a bitchy ironing board. Instead, she continued with, "...died. He died." *Where did that come from?*

"He died? I'm sorry." After a moment, Caroline asked, "Then why...?"

Plum sputtered helplessly.

"Oh, I understand. You're buying for yourself the things you would have wanted for him in your trousseau. How utterly romantic."

Considering how much fun Plum had been having only moments earlier, her enjoyment vanished in a flash. She changed back into her cook's things and went to the counter to pay, unsure now whether she'd actually wear any of them. She'd racked up a heftier bill than she had ever before produced from buying underwear, but she found that she could feel nothing about it. Neither joy, nor guilt.

"My dear, you will find love again. You're too beautiful a girl not to."

Ol' Caroline must have been looking at someone else.

"I know how much you're hurting now, but take it from a much older widow—in time this will pass. You will feel whole again."

Really? When? Because right now, Plum felt like roadkill.

CHAPTER SEVEN

The next day brought a sliver more hope. The prior night, after buying out the underwear store, Plum drove around on surface streets until she found a supermarket. She filled her cart with enough toiletries for a month, while trying to ignore the clenched fist her stomach seemed to form when she thought about having to go back in mere days and pick up a life in shreds.

A yawn in the toothpaste aisle told Plum that she felt more tired than she knew. She'd have to stop for the night—she couldn't make it all the way to Arizona in one stretch. That meant she should think about dinner, too. For a chef, she'd developed some awful eating habits lately; all of her meals seemed to come out of the chips aisle. She couldn't even remember the last time she'd cooked for herself. While she couldn't face a restaurant tonight, not after what happened to her when she'd shown up to work in one earlier today, she did consider buying something substantial at the market's deli counter. In the end, she bought a big enough bag of Cheetos to feed a family of four for a year, a cold bottle of wine, and a corkscrew.

Remembering the glass of Jack she'd left on the den coffee table, she decided once again that if ever there was a night to get hammered, this was it.

She almost fell asleep watching the checker sweep her products past the scanner, though she snapped awake when the checker spoke to her.

The big girl with the short Dutch boy haircut, said in an unexpectedly Southern accent, "You surely did need lots of toiletries. I hope we still have some left on the shelves for other folks." She grinned to remove any sting from the remark.

Plum supposed she had picked up a lot. Toothpaste and mouthwash, of course, along with a toothbrush, and a hairbrush, not to mention deodorant, moisturizer, and hand lotion. And, of course, she had to get shampoo and conditioner, in case she didn't like the shampoo the hotel provided wherever she might spend the coming days. Plum rarely wore makeup, though now, since she'd be getting gussied up in Crystal's things, she figured buying some makeup was also in order. Since she wasn't too sure what she'd need, she bought lots. She might have gone overboard.

Plum shrugged. "Just ran out of everything at the same time." If by "running out" she meant "left behind" in her effort to put other people's naked bodies out of sight.

"Who-ee. Look at the size of this bag of Cheetos," the cashier went on. "Your kids must really love these things."

Another unexpected remark sailed out of Plum's mouth, as it had when she told the undies saleswoman that her fiancé was dead. "Those little devils. I make them stretch it out over a month." She'd probably eat the whole thing tonight.

Apart from agreeing to Dylan's little charade, Plum had never taken to lying. Some of Crystal's boyfriends had been pretty loose with the truth. She'd always hated that you could never trust anything they said. She'd just relearned the same lesson from Noah. And yet, here she was dropping untruths to strangers she met along the way, and enjoying it. It was like a game. When had she ceased to be a girl who would find fun in this silly role-playing? Maybe when she started trying to be what everyone else wanted her to be; mostly, what Noah wanted her to be. Plum felt as if these silly fibs were nothing more than shedding the woman she was, and trying on new possibilities for the one she could become, now that she wasn't someone's out-of-step ball-and-chain.

Plum made the bagger put her purchases into a paper, not plastic, bag because a plastic bag really doesn't rise to the level of luggage. A national chain motel, not far from the supermarket, presented the ideal place to begin the drunk she intended to tie on tonight.

To her surprise, though, she didn't jump into the hooch right away. She turned her cell phone on briefly. Twenty-two messages from Noah. At this point, how much did they have to say to each other? Not enough to fill twenty-two messages. She shut the phone off again. When a wave of paranoia swept through her, even though

Noah wasn't particularly tech-savvy, she pulled out the battery. He wouldn't know how to trace her, but he might know someone who could. She wasn't taking any chances.

She brought into her motel room the satchel she'd snatched, and finally counted the moolah. Adding in what she'd spent and guessing at what she'd probably given Roy, she came up to around forty thousand. Forty! Noah sure had become a compulsive saver. And speaking of savings, she had doubled hers. She found, though, that she felt no sense of avarice about it. No triumph, either. Victory seemed impossible after Noah and Claire used her heart as a trampoline. All the money gave her was a bit of freedom. And that was exactly what she needed now.

Since she worked long nights at the restaurant, Plum wasn't used to watching much TV. Deciding that would make this outing more fun, she channel surfed for a while. Then because she decided she deserved even more fun, she lugged in some of Crystal's clothing, to play dress up while watching the tube.

She didn't actually break into the wine and Cheetos until later, after she'd picked out an outfit for tomorrow. By then she felt she looked good enough in some of Crystal's garments not to need to get drunk, after all. She only washed down a few handfuls of cheese curls with one glass of Chardonnay.

Reminding herself that, for the next few days at least, she didn't have to do anything she didn't want to, she surprised herself by sleeping better than she had in ages.

*　*　*

Now, she had passed from California into Arizona, and was well on her way to Applewood. Sometime back the sunlight had changed, taking on a clearer, more golden quality. Quite a change for Plum, who was used to the brownish smog of the LA Basin and the misty air of the California coast. It felt considerably drier, too. Accustomed to the feel of the higher humidity of her seaside home, Plum didn't normally like arid air. On the rare occasion when the Santa Ana winds swept the humidity away from Santa Monica, she'd always complained about the drying out of her skin and lips. But here, today, the dryness didn't merely wick away the moisture she was used to, it felt as if it also carried off the burdens that weighed her down, making her feel lighter and more hopeful.

After taking a quick glance at the map beside her on the passenger seat, Plum made the choice to bypass Phoenix, figuring she didn't need to drive through another city. What she needed more than anything was to leave everything familiar behind her.

Besides, the two-lane blacktop she took instead offered much more in the way of diversions than the relentless Interstate that brought her there.

"New Dead Things," one rural store's sign declared. She didn't bother to stop, since a bug-eyed stuffed raccoon in the window told her what she'd find inside. The sign sure gave her a laugh, though. "Warm Beer & Lousy Food," a restaurant's sign proclaimed. That tickled Plum, too, although she valued good eats too much to risk discovering that restaurant's highest appeal was truth in advertising.

The road climbed steadily. The higher altitude gave Plum a breathless quality. That strangely translated into anticipation in her mind. The high desert terrain, with its hillsides filled with prickly pear cactus and broad expanses of mesquite and juniper, wasn't quite as breathtaking as the waves crashing along California's coast. Still, its quiet natural beauty did stir her senses. And one aspect of this landscape did rival the ocean's stretch all the way to the horizon. The sense of space. She had rarely seen a sky as blue, or so vast. It stretched as far as the ocean did at the horizon, and looked even clearer.

Apple trees popped up here and there, too, sometimes whole fields of unworked, overgrown orchards, with their wild, twisting trunks and trees heavy with fruit. Their scent filled the dry air.

Plum pulled into a gas station for a fill-up. When she was younger, Plum harbored a secret fantasy that she called, "living life on the fly," that of escaping her regular life and setting up anew wherever she happened to run out of gas. Of course, with the Jeep's meager gas mileage, there was no question of that—it would have meant setting up shop on a neighboring street, not a different locale. She hadn't bought the old road warrior because it promised good gas economy, but for its distinctive profile. Noah had always complained that if his coworkers saw it, they'd think some gardener had parked in their driveway. Plum loved its individualistic statement. Its lines were its own, not the rounded curves of every car on the road, indistinguishable from every other.

A dented blue pickup screeched to a stop on the other side of the pump island. Wearing skintight jeans and a form-fitting white T-shirt, a twenty-something man stepped from the truck. Even Plum could see that a fine ass filled those jeans and a strongly muscled chest stretched the shirt. Too bad her own motor had stopped dead the instant she took in the sight of Claire riding Noah.

A rifle hung from a gun rack in the pickup's rear window.

Toto, we're not in La La Land anymore.

The guy offered her a slow sexy grin across the gas station island. Plum didn't get hit-on that often. Unlike Noah, obviously, she didn't invite it. Had she changed her signal somehow?

A moment later, she realized she sure had. She wore some of Crystal's designs today. Her off-white pants were snug, ending right above her ankles. And there were cutouts going down the outsides of both legs, like dotted lines drawn in flesh. Topping the pants was a forties style fitted blouse in cherry, with a deep halter neckline. By combining that neckline with one of her new Victoria's Secret bras, her full breasts were well displayed. No wonder the redneck Lothario had noticed.

He pulled a crumpled pack of cigarettes from his T-shirt pocket and lit up, allowing the butt to dangle from his full lips.

Who smokes while pumping gas? Was Arizona another state or another planet? Plum found that either would work equally well. She simply didn't care.

While she filled her thirsty Jeep, she ignored the guy's come-on, and just asked him how close she was to Applewood. But the altitude, which was much higher than the sea level she was used to, made her voice sound breathless. He probably thought he was making her hot.

Taking the cigarette into sturdy, nicotine-stained fingers, the poor man's James Dean gave her a wicked squint. "Why, darlin', you're there. Applewood's a big, ol' sprawl of a place."

While the words themselves might have been those sprouted by a lazy tour guide, the underlying sentiment radiated pure sex.

Man, are you barfing up the wrong tree. Though…it might serve Noah right if, instead of deciding it was lights-out for her vagina, she found someone else to fill it…though only if he cared. All those messages said he cared about something, though probably not her. More likely it was that she'd swiped his money. Or he worried she'd tell the bank he'd forged her signature on the second mortgage he'd taken out on their house.

The Arizona hottie was still talking. "You probably mean Old Town. All the tourists do." With a toss of his head that threw a shock of blue-black hair over his forehead in an appealing forelock, he said in a drawling Southwestern twang, "You'll find it on the far side of town. Applewood grew from the East side."

Plum nodded her thanks, leaving the smoking bad boy, with his muscled arms crossed over his chest, leaning against his pickup's battered fender in a decidedly calculated, determinedly casual pose. Probably waiting for a more agreeable honey to take the bait.

As for Plum, she was *there* at last. At the pointless destination she'd chosen from a dot on the map and a return address scribbled on loads of empty envelopes.

What did it matter? It was a diversion, nothing more. Tracing Crystal's connection to that West Pony Lane address might give her something to do, though tracking down the land in question in Budget-Mart's obsessive manifest destiny would be like picking a scab. After all, it was Budget-Mart that brought Noah and Claire together, allowing them to shit-can Plum's life.

It wasn't as if this excursion would change her life or anything.

CHAPTER EIGHT

Old Town Applewood absolutely charmed Plum. It looked like a town out of the Old West, complete with wooden sidewalks and hitching posts for horses. One of the local bars even featured a swinging door, like a Western saloon. Though more cars than buggies parked beside those hitching rails, there were several horses tied to one, part of a horseback guided tour. And horse-drawn buggies did carry tourists from one end of Old Town to the other, stopping at spots along the way.

While many of the locals and all of the tourists were certainly in modern dress, some of the shopkeepers had donned Western wear. Despite the contemporary touches, Plum felt as if she'd been transported to another time. With the drifting away of the modern world, it seemed as if her troubles had been carried off, too.

The fresh apple smell wasn't as strong here as it had been outside of town, especially with the pungent odor of horses offsetting it. But a couple of times, when she passed a café or bakery, the scents of apples and cinnamon made her feel oddly comforted.

Plum wandered through the shops. The altitude and thin air winded her if she moved too fast, but some leisurely shopping was what she needed anyway. Plum tried to remember when she'd last done something like this, apart from the undies and toiletries shopping. It was usually only a matter of squeezing in an overdue errand on the way to something else. Why hadn't she realized that before she could take care of someone else, she had to first take care of herself?

Despite the carefully calculated Western mystique, Plum noticed that strange posters—contemporary, commercially printed ones— hung in most of the store windows. "No!" some read, while others said, "Hell, no!" Every now and then Plum spotted a hand-drawn, "Yes," and there were even a few places without any signs, though those were rare. She wondered what they meant.

The stores were mostly geared to the tourist trade, with loads of antique and gift shops, and visitor tchotchke stores. Clothing shops, too. Most of those offered contemporary clothing, though a few were more geared to cowboy wear.

In one of the contemporary women's wear shops, the owner said, "Cute outfit. Where did you get it?"

Plum was still wearing Crystal's sexy duds, the one the redneck hottie had reacted so strongly to at the gas station outside of town. As part of her determination to continue reinventing herself, Plum made up a shop in one of the desert towns she'd driven through along the way, rather than revisiting a mother who had lapsed into a coma.

Plum wandered through some of the shops selling Western wear. Though Western clothing was offered everywhere these days, Plum had never really thought about dressing that way. Now that she glanced at a row of women's cowboy boots in an unexpected array of colors, and she remembered one of Crystal's outfits packed into the back of the Jeep that would be perfect for a particular pair of those boots. She considered coming back for them before she left town.

Some of the shops there even addressed everyday needs, more geared to the locals than tourists, such as an above average cheese shop, an olive oil vendor, and a vitamin store.

Vitamins! Given how erratically Plum ate and all the demands on her, supplements were a must. Another thing she flew out of the house without giving a thought to. She had no idea how hard living life on the fly would be—so much to consider. She might have checked the vitamin shelves when she raided that supermarket's toiletries department, though Plum never gave it a thought. Besides, she saw when she drew closer to the large store, plastered with several "Hell, no!" signs on the front windows, these were Rite-Health supplements, her favorites; she always looked for those at her local health food stores. She had no idea that Rite-Health had any storefront operations.

When she opened the door, a chime played a couple of cheerful notes, and a sign invited her to use one of a mismatched pile of baskets for her shopping. Plum loved the quirkiness of the unmatched baskets.

While she browsed, occasionally popping vitamin bottles into the spacious basket she chose, an elderly man came through a door at the rear of the store and sat on a stool behind the counter. Plum absently glanced his direction at the same moment he looked her way, and she found her gaze fixed there longer than a casual greeting with a stranger usually did. A fan of wrinkles on his aging face and a sense of peace that seemed to flow from his warm blue eyes reached out to her. He was a small, wiry man, maybe sixty-something, who radiated a bristling energy even while in repose. He wore a black cowboy hat, with a strip of silver studs around the band. A bolo tie dangled from his shirt collar. Though Western wear seemed to be the norm for lots of shopkeepers in the area, his seemed less affected, as if that was what he'd wear even if he didn't work in this Western town.

Plum couldn't say why, but she felt an instant connection to this stranger.

When she drew close to the counter, the older man asked, "Are you just visiting our little town, or relocating here?"

Relocating? What a strange idea. Plum had never lived outside of Southern California. Never even considered living anywhere else. "Only a short getaway," she said at last.

"Even short getaways are good for the soul."

That's what she felt—as if being somewhere else, with no burdens and responsibilities, not to mention no cheating lover—was good for her soul.

While she transferred her purchases from the basket to the counter, she said, "I didn't know Rite-Health had actual stores."

"Only one," the man with the cheerfully comfortable face said. "Our manufacturing plant is out back. We ship all over the world from here."

Plum asked if he was the owner.

With a courtly bow he said, "For my sins," though he said it with quiet pride.

She told him how much she trusted his products. "I always buy your supplements back home."

"And where is home? Somewhere closer to sea level, I'd say. You sound winded here."

For once, she didn't even consider fibbing. "Santa Monica, California."

"Ah, that would be Crowley's and Better Health. Good stores. Good customers."

After bagging her purchases, the old man took a moment to study her. Then, as if he also felt a kindred connection, as Plum did, he abruptly thrust out his hand. "Jake Gold."

Plum shook his hand. "Plum Tardy."

"Plum Tardy? What a delightfully unusual name you have, my girl."

With a sigh, Plum said, "Tell me about it. My parents didn't give a thought to how much schoolyard fun that would generate."

"Oh, children don't get originality. It's something you have to grow into."

Plum wasn't sure if she'd ever grow *out* of it.

She caught sight of some of the "No!" signs that also hung inside the store, and she asked about them.

Jake's happily comfortable face suddenly stiffened. "That's part of a campaign the merchants and residents are mounting against the town fathers' social engineering. We're trying to keep them from putting our businesses and the character of this town six feet under."

Plum gave her head a tiny shake to show she didn't understand.

"They want to bring a Budget-Mart here."

Clearly, it wasn't going to be such a cakewalk for Noah and Claire. The idea thrilled Plum.

An instant later, she realized what a fool she'd been. She had fled straight to the heart of the Budget-Mart war, after all. She'd even followed one of Noah's maps to do it. How long would it be before she came face to face with the louse himself, or his grapefruit squeeze? What had she been thinking? Why, in the course of her long drive, had that never occurred to her?

Should she leave now? This time truly not stopping until she ran out of gas?

CHAPTER NINE

In the end, Plum decided against fleeing. Odds were she wouldn't run into Noah here, after all. He was working on deals in multiple states. At the time she caught him and Claire *in flagrante*, he hadn't had any travel plans for the current week at all.

Besides, he wasn't going to see her, if she saw him first.

Still, she was going to have to deal with him soon. When she returned to California, she'd have to begin picking up the pieces of her life, not to mention having to deal with the issue of his forging of her name on those loan papers. She'd worked too hard to maintain a good credit rating to allow Noah to take that away from her, too.

For now, though, she was here, where this short getaway was giving her soul a lift, as Jake had said. She wouldn't give that up, either.

Anyway, she had a better offer—better than fleeing, that is. Before she left Rite-Health, Jake unexpectedly asked, "Plum, would you allow an old man to buy you lunch?"

Since more time spent with him promised to keep her spirits high, she quickly agreed.

"Great. What kind of food do you like?" he asked.

Does anywhere serve Cheetos? As a chef, it embarrassed her that her preferences didn't automatically spring to mind. She managed to say she liked everything.

Jake went on to describe some of his favorite lunch spots, and the food they served: authentic Mexican, great salads, burgers. Even an above-average Thai restaurant.

After a moment, Plum had a another thought. "Are any of them near 428 West Pony Lane?"

Jake's friendly eyes narrowed in suspicion. "That's pretty specific. You know someone there?"

Plum kept her answer as truthful as she could. "My mom used to know someone, but it was a long time ago." Well, the communication had started long ago; the postmarks on those envelopes actually covered decades.

Jake seemed to buy it. The suspicion faded anyway. "As a matter of fact, one of those places I told you about couldn't get any closer."

After he found an employee in his manufacturing plant behind the store to spell him, they walked a couple of blocks and around a corner to a part of Old Town she hadn't explored yet. Jake stopped before a café called Cup o' Joe, and held the door for her. Plum noticed in passing that this was one of the few establishments without a "No!" sign. In fact, its hand-drawn poster read quite emphatically, "Yes, dammit!" Another small sign announced the business to be for sale.

Despite a name that seemed to describe it as a coffee house, the bustling little restaurant served lots more than just "Joe." On the colorfully painted offerings sign, hanging on the wall above a glass bakery case, Plum saw an engaging menu. There were different breakfast items and baked goods for the morning, and, along with the usual sandwiches, burgers, and salads for lunch, were some appealing comfort food items.

Needing all the comfort she could get, Plum chose macaroni-and-cheese for her lunch. Possibly wanting a bit of comfort himself, Jake ordered a cup of tomato soup and a grilled cheese sandwich. They took the last empty table in a corner of the busy café.

"You surprised me, Jake," Plum said once they were seated. "I thought...you know, with you owning a vitamin store...I figured you'd have ordered something super healthy. Maybe vegan."

"I am a big believer in getting the nutrients we need, of course. The machine needs fuel. But I'm not a proponent of denial. I lived like that for too long. Now I understand that when it comes to feeling bad, it's not what you eat that matters, it's what's eating you."

Whoa! Jake's homespun philosophy hit Plum hard. She thought about how indifferent she had become to both cooking and her meals. She didn't have to wonder how long it had been that something had been eating her. She knew too well. No matter how many times she slammed the door shut on that memory, something kept opening it again.

"Jake, give me your story. Were you born here in Applewood?"

Shaking his head no, he said, "As far away from here as you can imagine, in both miles and attitude." He removed his cowboy hat and rested it on the extra chair at their table. "I came from New York, born to parents who were poor immigrants from Eastern Europe. Growing up, all I thought about was achieving success. The trouble was I didn't know that you could define success in lots of ways. My only focus was in terms of money."

He went on to describe his climb through the ranks of a cutthroat, international corporation, with his aim always on the CEO spot.

"I worked eighty, a hundred hours a week, never taking anything for myself. Never had a wife or family. Even my apartment wasn't anything special. I banked most of what I made. The money meant nothing to me, apart from using it to measure how far I'd come, and how far I still had to go."

A harried waitress, with a sweaty face and hair escaping from her messy bun, rushed over to their table, plopping down coffee mugs hard enough to splash some of the coffee onto the table. She dashed off without a word.

"I was a vegan then, eating what I believed to be healthy, though really just engaging in more self-denial," Jake went on. "Our CEO was rumored to be retiring, and I thought that was my chance to achieve what had always been my goal. Then I had a massive coronary and the doctor ordered me to take six weeks off from work. My spirits went into a downward spiral. I thought for sure that the board would appoint someone else, that this heart attack had put me out of the running for the only thing I'd ever wanted. With the walls of my apartment closing in on me, I started driving across the country, until I ended up here."

Though Jake seemed engaged in his story, Plum noticed as he spoke, his gaze kept drifting to the café's front door, as if he expected someone to come through it. Or maybe hoped.

"After that heart attack, I did lots of soul searching. I honestly don't think I cared if I lived or died. Here in Applewood I met lots of people who weren't successful by the standards I'd always held, though they felt a level of satisfaction I never had." He shrugged. "At the end of my forced vacation, I returned to work." He choked out a little laugh. "Apparently, during those weeks without me, the board realized how valuable I was, and when the CEO announced his retirement, they offered the job to me. Instead of feeling elated, I felt trapped. To their surprise and mine, I turned the job down."

"And you returned here?" Successful men like Jake had always intimidated Plum. Sunni's wealthy lawyer father did, and it went on from there. Yet even if Jake was the same kind of guy, albeit in radically different duds, Plum didn't feel the least bit uncomfortable. If anything, she felt as if they were best friends, who simply hadn't met until now.

"I did. My storefront and the plant were for sale, and I snatched them up on the spot. I didn't even know what I intended to do here, but I had learned something about supplements thanks to my heart attack. I saw what a perfect fit it was for me. According to my old standards, I've actually been quite successful." He shrugged. "What can I say? I must have the Midas touch. Now, I'm truly a success in more important ways. I dress the way I want, instead of adhering to some corporate code. I've made great friends, instead of merely having co-workers who'd cheerfully slit my throat before I slit theirs. I have a home I love and lots of interests." That stern look came over his face again. "And I have no intention of letting some corporate monolith take it away from me or anyone I care about."

At the sound of the door opening, Jake looked that way again.

"A woked pot never boils, Jake," Plum said with sage resonance. "You keep glancing at the door. Are you waiting for someone to come through it?"

Jake burst out laughing. "Oh, Plum, how funny you are. Surely that's *watched* pot."

"Really?" That didn't sound right.

"It's not that I don't love your company, my dear. I haven't enjoyed meeting someone as much as I've liked getting to know you in some time. It's that...I'm watching for a friend... Someone I think you'd enjoy meeting." He paused. "Especially given your Pony Lane connection."

So, he hadn't forgotten that. "My mother's connection." This time she kept it totally honest. She told him about Crystal's medical condition. "We're losing her. I need to hold on however I can... Anyhow, I found a letter she'd written to someone at that address. Just a newsy thing, but it's not like I can ask her about it now."

Jake studied her thoughtfully. Plum would have given anything to know what he was thinking.

A burly teenaged kid brought out their lunches, plopping the plates down heavily on the table. He left without ever acknowledging that those dishes were placed before people. Plum thought someone should tell the café's eager-to-sell owner something about service. Something about cooking, too, she discovered when she took her first bite. Plum's mac-and-cheese was good enough, but it lacked the creative wow-factor. Yet, who was Plum to talk? Her own creative spark had vanished months ago.

"Well, Plum, I've told you my story. What about yours? Tell me why a girl as pretty as you is traveling alone."

A red flag shot up for Plum. She hadn't considered this lunch to be a come-on. For one thing, she always gauged older men in terms of their dad-potential, not date-potential. She'd learned the hard way that they didn't necessarily see themselves in that role, which invariably brought an icky factor into the relationship. "Uh...Jake, I *just* got out of a relationship. I mean as nice—"

He held both hands out before him in the stop position. "Whoa, honey. I'm old enough to be your father. I assure you I don't rob the cradle. Besides, my heart belongs to another."

She liked Jake's unusual combination of Western ease and formal courtliness. "Does hers belong to you?"

He sighed. "If she even recognizes my feelings, then her portrayal of denial is nothing short of Oscar-worthy."

Whoever she was, Plum figured she had to be the one *not* coming through the Cup o' Joe door. She was one foolish woman, too. Plum pinched together her lips in sympathy.

Jake shrugged. "What can I say? Unlucky in love. Always have been."

Plum knew for sure that expression was *unlusty* in love, but she was too polite to correct him. She silently thanked Crystal for teaching her the way to quote proverbs.

He took a bite of his sandwich and chewed slowly. "As I said, I have a great life. More than I ever imagined I could have. But it would be better if I had someone to share it. I'm tired of living alone."

Plum offered him a compassionate smile. Still, she knew too well that you could live with someone else and still be alone.

"Let's get back to you," Jake said. "Tell me your tale."

"To give you the quickie version...I guess you'd have to say he done me wrong."

"Then he's a fool." Jake slapped his hand down hard enough on the table that he attracted the attention of diners at other tables, who briefly glanced their way. "If he doesn't appreciate you, he doesn't deserve you. You're better off without him."

Plum gave off a half-hearted shrug. "Maybe...there was something he needed that...I should have given him." Why was she still willing to cut Noah a break? She'd always believed he was out of her league, yet surely his cheating ways should have lowered the pedestal she had put him on.

"What about you? Was he there for you?"

A hole deep in her heart admitted he wasn't. Not when she needed him most.

"Plum, take it from an old man who didn't claim enough from life for too long. We all deserve a certain amount of space in the sun. Too many people live too small. That's wrong. You have to live bold, live big, taking everything life wants for us."

Living big. The idea resonated within her. She knew that living small was exactly what she did. Small? Hell, living shrunken was more like it. She knew that was exactly what she needed to turn her life around.

She wished she knew how.

CHAPTER TEN

Some problem in his plant took Jake back to his business, though he promised to rejoin Plum as soon as he could. With a sparkle in his eyes, he'd told her that when he returned he'd have a surprise for her.

Since they had spent so much time chatting, most of the lunch crowd had left. The harried waitress who'd served them proved to be Bonnie, the owner. With the lunch rush over, Bonnie came out from the kitchen and made herself an espresso at the machine behind the bakery counter. While Bonnie sipped her drink, Plum moved from the table to a stool at the counter and asked for a refill of her own black coffee.

Bonnie looked even messier now, with hardly any hair stuck in her bun. But who was Plum to criticize anyone else's appearance? She wondered how she'd looked when she asked that snooty Gordon to allow her to take over a new rendition of Dylan's on Montana. Why hadn't it occurred to her that if you look like a schmo, nobody is going to take you for anything else?

When did I simply stop trying?

"Nice place you have here," Plum said after introducing herself.

Plum did briefly consider how she might politely pass on some tips on how Bonnie could improve her service, or bring more flair to her cooking. Mac-and-cheese was always better with the addition of unexpected ingredients, she believed—Plum's own favorites were leeks and bacon or pancetta. Yet maybe she had no right offering advice to anyone. It wasn't as if she was holding her own life together.

Instead of blasting Bonnie with unsolicited opinions, she allowed herself to wander lost in thought again. Plum wondered why she hadn't ever considered opening a café like this, which would surely have required a smaller investment, instead of chasing the impossible dream of a frou-frou dinner house. Was it simply because Noah wouldn't have respected a café this humble?

Oh, Plum, how much did you give up for him?

Having told Jake the truth about herself, she kept the honesty-bit going with Bonnie. "I cook for a living in California."

"Want a job?" Bonnie said too fast. After a sick laugh, she added, "Forget that. I can't afford you. Hey, if you decide you miss cooking while you're here, you can spell me anytime. Me and my kids could use a day off."

Fat chance. This trip was all about giving Plum some rest. "You don't even know me. I could destroy your reputation and wipe you out."

Bonnie blew out a slow breath, like a smoker exhaling. "Yeah, that'd be a real change. If anyone ever suggests you go into business for yourself because you'd love being your own boss—shoot him."

"A rolling stone gathers no boss." Plum had learned that the hard way. Even if Plum had lost her love of cooking, and Bonnie was skirting by financially, Plum knew she still envied what Bonnie had built here.

Plum pointed at the "Yes, dammit!" sign in the window, and asked about it.

"That's yes to the Budget-Mart store, of course." Bonnie's face instantly took on high color and became more animated than Plum had seen her before now. "Don't give me Jake's argument. 'When Budget-Mart comes in, within a year, most of the local independent stores have to close. Within two years, the only jobs that exist are for low wages,'" Bonnie said in a snide imitation of Jake's New York accent. "I've heard it all too many times."

"You don't believe it's true?"

Bonnie shrugged. "I don't see how it can be. Budget-Mart stores draw people from neighboring towns, right? More shoppers?"

"But—"

"Look, it's a chance, all right. Which is more than I have now."

Plum didn't know what to say. She just nodded and left too big a tip for her coffee refill. Jake had already paid for lunch.

Since her conversation with Bonnie had wound down, Plum rose with her mug of coffee and meandered about, studying some of the Southwestern furnishings Bonnie had repurposed into restaurant fixtures. A rustic hutch held a selection of Cup o' Joe-labeled T-shirts and mugs.

When she paused near the front door, Plum noticed the storefront street address posted on the doorframe. "Bonnie, wait. This store's street number is 428-A. Is that 428 Pony Lane? West Pony?"

Bonnie nodded, making all her messy hair bounce amusingly.

That they were at the Pony Lane address Plum had asked about must have been Jake's surprise. Plum returned to the counter. "How long have you rented this space?"

"Eighteen glorious months," Bonnie spat with venomous sarcasm.

O-kay. "Then you wouldn't know who rented in…" What year should she give?

Bonnie shrugged.

Hmmm…momentarily stymied. Plum had always figured the correspondence involved some guy, although Crystal never stayed interested in any of them for long. And, usually, the less Plum knew about them, the better. But the letter Plum had found about the novel with the baby compounded the mystery. Crystal had never even joined a book club. Would she really have written endlessly about novels? If only Plum could have found other letters either from or to the mystery letter writer.

"But the landlady should know, right?" Bonnie said after a pause. "You'll find her next door at 428-B West Pony. Her name's Flo Gallagher."

Sure, the landlady would have to know. Plum decided she wouldn't wait for Jake after all, and just asked Bonnie to send him next door when he came back for her.

Scoping out the identity of Crystal's secret correspondent took on the feel of a treasure hunt. It gave this jaunt a more positive purpose than simply staying away until she could handle Noah's pity. Of course, it wasn't as if unearthing Crystal's secrets would matter at this point in her life.

CHAPTER ELEVEN

Ooh! 428-B was a *bookstore*. Did that mean that Crystal and her mystery pen-pal really did just discuss books? Plum found that disappointing. *No treasure there.*

Still, discovering a bookstore was always good news. Even if Plum hadn't had time to read since this trip began, she was going into book withdrawal—her fingertips itched with the need to turn pages. It was her own fault that she found herself without a book. A really devoted reader keeps a contingency book in her purse or car. It simply hadn't occurred to Plum that she'd need one in case her fiancé cheated on her with a coworker.

Even if she was Jonesing for a good book, Plum kept her expectations low. While she found the construction of the building, with its odd-sized river rocks, quite appealing, the outside of the bookstore itself wasn't as inviting as most of its neighbors. Painted on one of the two front windows, in a simple font whose letters were peeling, were the words, "High Desert Books." The most interesting thing about the place might be that it was one of the only stores lacking either a "Yes" or "No" sign. Didn't this business owner care? Budget-Marts do sell books, as long as you don't need an imaginative selection. If Budget-Mart got its way, this store could be one of the first to go.

On the second window, a tattered sheet of paper, held in place by yellowed strips of tape, indicated that this business was also for sale. The two shops of 428 West Pony Lane were both for sale? Was this building's mojo so bad that everyone wanted out?

Plum stepped through the door. After a quick glance, she determined that High Desert Books sold both new and used books. Plum's favorite kind of bookstore. As eclectic as her reading tastes were, she couldn't always find what she wanted in stores devoted to one type or the other.

Too bad the inside of this bookstore was as haphazardly arranged as the outside was unappealing. With its floor-to-ceiling shelves, constructed in bare pine, and the mismatched collection of chairs and display tables, it could have been attractively set up in a shabby-chic style. Instead, empty tables, where nobody had bothered to make new displays after the old ones had been dismantled, were coated in dust. The floor space was badly used as well, with shelving and merchandise crammed together, when there was plenty of space to spread things out.

Plum didn't see any clerk present when she slipped between two towering bookshelves. There was a customer there: an older woman, most likely in her seventies. She wore one of those stodgy knit suits favored by the moneyed dowagers on LA's chic westside. They probably cost thousands, though Plum always thought those dreary suits should have been reserved strictly for wearing in coffins. The older woman was attractive, though, with large brown eyes ringed by thick, dark lashes, and while some hairdresser had tried to tame her red-brown hair into the helmet-head look the knit suit crowd preferred, her natural waves kept breaking through in irrepressible curls.

The dowager turned toward a doorway on the back wall and cleared her throat. "Florence, thank you for agreeing to order those titles for me," she called in that direction, in a diffident tone that seemed at odds with her rigid bearing.

Sunni had always been great at reading people. That was a legacy from their childhood. Given her need to be prepared, she'd learned to be alert to when one of Crystal's men or her friends was about to toss them out. Today, that ability to read nuances was what made Sunni such a killer lawyer; she always knew when the other side was bluffing. Plum didn't read those signs nearly as well—just look at how Noah and Dylan had fooled her. Now, even Plum grasped that this was a woman used to dressing down service people for microscopic infractions. Yet here she was struggling to curry favor, something Plum would have bet anything that she wasn't used to doing.

"So…you'll call me when the books come in?" the older woman

asked.

"Don't I always, Hannah?" someone in the backroom barked.

"No, dear—you don't," Hannah said, with a trace of annoyance finally creeping into her otherwise obsequious tone. "Not that I mind stopping by here."

Liar, liar, cans on fire. This Hannah minded dreadfully, Plum felt sure. Still, for whatever reason, she didn't feel entitled to say that. The voice calling from the rear of the store just grunted. Plum grinned to herself, finding fun in watching this little theater production.

Despite the indifference of the bookstore's setup, the selection proved to be exceptional. Plum immediately found several old favorites that she used to own before Crystal made off with them. They all represented the kind of comfort re-reads that she needed right now.

Plum carried her selections toward the soiled raw wooden counter, situated midway along the far wall, where Hannah stood. Just as she approached it, the older women turned away, causing them to block each other's path.

After a bit of shuffling, Hannah asked, "Do I know you? You look familiar."

"I don't see how. I'm only passing through town."

The older woman nodded sadly. "You look a little like…someone I used to know."

Plum smiled, but shrugged to show she didn't know what else to say.

The grunter from backroom came forward. Only she, too, stopped in her tracks and stared at Hannah and Plum. She was also attractive, despite being a little on the plump side, though in a far more individualistic way than Hannah. Probably no more than her early fifties, her short brown hair looked like she cut it in hunks with a nail clipper.

Yet the quirky toss of the choppy layers worked. Her clothes, however, looked as if she fished them out of a Dumpster behind a thrift shop—the stuff even they wouldn't try to sell. Her well-washed jeans were at least two sizes too big for her, and her sweatshirt's sleeve was torn. Not an artful tear of the sort that brought big prices in trendy shops, but a real ragged slit. And Plum thought *she'd* allowed herself to become too indifferent about what she wore. Compared to this woman, she'd always been a fashion plate.

The newcomer stared at both Plum and Hannah, her rounded cheeks going pale, while red spots burned on her cheekbones, which matched the color of her unadorned rosebud lips.

Plum thought that she had either gotten loads better at reading people, or these two were easy. That the woman from the backroom *really* disliked Hannah radiated off of her.

Jake strode through the door at that point. He, too, paused beside them. With a curt nod, he said, "Hannah," in a voice so cold it could flash-freeze a side of beef.

"Hello, Jake," Hannah said, in a not-much-warmer tone. "I'll wait to hear from you, Florence," she sniffed, as she sailed out the door.

Once Hannah left, Jake's friendliness spiked. "Flo, I'd like you to meet my new friend, Plum Tardy."

From the warmth he directed Flo's way, Plum had no doubts that she was the woman he'd fallen for. Why exactly, she couldn't say, since Flo continued to stare rudely at her without comment. Plum finally offered her own hand for a shake, only to find in return a dead fish in hers. Jake continued on, rattling out a little of what he'd learned of Plum's circumstances, while Flo didn't react. *Jake, you can do better.* Still, Plum, of all people, knew there was no accounting for love.

Even while ringing up Plum's purchases, Flo didn't utter a sound. Though an ornate, old-fashioned cash register sat on the countertop, she processed the sale on a computer that rested in a well below the counter level. Flo remained in silent mode when she bagged Plum's books.

Jake didn't seem to notice; he'd taken a cell phone call from one of his employees, who apparently was still wrestling with whatever problem kept plaguing them. With a wave to both of them, he blew out the door.

After having built up her curiosity about Crystal's letter friend,

Plum now found that Flo's rudeness put her off. What was the point of asking questions if the woman didn't talk? Maybe Plum would find a sneaky way to get the information out of this disagreeable woman later. She decided to bide her time. She muttered a stiff farewell and carried her bag away.

Before she reached the door, Flo stopped her by suddenly asking, "Where are you staying while you're here?"

So she does talk. Plum shrugged. "Don't know. I guess I'll figure something out. I saw a cute B&B here in Old Town. Maybe I'll try there." Should she ask about Crystal's letters now? No, the timing still didn't feel right.

"Booked," Flo said hastily. "Totally booked." She cleared her throat. "Some group…you know."

"O-kay," Plum said, dragging the word out. "Well, I saw some motels out by the highway." It disappointed her, though, to learn that the B&B wasn't an option. Why hadn't they turned on the neon "No Vacancy" sign she'd seen in their window?

"You could stay here." Flo said, shooting the words out like a series of fastballs.

Plum looked down at the hard Mexican tile floor.

"Upstairs, I mean. I have an apartment there. It's not fancy, though it is comfortable. I use it for guests all the time."

This woman had guests? But Plum considered it. This could be a good spot for her. "How much?"

"Oh, no charge. I meant as my guest."

What was with the people in this town? Didn't they ever get burned trusting strangers? This seemed a whole lot more generous than Bonnie's offer to let Plum cook for her. That was, after all, for Bonnie, not Plum. It also seemed uncharacteristically generous for this woman who didn't give off even a whiff of warmth. Still, Plum couldn't find anything objectionable about Flo's offer. Living life on the fly must be all about seizing unexpected opportunities, the kindness of strangers and such. Deep inside, she knew this was another hopscotch move, but she hastily dismissed that thought.

"Sure, I guess that would be okay." She made herself sound more enthusiastic. "Thank you for your hospitality."

Flo responded with a satisfied nod. "I close at six. Come by then, and I'll get you set up."

"Cool beans." Plum burst out laughing at her own remark. "My mom used to say that when I was a kid. I haven't thought of it in years."

A frosty curtain suddenly slid down over the bookseller's features. She turned and went through the doorway to the backroom without another word. After a moment, Flo called, "You can leave now."

What was that about? It confirmed for Plum that this was the wrong time to question Flo about Crystal, but would there ever be a right time? Crystal always said, "Home is where the heartless are," and Plum hoped that wouldn't be true this time.

CHAPTER TWELVE

The apartment proved to be bigger than Plum expected, covering the upper floor over both High Desert Books and Cup o' Joe. Despite Flo's insistence that she frequently housed guests there, it seemed more like a storage unit. Two of its three bedrooms were stuffed floor-to-ceiling with boxes of books. Plum felt quite relieved to find an actual bed in the third.

Flo's protest that it wasn't fancy might have been an understatement. In the kitchen at the top of the stairs, only two of the four burners worked on a white stove whose enamel was so dotted with chips, it looked like a Dalmatian. Even the feeble flames flickering on the working burners seemed ready to give up the ghost. Still, Plum couldn't complain. The gold refrigerator hummed a bit loudly, yet it chilled the bottle of wine she brought in from the Jeep faster than she expected. The mattress in the room where Plum would sleep probably hadn't been new since the Carter administration, yet when she tossed herself onto it, it felt remarkably cushy. There was even a TV. No cable or satellite, but an antennae wrapped in aluminum foil produced surprisingly good reception.

In its understated way, the apartment did feel comfortable. The window in the eat-in kitchen looked out over rooftops, and in the distance, offered a nice view of brush-covered hills. The clip-clopping sound of horses' hooves drifted in from Pony Lane, where buggies toted tourists around Old Town, and made for an appealing background rhythm.

The kitchen fed into a living area that faced Pony Lane. Though its walls were faded, the sunny yellow they'd once been painted gave off more warmth than Flo, making Plum feel unexpectedly welcome. A sofa in worn, flowered chintz, which stretched across the front window, sported a strictly old-lady design. But an attractive Southwestern throw in brilliant earth tones covered most of the fussy chintz.

Plum figured if this room wasn't used often, the throw might be dusty and need a good shaking. Surprisingly, it smelled clean enough to be new. Was it new? The colors looked too crisp to have seen too many washings. Nah, Plum decided; crazy idea. Why would that curt woman provide her with a new throw? An equally perplexing question was why would she have invited Plum to stay at all.

Despite the apartment's quirky limitations, Plum felt good holed up in it. Its funky spirit appealed to her. While stretched out on the couch, she chomped lazily on a couple of Cheetos from her never-ending bag, and washed it down with a sip of the wine she'd poured into a juice glass she found in the kitchen.

More importantly, she felt safe. Even if they did show up, nobody from her old life would think to look for her here. Then she heard a noise downstairs, and she decided she might have been a mite hasty about celebrating that safety.

Plum crept to the top of the stairs, demanding in her voice's deepest register, "Who's there?"

"It's only me," Flo called almost happily from somewhere downstairs. "Sorry to intrude on you, Plum. I got home and realized I forgot something."

Plum inched down the stairs with cautious interest. Flo stood there, in that messy backroom, holding some fat book. A quick look at the book's spine surprised Plum. *She came back for an old high school history book?* Had Flo snatched up the first volume she could find, to lend a lie some credibility? Plum couldn't blame Flo for checking on things. This bookstore was her business, and Plum was a stranger. Why then had she invited a stranger to stay, if it worried her?

"I don't want you to think that I'll be coming back often, but I..." Flo's voice trailed off.

"No problem." Plum started up the stairs, but stopped with a sudden thought, and turned back. "I've been snacking. Would you like to join me for a drink?"

Flo looked stricken at first, as if she found the idea of sharing a drink with Plum about as appealing as brushing her teeth with sewage. To Plum's surprise, she quickly agreed. *What is it with this quixotic woman?*

Flo had changed from her ragged sweatshirt and baggy jeans into a rose-colored velour tracksuit. Some sparkly studs were scattered across the bodice, though, unless they were meant to be unevenly spaced, a few must have fallen off. Was that what Flo considered being dressed up? The rose tone did flatter her complexion. Unless something else had given her a flushed glow.

Plum found a bowl in the kitchen and a glass for Flo. After carrying them to the living room, she poured what was left from the monster bag of Cheetos, and placed the bowl on the ancient maple coffee table in front of the couch.

"You're eating snack food for dinner?" Flo asked. "I should have thought to tell you where you'd find a supermarket."

"Not to worry. I asked Bonnie. I even bought a little actual food there." Well, she bought a couple of frozen dinners, more junk food, and some carrots for the horses that pulled the buggies through Old Town. And dessert. Plum shrugged. "This seemed to hit the spot tonight. I'm planning to have cheesecake for my next course—balanced meals matter to me." Plum grinned. "Want some wine?"

Flo smiled for the first time. Plum found it an unexpectedly lovely feature. Maybe it was her smile that had captured Jake's heart. "Love it. Could you pass the Cheetos?"

* * *

A couple of hours later, with all the cheese curls gone, along with more than a half of the cheesecake, and most of the wine, they were still talking.

"Your mother really did all those wacky things? Woke you up in the middle of the night to paint rooms, or to decorate the house for Halloween in July? Was she that crazy?" Flo drowned an anxious-sounding giggle in a sip of wine.

"Bipolar was the official diagnosis, though she really only had a manic swing. Wouldn't take the meds, either."

"At least she didn't suffer from depression."

"No, but she was a carrier." Plum snickered, as she had when she and Sunni used to say that.

Flo produced an artful little frown. "And you say Crystal had been getting letters from this address for years? How funny. No wonder you wanted to come here."

Plum shrugged. "Envelopes anyway. I assumed there had been something stuffed in them originally." After a moment, she added, "Well, I did find a copy of one letter Crystal sent." She went on to describe the content. "Sounds like it was about some novel, right? You sure you don't know who the tenant was?"

While chugging a full glass of wine, Flo shrugged. "Probably before I owned the building. Anyway, I'm not the most fastidious landlord. I don't even use leases."

Plum would have felt sorry Flo had no answer for her, only the wine had made her too mellow to care.

"And your dad—was he nutty, too?"

Plum shook her head no. "Ben was great. We lost him too soon. He was a race car driver, and he went...you know...the way they do." She squeezed her eyes, the way she always did, to block out that vision. "He wasn't just my father, he was my best friend. Really like a big kid."

"Would he have grown into fatherhood?" Flo asked. "Into adulthood?"

"Fatherhood, yeah. But adulthood? Not a chance." Plum stared off into the distance, smiling fondly at the warm memory.

Flo poured the last of the wine into her own glass. "Want more wine?"

Plum stuck out her lower lip. "I didn't buy any. An obvious oversight on my part."

"There's a bottle in the mini fridge in the backroom of the store. I'll get it." Flo rose and went downstairs.

As Plum listened to Flo tapping her way down the steps, she realized that she hadn't felt this snug and cozy since she and Sunni shared the upstairs rooms in their grandmother's home. This was what she'd always tried to replicate in places, but never found after she left the family house in Venice. Not in any of her own apartments, and certainly not in the McMansion she'd shared with

Noah. She suddenly wanted a place like this to make her own.

Not that she would leave this one in its current primitive state if it were hers. Oh, she'd keep some things. That inviting throw, for sure, though she might move it to the bedroom—after which, she'd chop up that couch with an ax. Then she'd probably build up a layered wash on the pale yellow base on the living room walls. The recliner whose seat held the impression of Flo's butt would probably suffer the same fate as the couch.

Plum glanced around, seeing in a flash the way she'd transform it, if it were hers. Not like some decorating magazine showplace, not what anyone else would choose. She would make it into a unique, artsy gem. The kind of place that, when people who knew her saw it, they'd say, "Plum, this is so you!"

But it wasn't her, she thought, as reality crashed in with painful impact. It wasn't her space. She wouldn't even have more than a few days of pretending it could be.

Disappointment instantly crushed all the mellow feeling that wine and the comfort she'd found there had built. The idea of having to leave this place in a few days felt intolerable.

But...home was where you felt safe, right? Where a cozy sense of belonging closed around you, cocooning you from a cruel world. Had anyone ever said home had to be the place where you were born?

No! What was she thinking? She lived along the California coast. *That* was her home.

Okay, so she didn't have an actual physical place to live in now. Sure, she'd find one. Maybe she'd look for something like this, rooms over a storefront. Now that her Applewood temporary home had given her some direction, her California apartment search should go smoother.

But...would she really find the same funky spirit, the same safe feeling somewhere else?

Flo walked through the doorway, carrying a frosty bottle of white wine in one hand and a corkscrew in the other.

"Your bookstore is for sale, right?" Plum asked. She only heard those words when they came out her mouth—they had never been processed through her brain. "If it included renting me this apartment...I have almost forty grand. I can't take out a loan, for reasons I'd rather not explain, but I'm good for—"

"It's thirty thousand," Flo said. "Not thirty. I forgot—I lowered the price. It's twenty. No, ten. The apartment would be free."

"Flo, you know how negotiations are supposed to work, right?"

Flo's eyes grew so wide, she might have just witnessed a miracle. "Wait here!" She thrust the wine bottle and corkscrew at Plum. "I'll only be a minute." With that, she raced downstairs.

Plum absently clutched the wine bottle to her chest, scarcely noticing the cold. Was she really going to do this? She had a life elsewhere. Though...it wasn't much of a life. Was anything really holding her there?

While the thought of claiming this apartment as her own had drawn her first, the idea of running a bookstore now began to appeal to her as well. She'd always loved books. She hadn't liked the way libraries were run, and she found bookstores nearly as regimented. This might be her chance to show the world how it should be done.

Some noise downstairs broke into her thoughts. Was that the sound of a printer running? Flo was sure taking her time.

The proposed price for the store distracted Plum. Ten thousand bucks for a bookstore, along with free rent on the apartment? Was that really possible?

Flo barreled up the stairs. She burst into the apartment clutching a few sheets of paper, which she thrust at Plum. Plum noticed she'd stuffed a pen over her ear.

When Plum grasped the copy of the sales contract, the pages held a trace of warmth, as if they had just passed through a printer. Plum was right—Flo had printed out a fresh copy of this contract. Even as Plum wondered whether she'd made any changes in it, with one glance she saw that Flo had added to what Plum would be buying.

"Hey!" Plum said. "This isn't only for the business, it's for this building, and even some land. Where's the lot located?"

"Outskirts of town."

The property, identified by its plot identification number, wasn't a tiny lot, either—it stretched to numerous acres. Did she know that number? She'd stared at so many on Noah's maps. And this building contained an apartment, a retail store, and restaurant space. Had Flo changed the price? Plum flipped to the second page of the short contract until she found it listed. Nope, Flo still only wanted ten thousand bucks for all of it.

"Flo, this isn't possible. It's not enough money."

"You're used to California prices," Flo said. "Things are lots cheaper here."

So cheap as to practically be free? If that were true, wouldn't everyone live here?

Plum knew she should study this contract much more carefully. Well, as carefully as someone fairly buzzed could study anything. And there were probably other things that people considering buying a business typically did. They probably looked at the books, or talked to the accountant, or some such thing.

Those thoughts flew right out of Plum's head.

Flo held out the pen to her. Plum's hand slowly drifted toward it. "If I sign this, you have to agree to something else." Plum bit her lip. "Something you might find a tad unconventional?"

"I'm all about unconventional," Flo insisted. She gave her choppy hair a toss as if to show how much.

"No, I mean it. This is important. I don't want my name recorded on the deeds, not yet anyway." Wouldn't Flo question that? "It's not like I'm wanted by the law or anything. You see, there's a guy…" If she had to deal with Noah and Claire, Plum wanted to have the surprise factor on her side.

Flo grunted. "Say no more. None of them are worth the bother."

Plum decided that statement was close enough to an agreement. She took the pen into her hand. She hesitated for a moment. She realized she felt excited, the first excitement she'd felt for ages. *In for some penne, in for some pounds.* Plum quickly scratched her name on the contract.

"I'll get you the money," Plum said, starting to rise.

Flo shook her head. "Plenty of time for that." She reached for the unopened wine bottle.

Plum's excitement soared as she watched Flo open the wine

bottle and pour a measure into each of their glasses. Flo extended Plum's glass to her. She felt outright dizzy when they clinked their glasses to Plum's bright new future.

It didn't take more than mere moments for reality to come flying through on a gale force wind, forcing the excitement out.

She bought a bookstore in another state. With money she took from her cheating ex.

What had she done?

CHAPTER THIRTEEN

What had she done?

The shocking question that Plum kept repeating, until she finally drifted off the night before, still bounced around in her head the instant her eyes popped open the next morning: what had she done?

She'd bought a bookstore in a town she'd never seen before yesterday, simply because she liked the coziness the rooms over that store offered her. Only…she was already occupying those rooms as a guest. She didn't need to *buy* any of it.

After several minutes of staring at the water-stained bedroom ceiling, Plum assured herself that what she'd done wasn't *that* unusual. She'd known lots of people who made major life changes at the time of breakups. Breakups and divorces often provide the perfect occasion to start over.

Only…those other people researched the cities they considered moving to, deliberating judiciously between one choice and another. They looked into the available jobs in their new locale. They moved only after closing down their old lives in a sensible way. They didn't fly out the door, after catching their exes in the act, and take off to some places they'd never even seen, with nothing more than what they happened to be wearing and a big ol' bag of cash.

Hopscotch. While others strode ahead in life in a more focused way, Plum was always off somewhere jumping in offbeat directions. Even her vacillating now smacked of the way she'd flip-flopped while making other major life choices, such as before she went to cooking school.

And what about Noah? And Claire? It was one thing to feel confident she wouldn't run into them in Applewood if she only stayed for a few days, but quite another if she set up her new life here. Given the Budget-Mart connection, seeing them now was certain. Had the choices she'd made moved her far enough out of the victim camp to allow her to interact with them, while still retaining a shred of dignity?

Not likely.

Why, oh-why didn't she ever think before acting?

Plum rose from bed, in her pointlessly sexy Victoria's Secret nightgown, threw on her robe, and made her way to the bathroom, gathering along the way the empty wine bottles she and Flo had discarded the night before.

It occurred to her that while she had signed a contract to buy High Desert Books, she hadn't paid for it yet. She could probably still change her mind.

Plum had tried to pay for it the night before. She'd intended to count out ten thousand from the stash in the satchel, which she'd stuffed into an empty kitchen cabinet. But after they polished off most of a couple of bottles of wine, Flo realized she was too far into her cups to drive home.

"You could stay here," Plum said. "At this point, it's still kinda your place, and also kinda mine." She figured she'd give Flo the bedroom, while she'd sock out on the couch.

Flo's eyes had gone wide at that suggestion, while her lips pulled down at the corners, making her resemble a mask of tragedy better than anyone Plum had ever seen. That looked like outright revulsion. How could the place that offered Plum such warmth be so distasteful to its owner? Flo herself had described it as comfortable.

After a moment, Plum decided that she must have read that wrong. Flo insisted that she never slept well unless it was in her own bed. Well, sure. Everyone slept best in her own bed. Unless, of course, she'd caught some strange girl riding her fiancé in it. Flo said she only lived a short walk away, and after all that wine, she'd welcome the night air's clearing of her head.

"You can't walk alone at this hour," Plum had insisted.

Flo chuckled. "You can tell you're a city girl. We don't have much crime here in Applewood. If the cops weren't busy writing parking tickets, they wouldn't have anything to do."

Plum gave her lips a skeptical twist.

"Oh, it's not that we're all saints or anything. It's just that in a small town, you either know everyone, or you know of them. It's not as easy to get away with things."

"How nice," Plum said.

"Don't fall too in love with it. Believe me, we find other ways to stick it to each other. Lots of ways," Flo said with a bitter zing.

Yet, when Plum tried to give her the cash, Flo insisted she didn't want to walk home carrying it.

"If it's that safe…" Plum started to say.

Flo shook her head. "Like I also said, we're not saints. I'd be afraid I'd telegraph that I was carrying it. Someone could grab it and just take off. That's enough money to start over somewhere."

No kidding. It was enough money for me to start over here.

Flo told her they'd settle up the next day.

Now it was the next day, and the settling up was in question. While Plum brushed her teeth, and ran her fingers through her wavy, sleep-tossed hair, she thought she really could get out of the contract if she wanted to. She could simply refuse to pay. Flo would have to find her to sue her, and Plum herself had no idea where she would land.

Only…did she really *want* to get out of it?

Here I go again. Hopscotch! Or was it? Maybe it was just a reboot, something she'd encouraged Crystal to do.

Despite her apprehension, underneath it all, Plum still felt jazzed about the future that contract offered her, something she hadn't felt in too long. That day she and Sunni had worked on Crystal's house, she remembered thinking she might be stalled. What an understatement! If her life had ground any more to a halt, she'd have started moving backwards. Maybe this change would shake things up.

It would be tough on Roy if she bailed. But hadn't she done enough for Crystal already? Besides, what did she have to go back to? No home, no job, no lover. She'd miss Sunni, but they hardly ever saw each other. In Applewood, Plum had a chance to do work that offered her some fun, which she hadn't found in cooking for too long.

So? Was she really going to do this? Did it matter if she was playing hopscotch again?

Work—it isn't just for sleepwalking anymore!

* * *

Plum donned her cook's whites once again. She didn't want to do dirty work in Crystal's nice things, and her restaurant uniform was the only other garment she had with her. Though there was a drip coffeemaker and some ground coffee in the apartment's small kitchen, Plum decided to grab some instead at Cup o' Joe.

The alluring scent of sugar and cinnamon drifted under her nose when she walked into the crowded café. Plum decided on the spot to snag a cinnamon roll along with her coffee.

"Did you come to cook?" Bonnie asked too eagerly, her gaze going to Plum's chef's uniform.

Plum felt bad for dashing Bonnie's hopes. She hastily explained that she had bought the bookstore next door, and that the cooking things were all she had to work in. She didn't tell Bonnie that she was also now her new landlord. Maybe she'd give Cup o' Joe a free month's rent to help Bonnie out. Or offer to trade food for rent. There was no question that Flo had given Plum a deal. Maybe she could pass that generosity onto someone else.

"I can't let you ruin your chef's things with all the grime you're going to find over there. So pretty," Bonnie said with a wistful sigh. "I'm only a little bigger than you. You can borrow some of my old jeans and tees if you'd like—you'll find them in the office behind the kitchen. Go help yourself."

Plum sensed how much Bonnie admired her chef's whites. And they were a little baggy on her now, thanks to months of not eating much. The uniform would probably fit Bonnie well. "How about if we trade?" Plum said.

Though Bonnie's hair was still messy—to the extent that Plum questioned whether she'd even combed it since yesterday—the idea of trading clothes brightened Bonnie's harried face with the first real smile Plum had seen on her.

Back in the Cup o' Joe office, where the smell from the kitchen of some spicy Southwestern concoction captured Plum's senses, she shed her cooking jacket, leaving it folded on Bonnie's desk. She dove into the garments she found in a cabinet. She had to turn up Bonnie's jeans at the ankles, but her old T-shirt fit pretty well. Plum was good to go.

Back at the bookstore, after finishing her breakfast, Plum searched the place thoroughly to see what she had to work with. In a shed out in the alley behind the store, she found a colorful assortment of old paint cans. That was odd, since she didn't see any sign that the bright colors in those cans had been used in either the store or the apartment. The dried-out paint in those cans was thick, but she could work with it. She'd make good use of the stiff old paintbrushes she found there, too.

In the bookstore's backroom, she came across an amazing selection of cleaning products—amazing in the sense that Flo hadn't seemed to make much use of them in the grimy, dusty store. The Mexican tile floor looked like it hadn't even been wiped off in months, and the dirt worn into the bare wooden counter and shelving pieces must have accumulated over many years.

Before Plum dug in, she found some cardboard and hand-wrote signs for the windows that read, "Under New Management—Grand Reopening Soon."

After discovering that many of the bookshelves and display tables were on casters, she pushed everything over to one side. Then she tackled the floor, scrubbing those Mexican tiles until they gleamed. When she finished the floor, she began work on the counter, making unexpected use of some surprising paint color choices.

Hours later, a young guy came in, carrying a takeout container and a brown bag. "Howdy, Plum," he said, introducing himself as Bonnie's son, Davy. Plum recognized him from when she ate lunch at Cup o' Joe with Jake. He added, "Here's some lunch for you, courtesy of Jake Gold. He was sure you'd forget to eat."

"Thanks, Davy. How did Jake know I'd be here, that I bought the bookstore?"

"Everybody knows it. Flo emailed most of the town last night to encourage them to support you. That's a real surprise, too. Flo hardly even talks to anyone. She must really like you."

Plum's eyes stung unexpectedly. Back home, nobody ever took

care of her. She was the one always expected to be responsible for everyone else. They rarely even thanked her for it. Now two strangers had done more for her than her own family ever had.

"Hey, *that* looks great," Davy said, pointing at what used to be a dirty old counter, which now made a bold statement.

After scrubbing it clean, Plum had primed the wood with an undercoat of russet paint to pick up the tone of the floor tiles. Over that base, she dry-brushed turquoise enamel. Bold Southwestern colors. The effect was artistic and striking. *Thank you, Crystal, for making me paint spaces from the time I could hold a brush.* Because of Crystal's unusual decorating demands, Plum knew how to use even an odd collection of old paint colors to make a dramatic statement.

After Davy left, Plum sank to the floor and dove into her food. The container contained a chicken wrap with chipotle mayo and some garlic bread, while in the brown bag, she found a large soft drink and an oversized chocolate chip cookie. Discovering she was starved, she devoured most of it in minutes, leaving only half the wrap in the backroom fridge for later. She didn't even worry about how much better it might have been if she'd made it, rather than Bonnie. Maybe she finally felt ready to leave cooking behind.

After lunch, she went to work on the dingy walls. Plum didn't want to complain. If she hadn't found all that paint and those cleaning supplies, she could not have made such quick progress on revamping the tired old space. Still, would it have killed Flo to leave a ladder behind?

Of course, Plum could have found a hardware store in town and bought her own ladder, or borrowed one from another merchant. But she was making such progress, she couldn't bear to slow her momentum. Instead, she looked around and found a sturdy table, on which she placed another table. While climbing to the top, it occurred to her to wonder if the restaurant's group insurance still covered her. Now that she thought about it, if Dylan had been scamming his partner of everything he could steal, he probably hadn't sent in the health insurance premiums lately. While on those tables, Plum decided, it was probably best not to think about it.

While she was giving the walls a delicate paint wash from that precarious position, someone must have come into the bookstore. Plum didn't notice until a voice behind her said, "You up there, mind coming down?"

She found herself looking down on a short man, sporting a huge pompadour of inky black hair, over a small pinched face. While this guy didn't spend enough time in the barbershop, in Plum's opinion, he spent too much time in the gym. He was nearly as short as Plum, yet his overworked muscles made him look as wide as he was high. He could have been anywhere between forty and sixty.

"Actually, I do mind. It was too hard getting up here to come down. Who are you and what do you want?" Plum smiled vaguely to remove the rude sting from the words.

His facial features pinched together even tighter. "Diggy Long here."

Plum gave him her name.

"Plum Tardy! What kind of name is that? What were your parents thinking?"

Like that wasn't the pot calling the kettle nasty.

Diggy squinted up at her. "I'm trying to track Flo down."

Plum explained that she'd bought the store from Flo the day before and hadn't seen her since.

"Look, I'll be honest with you…"

Since Plum itched to get back to those walls, she'd rather he'd lie to her, if he could do it fast. Everyone did lately.

"You see, Flo and me got a big score going. Can't tell you about it, though." He actually mimed turning an invisible key in his lips, like little kids do. "Wild horses couldn't pull it outta me."

Wild horses weren't trying.

"Lately, it seems, Flo's out to get me. She already screwed me out of a piece of it. Still waters run deep, you know."

Why did everyone always quote that proverb wrong? It was *dark* that still waters ran.

"If she's cut and run—"

"She hasn't cut and run, she's just not here." Plum was the cut-and-run girl. Flo distinctly gave off a vibe that said nothing would ever move her out of her rut, except for a traveling rube with too much cash.

That muscular body moved faster than Plum would have thought possible. In three quick steps, Diggy stood at the base of her makeshift ladder. He reached up as if he intended to grab the upper table that supported her. Who did that?

Plum hit the deck—flattening her belly against the upper table, hoping it wouldn't collapse. Using the paint can still clutched in her hand, she swung it at his head.

"Hey, watch it!" Diggy complained. But he did back off.

Plum was so sick of everyone who had used her, lied to her, or pushed her around. She decided it was time she started pushing back. And this guy, who would cheerfully have thrown her to the hard floor, made the ideal starting point. "Hey, pal, if you don't want to be dressed in paint, you'll turn around and walk out that door."

"I have to find Flo," the lunkhead whined.

"Then ask someone else. I never met her before yesterday. Everyone in this town has to know more than I do."

He lowered that inky black head. "None of them will talk to me."

What a surprise. "Then it's unanimous. I won't talk to you, either. Now get out here before I turn you pink."

After the briefest of standoffs, the muscle sausage waddled out.

Plum climbed down off her makeshift tower, careful not to spill any paint. Diggy was sure not what she expected. She would have sworn the tough guys around here would be black-hat cowboys, not those who came off like Mini-Me enforcers for the Chicago mob.

While Plum scoured the floor for possible paint drops that might have spilled when she swung the can, Diggy returned, his tight face now more contrite. "Look at that, you did come down. Hey, Plum, I think you and me got off on the wrong foot, and that's probably my fault."

Probably?

"Do me a favor, huh, and get this note to Flo." He stuffed a crumpled piece of paper into Plum's hand. "Tell her to call one of these people, would ya? Only them—nobody else." With that, the little fireplug disappeared again.

She placed the can of paint down on the floor and looked at the wadded up piece of paper Diggy had foisted on her. Gasping aloud, she couldn't have felt more frightened if she'd found a scorpion in her hand.

One of the names on the sheet was Claire Denton. Skinny-ass Claire. Noah's partner in the Budget-Mart deal and orgasm generation. Coupled with her name was a telephone number with a West LA area code. It wasn't Noah and Claire's office number at Westside Homes and Offices, though, where they both worked.

The other name was Javier Silva.

Javier Silva? He owned another commercial real estate firm in Los Angeles. The firm Noah and Claire were competing against for the Budget-Mart commission, actually. Why would Claire's name be coupled with his? Why would they both be connected with Javier's phone number?

Staring again at the note that still felt repulsive, Plum decided that no one was calling Claire if she could help it. With determined strides, she marched through the bookstore and out into the alley. She viciously tore the note into dozens of tiny little pieces and threw them all into a Dumpster she found there.

And she'd seriously believed she might avoid any mention of Claire for a while longer.

With a sigh, Plum muttered aloud, "Flo, what did you get us into?"

CHAPTER FOURTEEN

After tossing away the bits of paper with Claire's phone number, Plum stood in the alley, feeling vaguely pleased with herself. Something under the Dumpster produced a squeaky little sound. She jerked away, fearful of finding herself standing too close to a rat, or something worse. To her surprise a small cat came out from behind the Dumpster's wheel, mewing softly in a scratchy voice.

She was a messy little thing, who gave off a faintly rancid odor. She hadn't been doing a good job of grooming herself. But, hey, she probably had to scour trashcans for food. Small for a grown cat, which Plum took her to be, with long hair in white, brown, and black. Her plumy tail only extended five inches or so, and given the other scars the cat sported, Plum figured the lost tail must have been a casualty of some street fight.

Plum picked her up and was surprised by how little the poor cat weighed. Beneath her thick coat she must have been quite thin. She wasn't wearing a collar or tag.

"You must be pretty scrappy to survive out here," Plum said softly. "You're small, like me, yet you're even tougher than I am. Think you might want to stay around and teach me how to be scrappy, too?" Despite some sticky fur, Plum nuzzled the cat's head with her nose.

Plum had always wanted a cat. It was out of the question when they were kids. Not only did they move too often, they could scarcely support themselves. More recently, Noah felt a cat would have been too much of a burden in their busy lives. Now, Plum finally had a chance. But was this cat the ideal choice? She gave off such a wild, street-smart air.

Then again, Plum herself had to give off a less-than-conventional vibe herself. Why not?

"Scrappy. I'll call you Scrappy. I'll leave the backdoor open for

you. If you want to stay, you're welcome to, but it's your choice."
Plum bettered the odds by taking pieces of chicken out of the partial
wrap she'd put into the bookstore's mini fridge, and piled those
pieces on the backroom floor.

The work went on, happily. A few times during the afternoon,
Plum found herself humming. To her surprise, Scrappy remained
even after she ate her snack. By late afternoon, the walls were
washed in a pale pink. At a glance, they still looked off-white, though
now they gave off a warm, comforting glow. And even though the
paint had been old and reeked of chemicals, once applied, it lent the
store a fresh smell. Amazingly, the cat wasn't covered in pink paint,
either, even though she'd climbed up on Plum's makeshift table-
ladder, and made a game of swatting at the paint can that dangled
from Plum's hand.

Too bad the warmly glazed walls were going to be mostly hidden.
While shifting fixtures around, it occurred to Plum that Flo hadn't
made good use of wall space, preferring to put tall bookshelves
back-to-back in the middle of the floor, creating tight aisles between
them. By using the walls more, Plum would open up spaces in the
center of the store, in which she could make seating arrangements
and other display space options.

The idea of rearranging the place gave her more of a charge than
she expected. This was fun!

The door opened and two women came in, both around Plum's
mid-thirties' age. One was tiny—shorter even than Plum—with a
delicate build. Her bright brown eyes and wide, engaging grin made
her instantly appealing.

The taller and larger woman wore the khaki uniform of the
Applewood Police Department. Plum remembered what Flo had
said about the local cops writing tickets. For an instant she panicked
when she could no longer remember where she'd parked her Jeep,
wondering whether it had already been papered with citations. Then
she remembered that she'd parked it legally in the alley out back.

"So Flo really did it. She went and sold out," the smaller woman
said, extending her hand for a shake. "I'm Becky Rodriguez. I work
for the local newspaper. Once you're settled, I'll interview you for

the *Comings & Goings* column I write."

"And I'm Ginger Maddy," the police officer said. The African-American woman actually looked gingerish, from the tone of her skin, to her reddish hair. She also sported a dazzling smile.

Plum introduced herself and invited both women to pull up chairs amid the chaos of a bookstore in the process of being remade.

"Look, Bec," Ginger said when Scrappy meowed to them. "It's that cat. The one I told you about that I thought would make a good article. All the patrol officers see her around here. It's amazing that cat has survived for so long, given the coyotes that raid the trashcans in these alleys."

Plum's gaze shot to the cat, seated on the arm of the battered side chair she occupied. *So you really are a scrappy survivor*. As if she could read Plum's thoughts, Scrappy blinked at her.

"I thought it would make a good piece, too, but my editor disagreed," Becky said with a suppressed sigh.

When the cat wandered off toward the backdoor, and probably out of her life, Plum tried not to feel disappointed. "Am I the first sucker to express an interest in High Desert Books?"

Both women insisted she wasn't. "The idea of running a small town bookshop has appealed to several people, but talks always broke down," Ginger said. "I think Flo kept upping the price."

Funny that she went the other way with Plum.

"And, inevitably, Flo's grouchy side always emerged. She must like you if she went through with selling the bookstore to you," Ginger added.

Davy had said as much. Initially, Plum had found Flo dour. She'd become pleasant enough once she warmed up, though Plum didn't regard her friendliness as *that* over-the-top. By contrast, her grouchy side must have been *really* grouchy. And why had she lowered the price so dramatically? Had she decided to dump the bookstore once-and-for-all? Did she think she had to sweeten the deal with all those extras?

"What's the scoop on Flo?" Plum asked. She didn't just mean the moodiness. She also wanted to know whether she had entered into a business transaction with a crook—Diggy Long's insinuation had made her suspicious—even if she didn't want to come right out and ask that of a police officer. Ginger might stop writing tickets and investigate.

Becky shrugged. "Don't know. She's been ill-tempered for as long as I've known her, but I'm a relative newcomer here."

Ginger nodded. "My mom told me something happened to Flo when she was young, and she's never been the same."

Plum wondered if that was what people would say about her someday. That after some guy screwed her over, she turned into a wounded old cynic. In moving here had she just found a place from which she could sour for the rest of her life?

"She's lucky that so many people here are committed to shopping locally, or they would never put up with her rudeness," Becky said. "And speaking of shopping…we came by for our book club books. If you're not open for business yet, we'll come back."

"Do you see them here somewhere?"

Ginger nodded. "There's a stack of our next choice on that shelf." She pointed to one of the tall bookcases shoved into the corner.

"Then take them. You can pay me once I'm operational," Plum said.

The two women smiled at each other. "She's going to fit in here fine," Becky said.

Ginger went to the shelf and took a couple of trade paperback books. "Sure you don't want us to fill out an IOU or something? I'd arrest us if we didn't pay." Plum insisted she trusted them.

"Flo gives us a twenty percent discount on book club titles," Becky said.

Plum nodded to acknowledge that she would, too. It did occur to her, though, that she really didn't know anything about running her new business. All she thought about was changing the décor. Shouldn't she have arranged for Flo to train her in the basics?

Hopscotch!

Becky gave her head a tilt. "Plum, would you consider hosting our book club meetings here?"

That sounded like a good idea, giving readers extra time around the store's stock. "Sure. Why not?" Her first business decision.

"It's that Flo would never—" Ginger started to say. Becky gave her a slight nudge in the side to silence her, but not before Plum caught it.

Was Flo outright antisocial, or just sad?

"You know what, Plum? We need to take you out tonight, so you can get to know some of the locals," Ginger said. Becky jumped in to say it was a great idea.

"It sounds wonderful, and I'd love it. Although…I was going to ask Jake Gold if I could take him out tonight. He's been very kind to me."

"A perfect addition. Don't worry, we'll pop by his place and make sure he's in." Ginger glanced at her watch. "Oops! Gotta get back to the station house. Plum, we'll pick you up here tonight at seven, okay?"

As soon as her new friends left, the phone rang.

A phone? Naturally, her new business had a phone. The only problem was finding it. While the telephone wailed, Plum searched through the chaos she'd created by shifting things around. She finally came across it stuffed on one of the shelves under the counter.

Plum grabbed the receiver, but forgot how to answer it. "Desert High Books. I mean, High Desert."

Her caller was Flo. "Changing the name already, huh?"

"Not the name, though I've changed a few other things. I hope you'll be okay with that, Flo."

"It was overdue. I always meant to do more with the place."

Plum stretched the phone cord and sat on the floor, careful not to touch the counter. The turquoise enamel hadn't fully dried yet. "What's with all the weird paint cans you had in the shed?"

"I used to buy bargain paints at the hardware store. You know, colors they made that weren't quite right, which people wouldn't take. They really discounted them. I always planned to do something creative with those colors."

Plum figured she'd allowed Flo's paint choices to finally live out their destiny. It shocked her how drab Flo sounded. And how familiar the feeling was to Plum.

"Listen, Plum. My lawyer isn't happy about that demand you

were insistent on, about not recording your name on the deeds. Now, don't worry—we'll make it right for you. It's just a matter of finding a way to structure it. He said he'd stop by sometime today or tomorrow to iron out something we can all live with."

"As long as we do. You know, Flo, it occurred to me today how hasty I was. Not that I'm backing out or anything—I'm really excited by the prospect of owning this bookstore." She didn't want Flo to know how close she'd come to bailing. "It's that I realized I don't know anything. How you choose new books, how you order them. I'm going to need some training. I mean, there's a computer here—computers and I don't get on that well." Plum-logic wasn't anything like digital-logic.

While Flo spoke, Plum happened to glance into one corner of the shop and realized it would make a perfect spot for books for children. Maybe she'd call it "Kids' Korner." She'd seen a small table and some tiny chairs in the shed. All she had to do to create the space was add short bookshelves that little ones could reach. While she thought about the ways she might transform that area, she missed some of Flo's response.

"What…?" Plum asked.

"I said you don't need training because I left you a manual. After you fell asleep last night, I stayed there and wrote instructions for everything you'll have to do."

Plum couldn't believe that she'd actually slept with another person in the building. She must have felt really safe. Of course, she had also been pretty buzzed. She wasn't used to drinking that much. But Flo had been tipsy, too—that was her reason for not driving home. Yet she'd stayed and created that manual. Was that an indication how much she really didn't want to come back to the bookstore? Would Plum find after a while she'd become as disenchanted with bookselling as Flo, as she'd become with cooking?

More hopscotch?

"You're set, right?" Flo said, sounding eager to end the conversation.

"No, wait. There's something else I have to tell you. Some guy named Diggy Long came by, and—"

"Don't you worry about Diggy."

"Flo, he insinuated that you two were involved in something shady."

"I'm telling you, Plum, don't pay any attention to him. Diggy Long is a blowhard and a bully. If he bothers you again, tell him I kicked his ass in grade school, and if I need to, I'll do it again."

Only if she wanted to break her foot. Diggy could not have been as bulked up as a grade school bully, unless they'd added steroids to his recess milk.

"You know what they say about bullies caving," Flo added.

"Sure. The harder they are, the bigger they fall."

"…uh…right." Flo cleared her throat. "Was that one of Crystal's expressions?"

"Did I tell you about her proverbs last night?" Plum asked. How buzzed did Plum have to be that she didn't remember saying that?

"How else would I know?" Flo's voice hardened. "Plum, I really gotta go now."

"Flo, when will I see you again?"

"Soon," Flo said shortly, and she hung up before Plum could prolong the conversation.

It was crazy; before she hung up, Plum would swear that she heard Flo sob. Why would she? Was she that conflicted about selling her bookstore? Plum would have sworn Flo couldn't wait to get rid of it. Plum remained on the floor, trying to make sense of it, holding the phone until after the canned operator voice came on instructing her to hang up.

To her surprise, the cat walked in from the backroom. A wave of happiness swept through Plum because Scrappy hadn't abandoned her. How pathetic was she that her emotional equilibrium could be shattered by a strange cat's rejection?

Scrappy's staying made Plum want to take a risk for the little fur-ball. She decided she'd dash out to a pet shop she'd seen up the block and buy the supplies a new cat needed.

A half-hour later, after purchasing what the pet shop employee had called the "new cat startup kit," Plum headed back to the bookstore, carrying loads of food, toys, a litter box, and litter.

It was only when she approached the bookstore's locked door that she noticed Becky Rodriguez, her new friend, waiting there for her.

Becky held some of Plum's purchases while she unlocked the door, and followed her in. Once Becky deposited her bags on the floor, she said, "Plum, it occurred to me…you know, because you're okay with us having book club meetings here, that maybe you'd welcome another meeting." Becky's small hands fluttered nervously. "I work for the Russell newspaper."

Plum shrugged to show that she didn't know anything about it.

"Trust me, you'll learn what that means soon enough. The Russells are the richest, most influential family in the area. Gil Russell owns the newspaper, and he's on the Applewood Town Council. He also heads the Yes on Budget-Mart campaign. When he talks, he expects people to listen, especially local merchants."

Could Becky have sounded any more bitter?

"I'm squarely in the no-camp. A Budget-Mart store would be the worst thing that could happen to this town. If I'm asked, I won't lie about it. But I don't want to lose my job, either, so I don't flaunt it." Becky took a deep breath. "Your bookstore is below the radar at this point. I mean, people around here are used to Flo's being antisocial." She rushed into the next sentence. "Any chance you'd let us hold the No on Budget-Mart committee meetings here?"

The unexpected request startled Plum, and it scared her. She was flying under the radar, all right, but from the people back home. Yet she also wanted to stop the Budget-Mart train, for reasons that went beyond now being a local merchant.

Plum shook inside with a desire so strong it shocked her, though she tried to make it casual when she said, "Sure. Happy to help."

"Great!" Becky said with obvious relief. She made an excuse to leave and was gone in a flash.

While Plum unpacked her cat gear, she muttered to Scrappy, "The die is cast, girl. No turning back now."

Plum wasn't sure whether the idea excited her, or scared her out of her wits.

CHAPTER FIFTEEN

Becky and Ginger came by to pick Plum up as promised. They were both more decked out in Western wear than Plum expected. Becky wore a flared leather skirt and matching vest, along with scuffed cowboy boots that looked as if she actually used them to ride horseback. Ginger wore a dress with cream piping and rust fringe that complemented her skin and hair tones. She also wore cowboy boots, though hers appeared newer.

Plum thought they both looked so great, she vowed to buy a pair of those boots for herself.

Her own look was far more urban. She discovered among Crystal's things a pair of jeans embroidered with graffiti, using the style of lettering the homeboys favored back in LA. Both of her new friends raved at her sense of style. Plum was honest enough to admit her mother had designed those jeans, but she let them think she dressed this stylishly all the time.

That's what you do when playing hopscotch. Or even rebooting.

Plum showed them both around the bookstore, updating them on her progress. She'd now finished painting all the bare wooden bookshelves. Tomorrow it would be time to put them all into place, and then arrange the books.

She locked the cat in the store, and hoped her little friend was as well-behaved as she seemed. Plum would hate to come back and find her newish-looking store destroyed.

Together she and her new friends walked over to Jake's vitamin shop, where he was just locking up. He wore his usual well-worn Western duds, and like the others, he raved about Plum's look. Then, while Ginger and Becky took the lead, Jake offered Plum his arm in a courtly way.

Still feeling a bit winded by the walk, Plum asked, "How much longer will it take before I'm used to this altitude?"

"Not much longer. You actually sound more acclimated already. And wait until you visit Santa Monica again after being here for a while. You're not going to believe how strong you'll feel."

Strong how? If he meant stronger in any way other than her lungs, she didn't believe it.

After waiting for a horse-drawn buggy filled with tourists to pass, they crossed the street and walked to a bar named Dancin' Dan's. That was the place she'd seen when she first came to town, with the swinging doors of an Old Western saloon. Music from a Country Western band floated out.

Once they had taken seats at a round table with a good view of the stage, and were waiting for the beers they'd ordered, the talk came around to the Budget-Mart crisis. "I covered the Town Council meeting today," Becky said. "Gil tried to ram through a sales tax deal for Budget-Mart, but he couldn't get the votes. It was close, though. If some of the council members he keeps in his pocket hadn't been absent, it would have been a slam dunk."

"Isn't that always the way?" Jake said. "They claim Budget-Mart will bring in more sales tax, but then they give them a break, so the total revenue goes down, especially once Budget-Mart drives the other stores out of business. That's a deal none of the other merchants get. Is it any wonder why the independent stores can't compete?"

By mutual decree, they decided to make that the last of the Budget-Mart talk, and devote the rest of the evening to fun. From then on, it was all laughter. Becky and Ginger tried to teach Plum to line dance. Plum wasn't too good at it, since she wasn't good at any kind of dancing—she seemed to hear a beat that was different from what other people heard. She sure had fun trying, though.

"Don't worry. I'll get it if I practice. A little learning is a dancing thing, you know," she told the others in a profound tone.

At the end of the night, Jake said he'd escort Plum back to the bookstore, but she insisted she wanted to walk alone

"Flo says it's safe," Plum said.

Ginger bristled. "Sure, it is. We at the PD keep it that way."

From the grins the other two seemed to be suppressing, Plum

gathered Flo's assessment of the local police wasn't far off.

Finally, Plum set off on her own. She felt so relaxed walking back to the store. She liked her new friends and her new home, and now that she'd lived with it for a bit, the direction her life was taking, even if it had required a sharp, unexpected turn. If it weren't for the intrusion of Claire's name popping up that afternoon, and the secrets Plum knew she was keeping, it would have been perfect.

When she approached the bookstore, she saw a man standing before it, staring through the front window. Though it was still a mess inside, she'd left a light on in there, so she'd be able to find her way up to the apartment when she returned. It didn't throw much light outside, though, which meant she wasn't able to make out much about the man, other than that he looked tall and slender.

As a longtime city dweller, she felt a flicker of fear. Confronting a strange man encountered in the dark wasn't something to get too casual about. Then, the man turned her way, and in the pale moonlight, she got a look at him.

Stunned, Plum came to an abrupt stop. There, standing before her, smiling in recognition, was what had once been the cutest boy in her high school. All grown up now, naturally. And he had grown so good.

* * *

"Well, tickle my Elmo! Brian? Brian Coburn?" Plum asked, sputtering.

"It really is you, Plum. When Flo told me she sold the bookstore to someone named Plum Tardy, I figured there couldn't possibly be another one."

Yup, there's no invisibility with a name like Plum Tardy.

"I know should have waited until tomorrow, so I didn't scare you half to death," Brian continued. "I swear I wouldn't have pounded on the door. I would only have knocked if I caught sight of you in there."

Brian surprised Plum by picking her up and happily swinging her around. When he placed her down, Plum wasn't sure her rubbery legs would hold her. They did, thankfully, but she made another discovery, too.

Heat wave sweeping in south of the Equator.

Where had she gotten the idea that her girl-parts no longer worked?

Plum wouldn't have thought it was possible for Brian to look better than he had in high school, but he did. As a boy, he'd been nearly perfect. Whatever flaws he might have had only added to his appeal. Such as where one front tooth crossed over the other, which was revealed through a crooked, decidedly wicked grin. That grin still looked wicked, though today it seemed as if it had more to brag about. Those blue eyes, which contained flecks of gray that appeared silver in the light, were still so arresting—only now, when he flashed that naughty grin, an appealing fan of creases formed to showcase them. He was still tall and lanky, with wide shoulders and narrow hips, and his musculature had developed to a just-right degree. Plum couldn't wait until he turned around because nobody she'd seen then or since had filled out the seat of his jeans better.

Brian Coburn wasn't merely the cutest boy in her high school, however, he was the well-regarded, fast-track son of one of Venice Beach's oldest and richest families. And given Southern California beach communities' standards, that was saying something. Venice was a section of such stark contrast between the haves and have-nots. Naturally, given that Crystal and her brood made a habit of sponging off friends and relatives, they were solidly in the have-not category, while the Coburns held a pretty high perch in the haves arena.

So what was the Coburn fair-haired boy doing here, in this quiet little town, wearing a faded flannel shirt that looked as if someone else might have broken it in for him?

As if by unspoken consent, they walked together down Pony Lane, until they found seats beside a hitching post on an unoccupied bus stop bench. Along the way, Plum learned that Brian was Flo's lawyer, the one she had promised would contact Plum.

Questions threatened to make Plum's head explode.

Brian must have had as many questions about her, and he started first. "Okay…let's see if I understand this. You jumped in your car, drove to a small town in another state, and with no deliberation, decided to buy a business?"

"You're making it sound stupid." He obviously didn't know how to play hopscotch. "What about you? There has to be a story why you're here."

"Oh, the Coburns have deep roots in Applewood, longer even than our roots in Southern California. And you know we've lived in our Venice compound for generations." Brian absently smoothed out his faded flannel shirt. "My grandparents owned a cabin here that we all used for vacations and family reunions."

He was the one! The person she knew when she was young who talked about vacationing in Applewood. The memory came back to her now. She'd always sat at the geek table at lunch during high school, which had been positioned near the table favored by the popular kids. She remembered all of them talking about their trips, but especially Brian's getaways here. Whatever Brian said had always caught her attention; Plum would have listened to him reading the dictionary. There was always talk from that table about European excursions as well, and skiing in South America. Those jaunts seemed impossibly unattainable to a kid from a family that was never far above being homeless. The gatherings in Applewood, though—that was something Plum could dream about.

That still didn't explain why he lived there now. "Brian, the last I heard, you had finished law school and went to work at your dad's firm in downtown LA"

"Ah, yes—me. Of course you'd want to know how the golden boy fell on hard times." Brian brushed his hand through his wavy brown hair, hair that Plum had always itched to run her fingers through when they were younger. "I did go to work for Dad's firm. Made partner in only two years, thanks to Dad's twisting the arms of all the higher-ups. They gave me everything, you know. My parents, I mean. They thought I shouldn't have to work for anything."

Plum did know that. As a kid, she'd always envied how smooth the path had been made for him.

"Anyway, my partnership didn't go over that well with lots of others in the firm, but they accepted it. Until Dad upped the ante even more, forcing them to make me the managing partner of our Chicago office before I had dried out behind the ears. On the surface, my success seemed to go to my head. I must have appeared outrageously arrogant. Deep down I was drowning, and I knew it. I couldn't count on support from anyone else in the firm. Even Dad— when I tried telling him I wasn't ready for the position they'd given me, he accused me of being ungrateful."

"That had to be tough."

"It meant that I needed an escape from all the pressure, and I finally found it through the stuff I shot into my veins." In the glow of the streetlight, he looked directly at Plum when he admitted, "Heroin."

Though the admission shocked her, she just nodded.

"Long story short...I eventually OD'd. Passed out face down in the gutter—I'm lucky someone called an ambulance, lucky to be alive." He shrugged. "Dad's first thought was to get me into some hush-hush rehab place, hoping to keep it from the other partners. There was no chance of that—I'd been crashing and burning on the work front for years by then. Somehow I also knew I'd hit bottom, and I had to find my own way up."

A driver of a car going past honked his horn and sent Brian a friendly wave, which he answered in kind. The smile he sent that driver quickly faded.

"When I got out of the hospital, with the worst of the withdrawal over, I remembered my grandparents' cabin on the lake here. We were always coming to Applewood for holidays and festivals and whatnot when I was growing up."

Plum remembered. She'd always envied him those trips.

"As a kid, I considered Applewood hokey, yet after the fall I'd taken..." He shrugged. "I didn't have any money. I'd gone through everything I made and everything in my trust fund. I was busted, for the first time in my life."

Plum waited for Brian to go on.

"My grandparents let me stay in the cabin, and they gave me an old car. They also opened an account at the local mini-market, so I could buy food and gas. I couldn't have been trusted with any cash then—I couldn't say for sure that I wouldn't have bought drugs. And that was how I lived at first. I found the Narcotics Anonymous meetings here in Applewood and the neighboring towns, and every day I attended as many meeting as I could. NA, AA—anything to get me through. Along the way, my sobriety grew stronger. I met people, like Flo, who hired me to do some legal work. Flo must have known someone in Venice Beach, because as soon as I told her that's where I was from, it sealed our connection. Through Flo I met Jake Gold. Jake introduced me to his lawyer, who gave me my first job here."

"And now?"

"Now I have my own firm, which is doing well. I'm also on the Town Council." Plum heard pride in his voice for how far he'd come.

"Do you miss it, the old life?"

With a tilt of his head, Brian said, "Sometimes, when it gets hard, I miss the ease. Then I remember what that did to me. And when I lock horns with Gil Russell—if you stay here, you'll meet Gil—and I see what money and influence has done to him, I'm not sorry to be where I am now."

"Your parents…?"

"Don't understand. Never will."

They lapsed into silence for a while, both seeming to accept that the postmortem of the worst parts of the past should be over now.

Brian flashed her that wicked grin. "I suppose you know I had a powerful crush on you in high school."

"No, you didn't! Nobody had a crush on me. That's why I had to go to the prom with the son of one of Crystal's friends. Her *gay* son. I can't imagine what his mother had to pay him for that."

"You're wrong, I did. Hey, didn't you notice how often I drove past your house before school, even though it was out of my way?"

She had noticed. That was why she always got to the bus stop early, to make sure she didn't miss seeing him drive by. But she thought he must have gone that way to pick up some friend in the neighborhood, not to catch sight of her.

"You were different from everyone else, already so completely your own person, while the rest of us were all just parts of the pack." He gave his head a shake. "I didn't have the courage to be with you then. Even though I knew you were the prettiest girl I'd ever seen, and that hasn't changed."

Plum felt a wave of warmth flood through her, even if she didn't believe it.

"I hope the man you found appreciates that." With a nod of his head, he indicated the engagement ring still on her finger. A question seemed to crease his brow.

"Oh, no! We're not together anymore. This ring is just waiting there until I can find a pawn shop."

"It's a pretty ring, pricey. You won't get enough if you pawn it. Why don't you let me ask around town and see if there's a jeweler here who'll pay decently for it?" Brian cleared his throat and became a little more business-like. "Is the guy who gave you that ring the reason why you're demanding that we not record your deeds?"

Plum nodded, and told him the quickie version of how their engagement crashed and burned. "I can't deal with him yet. But Noah's in real estate—if you register those deeds, he'll find me."

A shadow crossed Brian's eyes. "Are you in danger?"

"Only from further humiliation. He didn't beat me, if that's what you're asking. He's a disloyal louse, not a criminal."

"What you're asking for, Plum, would be highly irregular, and it would leave you unprotected. What if Flo were to die before those deeds were recorded?"

"You could put it into her will or something. Please, Brian."

"I guess we could do it with a trust." He sighed in surrender. "Okay. I'll think of something. We'll make this work."

"Great." Plum grinned happily. "Let me ask you something else. The price Flo wants for all this—isn't it too cheap? I know I'm used to California real estate values, but even for rural Arizona, isn't ten grand too low?"

Brian seemed to deliberate before speaking. "Plum, you know what I always think makes for the best deals? When both parties get what they want."

That didn't answer anything, yet she sensed it was all she was going to get from him.

Brian directed a studious look her way. "That's really the reason why you're buying the bookstore, right? Because your engagement broke up, and you want to make a life change? That's the *only* reason?"

"Sure. What other reason could there be?"

While Brian didn't say anything more, Plum felt certain he had another reason in mind.

CHAPTER SIXTEEN

Plum awoke in her apartment bed the following morning feeling even better.

Last night, after their talk on the bus bench, Brian walked her back to the bookstore door. Before he left, he gave her a kiss. Only a soft peck on the cheek, but that was enough to send that heat wave sweeping through her again. If she'd had a moment to think about it, she might have panicked. Noah's betrayal had knocked her self-esteem down to dirt level. Thankfully, Brian's kiss took her by complete surprise, and that allowed her euphoria to soar. She floated through the bookstore and up the stairs to her apartment.

Had she found her rebound guy? Even as she wondered that, she admitted how much she hated relegating Brian to that role. Was it possible to skip the rebound step?

The cat proved to be as good as Plum had hoped while she was out last night. Before going upstairs, she opened the backdoor for Scrappy, offering to let her go. When the cat showed no interest in leaving, they went upstairs together.

Despite her dreamy state, Plum had become quite focused once she made it to the apartment. She remembered a pendant with a long chain among the pieces of Crystal's jewelry, and dug it out. With no ceremony, she yanked the engagement ring off her finger, surprised by her lack of feeling for that milestone. After slipping it onto the chain, she allowed Scrappy to bat it around a few times. Plum knew she'd have to keep a tight hold on it. As scattered as she was now, she couldn't risk losing that ring, which was one of the only assets she had left, beyond her diminished savings and the cash in the satchel. Still, she didn't want that ring sending a message that wasn't true anymore.

Maybe what the ring represented hadn't been real for some time. Plum thought about how Brian excited her. She couldn't remember the last time Noah had made her feel like that, sexually, or in any other way. Maybe his cheating was the way he expressed what Plum hadn't admitted, but now knew to be true.

As a couple, they had never worked as on paper. Noah had always been into externals, while Plum was oblivious to the things people like Noah valued. In the beginning, it made them feel as if they formed a world apart from either his connections or hers. And their chemistry and sexual heat had been good. Eventually, though, it must have been the differences that drove them apart. Plum often felt she embarrassed Noah before his friends and coworkers, even if he never actually said it. She felt she had to live up to some unspoken standard, and imagined she missed it by miles. She hung on because she believed he'd been too good for her, as if she'd scored the brass ring in the boyfriend biz. It had never occurred to her to wonder why he had chosen her. Maybe he simply felt daring for having picked an unconventional girl. Either way, now she saw that they'd both settled.

Wordlessly, in the deepest recesses of her mind, Plum admitted when things had begun to unravel for her. Once again she slammed the door on that time of loss.

Absently, while perched on the bed, she wrapped her fingers around the ring, almost as if she thought she could recapture what she now knew had been dead long before she walked in on Noah and Claire. When it didn't happen, with a sigh, she clipped the chain around her neck and slipped it below the neckline of her blouse.

It had also occurred to her that, despite having kinda bought a bookstore, she hadn't read anything since she left Santa Monica. She was going into reader's withdrawal. She'd actually bought a few books from Flo the first time she'd dropped into the store, which she now had stacked on the nightstand next to the bed. Comfort reads—a couple of cozy mysteries, a romance, and some fun women's fiction titles. Every true reader has books she turns to in her darkest times. Rereading one or two of those was sure to give her the peace she craved.

Plum so longed to get lost in one of those books that she didn't even bother getting undressed, she just plopped against her propped-up pillows and grabbed the top book. While she tried one after another in the stack, she couldn't seem to get into any of them. What was wrong with her? Was there simply too much story in her life right now to let any more in?

She clutched one of the books to her chest, almost as if she thought she could absorb the soothing calm she needed through the cover. She must have fallen asleep like that.

She awoke the next morning when the sun streamed through the window, to find herself still in her clothes, lying on top of the plaid cotton bedspread, with the cat curled up beside her. She spotted the book she'd been holding when she fell asleep on the floor beside the bed. The ring on the chain was still clipped around her neck.

Given how sad she'd felt about her lost relationship when she drifted off, she thought despair should have taken hold of her during the night. Instead, she felt great. She'd passed a milestone last night. Plum might not be all she wished she to be, but she wasn't that deeply wounded woman anymore.

Besides, Brian Coburn had come into her life. Before they'd parted the night before, he asked her to have dinner with him tonight. Plum knew she'd have to struggle all day not to glow.

When Plum went downstairs to the bookstore, dressed in her work clothes again, with Scrappy on her heels, she was surprised to see she had company. Becky and Ginger stood outside the door, waiting to be let in. Ginger held a tray of coffee containers.

"What gives, guys?" Plum asked when she opened the door.

"After you left last night, we realized we were both off today. We decided to come and help you whip this place into shape," Ginger said. "But first, coffee."

"Don't forget the goodies," another voice cried. Jake popped through the door behind them, carrying a brown bag. "Hey, it's that cat."

"Right," Ginger said. "I've seen her dashing across this street a few times when I've been on patrol."

Jake explained that the cat had been living in the alleys behind the Old Town stores for months now. "I heard her owners abandoned her after their house was foreclosed."

"And nobody adopted her?" Plum demanded, aghast.

"A couple of people tried." He shrugged. "She seems to want to be on her own. Must have a streak of wanderlust."

"Maybe the cat works with the pet store to boost 'new cat setup' sales," Plum said in a too-grumpy tone. Was it the bookstore that brought out the grouchy in people? She sounded more like Flo already.

"Maybe she's just been waiting for you, Plum," Ginger said.

That idea made Plum feel welcome.

The fun of the night before continued for the four of them, along with their furry little friend. After breakfast, Jake announced he had to return to work. "I'll check back on you later, Plum. You kids have fun today. You're doing a great job refurbishing this old place." His praise left her with a feeling of pride.

Plum heard sincerity in Jake's voice; she knew he meant it. Yet when his gaze paused on the counter, and the changes she had made there, she suspected that saddened him, too. Probably because he would miss seeing Flo standing there when he shopped. He must wonder if he'd ever see her again. From everything she'd heard, Plum considered it unlikely that Flo would stay involved with her old merchant neighbors, if she ever had been.

The three women pushed all the fixtures into the places where Plum planned for them to go. Then it was time to shelve books. Plum's original ideas didn't stop with the décor. She'd always had distinct beliefs of how books should be organized. She thought romances with dogs in the story should really be shelved in the pet section, and books about keeping the peace in multi-cat households would be better served in either Personal Growth or Current Affairs, while titles about UN peacekeeping efforts among rival factions in Third World nations should really be placed in Marriage. Her eccentric organization went on from there. Becky and Ginger shared a laugh, though they caught on soon enough.

They were all well into shelving the stock, when the door opened, and Flo stomped in. All three women stopped and stared at her. Plum noticed Flo's being there stunned Becky and Ginger as much as her. She would have sworn Flo never intended to enter this place again.

"What?" Flo snapped, while taking in their shock. "You said you wanted training."

"I do!" Plum hastily assured Flo. "I'm glad you changed your mind."

Flo grunted amiably. Then she stared around, slack-jawed.

Plum saw the dramatic changes she'd made to the bookstore as they must appear to Flo. "Flo, are you okay? You're not mad at what I did, are you?"

Slowly, Flo's eyes glistened with tears. "It's beautiful, honey, simply beautiful. I wish I were one-tenth as creative as you are, Plum." She sighed. "I'm so proud of you."

Plum felt an unexpected jolt of pleasure. First, Jake had praised her, and now, Flo. Back home no one ever did. Her nearest and dearest always acted as if she were something to endure.

A UPS deliveryman arrived with a dolly overflowing with boxes of books from publishers and wholesalers. Flo became instantly more business-like when she dragged Plum behind the counter and proceeded to teach her how to check new books into the computer point-of-sale system. Flo separated out the books that were customer special orders from those that were general store merchandise.

"These three are for Hannah Russell." Flo's lip curled in distaste. "Why don't you call and tell her they're here?" Flo said, indicating where Plum would find the telephone number.

Plum did as Flo asked. She recognized the voice on the other end of the phone as belonging to the older woman in the stodgy knit suit she'd seen when she first entered High Desert Books.

"Are you a new employee, dear?" Hannah asked. "Florence does keep trying to find helpers, but they can never seem to put up with her."

Hannah had turned nasty there. If Plum had been a new employee, wouldn't that crack have diminished the chance of Flo keeping her on? Plum explained that rather than working for Flo, she had bought the bookstore.

"Oh." A silence followed the sound of disappointment. "Good luck to you, my dear. I'll send my husband, Gil, to pick up the books," Hannah said before hanging up.

"She was sorry to see me go, huh?" Flo asked sarcastically, after Plum finished the call.

"I think she was, actually." Plum kept to herself Hannah's comment about Flo not being able to keep staff. "Hey, how can I charge her for the books? I don't have any change in the register." She didn't even have a bank account. She probably wasn't handling this business purchase the way anyone else would.

"Sure, you do. I left what was there on my last day. And I transferred the business checking account and credit card processing over to you today. You'll have to stop by the bank to sign some things."

Flo sure didn't seem to need money. Or want it. Plum still hadn't paid for the business. Brian insisted that Flo would wait until they'd hammered out the final paperwork. Shouldn't she want earnest money at least? And shouldn't the cash in the bookstore's checking account be Flo's, not Plum's? Plum decided it must be Applewood, not Disneyland, that was the happiest place on earth. The most generous anyway.

A couple of hours later an older man came in. Though he had to be well into his seventies, he stood ramrod straight, to the point that Plum wondered whether he carried a spine like everyone else, or had a broom up his butt. He was the first man she had seen in Applewood wearing a suit, a fine-looking silk that matched the wavy steel gray in his hair. Plum would have regarded him as outright handsome were it not for the paleness of his skin and the dismissive quality in his eyes.

He directed that indifference at Becky and Ginger, where they had stopped shelving books and stared at him. "Rebecca. Officer," he said without a shred of warmth.

"Hi, Gil," Becky said in a too-deferential tone. Ginger returned to shelving, yet the big woman seemed to have grown smaller under his gaze.

While completely ignoring Flo, and glaring briefly at the cat on the counter, he turned his attention to Plum. "And you are?"

Not curtseying, dude, though she felt he expected that. Men

who flaunted their sense of entitlement had always threatened
Plum. With one withering stare, Sunni's father had been able to
make Plum shrink to thimble-size. For once she held her ground and
simply introduced herself. She didn't even tell him she'd bought the
bookstore, figuring Hannah would do that if either of them cared.

Plum rang up Hannah's books and bagged them without saying
anything else. Gil walked out without another word to any of them.

"Every clout has a silver lining," Plum said with a sniff after he
left.

The others cracked up over that, and it peeled away the
uncomfortable pallor that Gil's presence had cast over the place.

"We're almost finished here, Plum," Ginger said. "Got any more
books?"

Plum turned to Flo. "There are boxes of books in the bedrooms
upstairs. Why are they up there?"

Flo shrugged. "Some of those can be brought down here, but
others are more rare. I always intended to look through them, maybe
list them for sale online."

Plum thought Flo's intentions should have been enough to pave
the road to hell in more gold than in Fort Knox.

"We'll keep going," Becky said. "Neither of us has anything on
for tonight."

Plum hesitated. "Uh…I do, actually. I have a date."

Ginger stopped and stared. "You've been in town for two
minutes, and you have a date? Who with?"

"Brian Coburn."

Ginger whistled.

"It's not what you think," Plum said.

"Girl, what I think is that you've bagged yourself a rock star,"
Ginger said.

"I didn't bag anyone," Plum said, a shade more defensively than
she intended. "Look, on the surface it's a crazy coincidence. Brian
and I actually went to high school together." She didn't mention that
Brian's teenage talk of vacationing in Applewood claimed partial
responsibility for her being there. "This isn't really a date-date, it's
merely two old friends catching up." Too bad they'd actually caught

up last night. Plum wasn't entirely sure she was telling the truth.

"Were you two an item then?" Becky asked.

Plum shook her head no. "He was a senior, while I was a sophomore. He was cool, while I was...not."

Her friends wanted to know what she planned on wearing. Plum shrugged. To be honest, even if he had taken a tumble down the social ladder, Brian Coburn still seemed way above her. Plum suddenly felt too ordinary to be flitting around in Crystal's flashy things.

"Why don't we go upstairs and see what you've got?" Becky suggested.

Before Plum knew it, her friends had swept her to the rear of the store. She stopped when she realized Flo hadn't joined them.

"Flo?" she asked. "Aren't you coming?"

"You girls go. I'll stay here and...and finish some paperwork for you."

What paperwork? Plum hadn't opened her doors yet. She didn't even have paper.

"Nope. If we're playing dress up, we're all playing," Plum insisted. Though the other two women giggled while racing up the stairs, Plum waited at the rear of the bookstore for Flo to join them.

A shy smile unexpectedly lit up Flo's hooded eyes. Plum suspected people didn't often include Flo in things, and she wondered why not.

* * *

The bedroom furnishings looked as randomly put together as everything else in the apartment. A walnut headboard, unconnected to the bed frame, leaned against the wall. Across from the bed, there was a small dresser in some whitewashed wood. But filling the corner was a lovely mirror, with rosewood trim, which hung from a decorative rack. The mirror itself pointed at the ceiling, since Plum had never adjusted it.

Everyone else draped across the bed, including Scrappy, while Plum lifted clothes out of the boxes. She'd brought all the boxes in when she moved into the apartment, and tossed them into the room's closet. She hadn't yet hung most of them.

"What a great sense of style you have, Plum. These are really gorgeous. Different from anything I've ever seen, though, to-die-for," Becky said, holding up before her one of the garments Plum had draped on the bed.

Plum couldn't maintain the charade that this was how she normally dressed. She had tried to keep a low profile here, not trotting out the full account of her gruesome story. Well, she'd told Jake, Brian, and Flo some of it. She hadn't told anyone the whole gory truth because she couldn't bear the weight of all the pity that was sure to generate. Besides, wasn't she supposed to be rebooting here?

Then again, she wanted these women to become real friends. And she'd always believed women form friendships by sharing their stories.

So, slowly, it dribbled out. She started crediting Crystal with the clothes they all loved, and moved onto what happened at Dylan's, and finally, Noah's betrayal. Before she knew it, she'd spilled most of it. It wasn't too bad. She saw more sympathy than outright pity on their faces. Maybe even outrage on Flo's. Plum decided she had to be reading that wrong. She couldn't imagine Flo getting that worked up about the plight of a stranger.

Ginger whistled. "That was quite a day you had there, Miss Plum."

Plum had to nod. "That's why I can't get serious about any guy now. Especially not Brian. I don't want to use him for my rebound."

Flo hadn't spoken up until now. "Plum, you do everything your own way. Look at how you came here and bought the bookstore. There's no reason to believe you'll have a rebound like other people. Brian Coburn has become very dear to me. I wouldn't encourage you to see him if I suspected you'd hurt him."

Plum found she wanted to believe that. But she had to wonder whether buying the bookstore made this her rebound life. Would she want to shed it when her real life came along?

Plum continued trying on the outfits they produced. She didn't take their gushing about any of them too seriously. As Crystal always said, you can make a pig sing opera, but it's still going to sound like a pig.

Finally, Ginger whistled at something she found. "Look at what we have here. What I wouldn't give to wear this."

It was Crystal's lime green handkerchief dress. Made with sections of soft fabric stitched together, the skirt sections draped at different lengths. Beside the plunging neckline was a cluster of cloth pieces arranged to look like a pressed flower. And all along one side, Crystal had painted in white fabric paint an impressionistic Hollyhock plant.

Before Plum knew what had happened, they had her dressed, and Becky was picking through the handfuls of the jewelry that Plum had also dumped into one of the boxes.

"Hey, check these out," Becky cried, holding up a pair of teardrop earrings in some green stone.

"Ooh, good find, Bec," Ginger said. "It's like 'something borrowed, something blue,' only green."

"I'm not getting married, Ginger! I'm just having dinner with an old friend," Plum said with barely suppressed exasperation.

It wasn't true, though. Brian had never really been her friend. He was a boy she once knew, a boy she'd had a desperate crush on. So why was the prospect of dinner with someone who wasn't even a friend making her giddy with excitement?

From the bottom of the stairs, Brian suddenly called, "Plum, are you there?"

Man, she had to either put a bell on that front door or start locking it. Anyone could walk in.

"She's coming," Flo shouted.

Flo and Ginger moved toward the bedroom door. Ginger turned back long enough to say, "You wait, Plum. Make an entrance."

Becky stayed with her after Flo and Ginger left, absently adjusting one of Plum's curls, which had tumbled over her forehead. Close up Plum noticed fine lines around Becky's eyes that she hadn't seen before. She was either older than Plum had originally believed, or the years she'd lived had been harder on her.

"There are some dashed hopes riding on you tonight. I don't

know you well, Plum, but you strike me as someone who frequently drops the ball right when you're in the shadow of the goalposts."

Becky hadn't read her wrong.

"Don't drop it this time, okay?"

"Not to add any pressure or anything," Plum said. They both laughed.

After Becky went down, Plum waited alone. Not to make her entrance, as Ginger had advised, but merely stalling. Could she really risk another man's rejection? She went to the mirror in the corner, absently tilting it into position. Slowly, a woman came into view. A woman with auburn hair and ivory skin, wearing a body-skimming green dress. Her striking good looks and small womanly body stunned Plum. Was that really how she looked to other people? Plum hastily scampered away, before she had a chance to scrutinize the image too closely, allowing a rare cloud of self-worth to propel her out the door.

Brian waited at the foot of the stairs for her. When Plum reached the midpoint of the stairs, he held out his hand.

In that instant, the scene became transformed in Plum's imagination, as a wordless fantasy played out for her. A long held fantasy. Only in her imagination, that wasn't Brian at the foot of the staircase holding out his hand to her, but Noah. It wasn't even this set of stairs, but the wide stairwell in Crystal's Venice house. The picture rolling out in Plum's mind's eye was the wedding scene she had always envisioned. Noah would be waiting there, when she swept down in an original gown that Crystal would have made for her.

She'd been kidding herself. Even if they had made it to the altar, even if they held their wedding in Crystal's house as Plum had always hoped, it would not have happened that way. Noah would never have directed the attention to her. He would have stood where all eyes would have remained on him. And forget that business about it being bad luck to see the bride before the wedding—he would have had a role in picking her gown, to make certain it neither overshadowed nor embarrassed him. As the vision drifted away, there was nothing remotely appealing about that fantasy anymore.

Still, Plum felt a pinprick in her heart.

CHAPTER SEVENTEEN

Plum figured Brian would take her to a joint like Cup o' Joe for a burger or salad. Instead, they drove in his pickup truck to a restaurant called Paddy's Lakeside, which was situated on a lake on the far side of Applewood. A fine dining spot, with white tablecloths and a gourmet menu. When the moonlight danced across the surface of the water, Plum hoped she didn't swoon too loudly.

An elegant waiter appeared at their table on the sprawling terrace and asked what they would like to drink.

"A Perrier for me," Brian said. "The lady will probably want something stronger."

The lady felt too weird asking for booze when her date couldn't. "Perrier works for me, too."

Brian reached his hand across the table. "Plum, alcohol has never been my drug of choice. If you would like wine, please order it. I don't consider it anything more than a slightly superior soda pop."

Since Plum rated it higher than Brian did, she asked for a glass of Chardonnay. Though she wondered whether she should be drinking any alcohol when she was already so intoxicated.

Once dusk crept across the sky, Brian pointed to a light coming from a sizable log home on the far side of the lake. "That's my place. I left a light on so I could point it out to you. I'd love to bring you there sometime."

"Your grandparents' vacation home? You're still there?"

"I bought it from them several years ago."

"Cool beans." Plum enjoyed reclaiming that expression. "They didn't mind selling the family getaway spot to you?"

Brian shrugged. "Nobody else used it anymore, even though our family was one of the original homesteaders here. Can't have family reunions where the outcast lives."

His tone wasn't bitter. Plum found it odd to think someone like

Brian could sound as out-of-step as she did. He wasn't, of course, she thought, dismissing that idea.

He sighed softly when he turned his attention to her. He told her how beautiful she looked in that hollyhock dress. Plum flashed again on the startling image of the woman in the mirror. If she could sneak up on her own impression like that more often, she might believe it.

Plum gave the menu high marks for being remarkably eclectic. She chose Chicken Kiev, which many chefs considered a dated choice. Plum never grasped the idea that food could go out-of-style. Hardly anyone offered it anymore because it demanded such exacting preparation, and it rarely came out right. The herb-butter mixture in the center was supposed to spurt when a knife was inserted, not leak out as it often did. But it, like the mac-and-cheese she'd ordered with Jake, was comfort food—albeit gourmet comfort—and Plum was still strongly in consolation-seeking mode

Conversation flowed easily for them once again. "So Sunni became a corporate lawyer?" Brian said. "I remember her slinking out of your house in those quirky outfits your mother made for the two of you, looking miserable. I bet she loves the suits she has to wear now."

"Are you kidding? I think she sleeps in them."

A string quartet played softly in the corner. Between courses, Plum and Brian made their way to the dance floor. Even while wearing heels, she was still much shorter. Yet she fit against him remarkably well. Finding herself that close to Brian made her heart and her hormones flutter uncontrollably. If this night ended in a bust, at least she had this wonderful time to remember.

After they returned to their table, Plum said, "I met your friend Gil Russell."

Brian choked. "Hardly my friend."

Plum relayed her impressions.

"You know, Plum, I don't think he's a bad man, he just has to control everything. And it's not as if he has all the answers, he only thinks he does. His life and Hannah's must be incredibly sad. They lost their son thirty-odd years ago, and they've never gotten over it."

"That's awful. How did he die?"

"On Billy Dean's high school graduation night, while driving drunk, he wrapped his brand new sports car around a light pole." Brian cleared his throat. "Having had my own troubles in that area, I'm not one to judge. Still, you'd think that would have caused them to rethink their values. Yet Gil is still determined to make this town into something most of us don't want."

"I noticed you all have other jobs, beyond the town council."

"That's because they only pay us a hundred bucks a year for serving on the council." Brian's eyes crinkled merrily. "I've lived on less, mind you. But most people find they need another job to get by."

Plum laughed. He really wasn't the Brian Coburn she remembered from high school. She had to admit the path he'd followed, and his erratic tumble surprised her. She felt certain that Brian must have gotten a copy of life's rulebook, the one she'd somehow missed. Maybe he neglected to read it.

"Do you ever see your parents?"

"Not often." Brian gave his head a sad shake. "They'd be happy to turn back the clock if I could pretend the last eight years never happened. I can't do that."

"For you, Gil Russell must be an uncomfortable reminder of what you left behind."

Brian held her gaze for a few moments, perhaps in acknowledgement of a keen observation.

"Yeah," he said with a sigh. "No matter how sorry I feel for him, don't think I let that scramble my brains. It makes me crazy how some people on the council can't stand up to him, purely because of his money and power."

Plum understood it too well. She was rarely able to stand up to people like Gil.

"When he can't be there for a vote," Brian continued, "I always say, 'The king has left the castle—it's time for democracy to reign.' Sometimes then we can pass a bill Gil would oppose."

"What about when he returns? Do the weaklings rescind their

votes?" She felt some shame for labeling others as weaklings, when she knew she was describing herself.

"Fifty-fifty chance either way. It's the best we can do."

"Then how did you get these people to create a stalemate over Budget-Mart?"

"We have Jake Gold and his campaign to thank for that. But I don't kid myself—it's still an uphill fight. Unless something unexpected happens to tip the scales, the No on Budget-Mart crowd is going to lose. All we're succeeding in doing is holding off the inevitable."

Didn't that make her crazy to move ahead with her bookstore purchase? Was this any better than the life she'd left behind?

After a leisurely dinner, Brian drove them back to Old Town. There, they ducked into a little jazz club a couple of blocks from the bookstore for a set. Afterwards, Brian walked Plum back to her door.

In the darkness of the bookstore's doorway, he took her into his arms. He leaned down to kiss her. A kiss that started out gently, but grew from there, eventually curling her toes, reaching all the way up her spine, and finally making her hair stand on end. A few more kisses joined the first, deeper, more demanding. Exploring each other with their tongues, and clutching each other tightly.

After some pretty heavy breathing, Brian held Plum a few inches away, and let an unspoken question form between them.

She'd wanted to say, "No, not ever. I'm never letting another man get that close." Instead, she said, "Not...yet." Yet? Did that mean that something would happen eventually?

"Then there's still hope," he said breathlessly.

Still hope? Damn right. Hope was giving her an orgasm.

Brian said good night after Plum unlocked the door to the bookstore. Once inside, she floated upstairs.

"Scrappy," she said to the cat who waited for her in the kitchen. "Is this for real? Or just some high school fantasy I'm living out?" Questions for another day. This night was truly one of the most enchanting Plum had ever known. She intended to savor that.

She changed into her sexy nightgown, feeling for once as if it were warranted. She also felt too happy to sleep. Plum decided she really should get started hanging up Crystal's things in her closets here, especially since many of them were spread out on the bed, where the ladies had left them when they dressed Plum for her date. Unfortunately, the closet in the bedroom that she slept in was small. She managed to stuff some of the garments into it, though she decided she might want to reconfigure this place.

She needed to look through more of those boxes of rare books that Flo had used to fill the other bedrooms. That might be too much for tonight. For now, it would be enough to think about how she might use the closets in those rooms. Though the rooms were packed to the ceilings with boxes of books, their closets were not only empty, at some point, they had been swept clean.

Recently, in fact, Plum thought. Had Flo swept them before Plum moved in? Considering how much dust coated most of the place, it would have a strange choice to limit her cleaning to empty closet floors. Maybe the cleaning up was part of the process of moving out some of her personal items, before Flo loaned those rooms to a stranger.

The closets in the other bedrooms were bigger, and all together, they should allow her to bring order to her new wardrobe. While deciding which types of clothes she would store in each space, Plum walked back and forth, studying the hanging options. Scrappy dashed in and out of all the closets.

Scrappy found something on a closet floor and began to knock it about. Plum saw the cat had found a photo, one that had fallen out of an album, given that an album corner mount still adhered to one side. She picked it up.

The picture was of a cute little girl, with two missing front teeth, who sported a mop of curly red hair.

Plum's jaw dropped in shock. That wasn't *some* little girl—that was *her*. Plum. She'd seen this exact photo not long ago. Crystal had documented every stage of her kids' lives in pictures. She hadn't put any of them in albums. Instead, another closet in an unused bedroom in the Venice house had been filled with her lifelong jumble of photographs. Plum had already sorted through them, filing them in boxes that each covered a period of time. She'd stuffed the whole lot of those boxes in her garage back in Santa Monica.

To sort them, she'd had to look at all of them carefully to determine when they'd been taken. And she remembered this picture in particular. While she'd studied it before boxing it away, it occurred to her that if she ever had a daughter, there was a chance that her daughter might look like this.

A sharp pain stabbed her right in the heart, making Plum reel as if from a body blow. She slammed that door shut inside of her, faster than ever.

There was no question about the identity of the subject of this photograph, however. The only question was: what was it doing here?

Logic kicked in fast. Crystal had been close to someone who'd might have lived in that apartment. With all those letters going back and forth over all those years, it wasn't strange to think some must have contained pictures of Crystal's kids.

But...why was it *still* here? Whoever Crystal's Applewood friend had been, she was gone now. Wouldn't Flo have come across this photo years earlier?

How long had it been since anyone lived in that apartment? Had Flo ever lived there? Plum thought the well in the recliner did distinctly mirror the shape of Flo's rear, though she admitted that lots of people could have worn it like that. Including Plum herself; while smaller, her own butt followed similar lines. Besides, Plum could easily imagine Flo coming up here to watch TV, while ignoring her customers downstairs.

And yet, even as logic answered the questions, a little buzz of anxiety began radiating out from deep in Plum's gut. Some things didn't come together as well. Such as why Flo sold the business to her at a giveaway price, not to mention throwing in all those other unnecessary extras.

Plum stared at the photo again, viewing it as she would a stranger's picture. Willing it to give up some answers. Making a wild, intuitive leap, she flashed on a crazy idea, of where she might find a clue to whatever history she and this apartment might have shared.

With nothing more to guide her than the memory of writing on the side of a cardboard box, Plum walked down the stairs. At the bottom, instead of turning right into the bookstore, she turned left. She went out the backdoor to where she had parked her Jeep. To where she'd left that box labeled, "Plum's birth certificate." By the time she reached into the Jeep for the box, the buzz of worry in her gut had spread clear through her.

She carried that box back upstairs and dumped its contents on the coffee table. Years of correspondence, months of legal papers— she shoved them all aside in her search for something that would signal the truth. Finally, she zeroed in on a document she found at the bottom. An official-looking document that contained a baby's footprint, along with the print of a mother's thumb.

It looked like a birth certificate. It couldn't be Plum's. She'd told Sunni the truth that day when they sorted through the papers in Crystal's closet. When Plum finished cooking school and went out on her own, Crystal gave Plum a packet including her birth certificate, along with all her various school and inoculation records. They were all still in a strongbox Plum kept on her closet shelf.

But this document, in a box labeled, "Plum's birth certificate," distinctly looked like another one. Plum's hand shook as she reached for it.

"Baby girl Gallagher," the document read, with a date and time that coincided exactly with Plum's own birth. "Mother: Florence Jean Gallagher. Father: unknown."

There was a question she knew she should ask: why would a certificate related to a baby born to Florence Jean Gallagher in Arizona be in a box defined as, "Plum's birth certificate," which she found in Crystal's house in California? The words refused to form.

Plum *knew*. She simply knew. Connections continued to fall into place, but she no longer needed them. Her sense of knowing quieted that buzz of anxiety within her. And strangely, rather than feeling shocked, given her hopscotch life, Plum saw how the situation she now found herself in was nothing short of inevitable.

CHAPTER EIGHTEEN

Plum finally verbalized the unspoken understanding screaming the truth in her mind: she had been born, not to Crystal, but to Flo. Florence Jean Gallagher.

Plum understood now what Flo must have removed from those cleaned-up closets. Years of letters from Crystal, perhaps copies of what Flo had sent to her. Evidence of a child shifted from one mother to another.

No wonder Flo had stared at Plum when she first came into High Desert Books. What a shock Plum's presence there must have been for Flo.

Something else hit Plum like a thunderbolt. The copy of the letter she had found in the Venice house, the one from Crystal, the bad copy, missing so much text—that letter wasn't *all* about the novel about the couple who took on someone else's baby. Plum went to where she'd left her tote bag on the recliner and fished out the letter. Rereading it, she understood it now. Crystal had written about the novel she'd read because that couple's situation was like hers and Ben's. Those other lines, which Plum had thought related to the book—"baby always cared for" and "never want for anything"— related instead to Flo's actual baby. Plum.

When Plum objectively studied that photograph of herself as a little girl, it became undeniable. In a purely physical sense, she had never fit with Crystal and Ben, as Sunni fit with Crystal and Alan Meadows. Plum had always believed herself to be a throwback to some dead relative. That wasn't it at all. She resembled Flo. Flo and someone else.

"Father: unknown." What reason would Flo have had to keep that man's identity secret? Had she been protecting some guy who didn't want his paternity known, such as a married guy. Or denying him what was his? Plum admitted that it was also possible that Flo had been promiscuous enough not to know who her child's father had been. Somehow, that didn't seem possible with the wounded, prickly woman Plum had come to know.

With the shock of her discovery finally fading, Plum moved on to studying the rest of the material in the Plum's birth certificate box, in search of more answers to the progression of her life.

Many of the legal papers appeared devoted to selling the fiction that Crystal claimed she'd given birth to Plum in what those documents called "an unattended birth." A birth, apparently, with no doctor or midwife in attendance. Crystal's friends had provided affidavits swearing they'd been present at that birth. They'd fudged on that, though it didn't represent big-time lying in Crystal-land.

Was there any question why Plum was as goofy as she was? Yet, could she really assume she'd be any different if her own birth mother had raised her?

Lastly, Plum went through copies of decades of correspondence between Crystal and Flo. These were only a fraction of the letters exchanged, given all those empty envelopes. Had Crystal gathered them together in the hope of giving Plum a representative sample someday? Had she simply gone silent too soon for what she always intended to tell Plum? In most of the copies of Crystal's letters to Flo, Crystal consistently shared with Flo how her little girl was getting on. That was the way Crystal always referred to Plum in the letters to Flo, as *"your* little girl." Never as Crystal's, and never their joint-daughter. That explained a lot. Flo's letters to Crystal always expressed a needy, but also curiously curt, gratitude for the care Crystal was giving to Plum, and what she shared with Flo about Plum's life.

What wasn't contained within that box was any adoption paperwork. Curious. Given Crystal's unique thought patterns, that stuff could easily be filed away somewhere else in that big house with an entirely different label. Or lost forever.

Plum's mood this night had ridden a roller coaster. The enchantment she'd felt with Brian now seemed so far in the past, she had to remind herself it had only occurred a couple of hours earlier. She'd moved at lightning speed from that, to anxiety, to shock. And now, she found, to anger. Anger at a life filled with lies. Lies that ran right up to the present—Flo could have told her all of this. Plum no longer questioned why Flo wanted to sell her the bookstore and the rest of the properties at a bargain price. If Plum had demanded it all for free, she'd bet Flo would have agreed.

Plum's love and loyalty wasn't bought that cheaply. It wasn't just a life of lies she had lived, but a life of abandonment, too, in which nobody had ever loved her enough.

A sob escaped from her throat, surprising Plum. No, she couldn't allow herself to sink into hurt, or she'd drown in it. Not after what Noah did just days ago. She couldn't deal with one more rejection. She had to keep herself firmly in the anger.

It mushroomed within her, building until it encompassed a determination to take some action on this. Tonight. She'd never be able to sleep until she did.

How? She didn't know where Flo lived. All the letters from Crystal had been addressed to the bookstore address.

She *had* to find some way to reach Flo. Plum went back downstairs for the phone directory she remembered seeing shelved under the counter. Too bad Flo wasn't listed. Dammit! Another idea quickly sparked in her brain. A second search confirmed that, unlike Flo, Jake's number was listed.

With the open phonebook clutched to her chest, Plum stumbled back upstairs to the apartment. Then, she hesitated. Could she really make that call now? It was after midnight. Most people consider it rude to call anyone that late. Did that rule apply to nights involving life-altering revelations?

Plum yanked the receiver from the yellow kitchen wall phone, and dialed quickly before she could change her mind. Jake answered after a few rings, and fortunately, he didn't sound sleepy. Maybe she hadn't awoken him.

Plum skipped the apology for calling at that hour, in case he only gave her a moment. Instead, she spat out, "Jake, I need Flo's address."

"Has something happened there in the apartment? Some emergency?"

How would he define *emergency?* "...No."

"Then I can't let you have that information, Plum. If Flo wanted you to have it, she'd have given it to you."

They went back-and-forth on it for a while. Plum sensed she wasn't going to convince him. Finally, switching gears, she insisted he come to see her.

"When? Now?" he demanded.

"Yeah, I think it has to be now."

Jake hung up with a heavy sigh, which Plum couldn't interpret at all. But he showed up about ten minutes later at the bookstore's front door. He still wore the same clothes she'd seen him in earlier, when he dropped by the bookstore, a worn leather vest over a denim work-shirt and jeans. Maybe he really hadn't undressed for the night. She felt a little less guilty clinging to that idea.

"This better be important," he said gruffly. "I was up to the final few chapters of a mystery novel that had kept me guessing for three hundred pages."

"Don't worry," Plum said. "We have some major plot twists for you here, too."

"No murders, though, right?"

"Not yet."

Though Jake shot her a startled glance, he said nothing while she led him upstairs.

When they reached the kitchen, and he spotted Scrappy on the counter, staring out the kitchen window that overlooked the alley, he said, "Look at that. The cat's still here."

Plum refused to be distracted. She hadn't told him everything to do with her leaving California. After they were seated, she went through it all. Every gory detail of her encounter with Noah and Claire.

"I'm sympathetic, kid. If that sombitch Noah were here, I'd knock him on his ass. Still, I don't understand—"

"Stay with me, huh, Jake? I'm trying to give you a full picture."

She moved onto Noah's working for Budget-Mart's commissions, his maps, some of which depicted Applewood in detail, and then, onto Crystal's circumstances, and the envelopes with the Applewood return address filling that closet. She gave him the most complete picture of anyone there—she hadn't told Ginger, Becky, or Flo about Noah's Budget-Mart connection. For Jake to fall in with her plans, Plum guessed he'd have to know it all. Finally, Plum showed him the photo she'd found earlier this evening and went through the contents of that box, especially the birth certificate, and the letters from Crystal describing for Flo her daughter's life. His eyes widened in surprise.

"Flo? *Our* Flo? *Flo* is your birth mother? Is that your theory, Plum?" he asked. "Assuming it's true, are you telling me you didn't know that when you arrived here in Applewood?"

Plum shook her head no. "I always knew I wasn't Crystal's favorite, that Sunni was special to her, in a way I never was. Yet I never doubted that she and Ben were my parents. It didn't even occur to me that I might have been adopted."

What she really couldn't imagine was any adoption agency giving Crystal a child. That part of the story needed further study. Maybe someone took a bribe.

Jake briefly stared off. "That's why you asked about the West Pony address. I worried about that."

"What did you think?"

Jake shrugged. "That you were a process server, maybe. When you didn't do anything to Flo, I forgot about it." He gave his head a shake. "Your coming here by chance—that's a helluva coincidence."

"Not really. The coincidence was Noah pursuing a Budget-Mart deal here. But this is precisely the kind of small town that Budget-Mart favors. He's also trying to put together their deals in similar towns in other parts of the country. Besides, there's Brian Coburn. When we were in high school, I overheard him talking about vacationing here. For a kid who lived an unstable life, Applewood sounded heavenly. Put that together with all those empty envelopes, which left a trail of breadcrumbs, and when I needed to escape someplace, it was the only place I could think of."

Plum didn't add that by living a hopscotch life, odd circumstances often came together for her. But she was too embarrassed by her own weirdness to confess that. Would she have been more like everyone else if she hadn't been tossed aside like…? She caught sight of Scrappy, now perched beside Jake on the couch. If she hadn't been abandoned like some unwanted cat?

Jake ran his hand roughly over his face. "You want to confront Flo with it tonight? You can't give her until tomorrow morning?"

"Would you, if it were your life?"

He sighed in surrender. "Do you have a navigation unit in your car?"

Plum snorted. "I'm lucky my Jeep has wheels."

"Okay," Jake said. "Get me some paper, and I'll draw you a map. It isn't far."

Plum dashed to the kitchen, where she'd left a pen and pad, which she extended to him on her return.

As Jake set to work on his map, Plum went to the kitchen window, where the cat waited to be let out. With her heart in her throat, she raised the window. The cat bolted, as if she'd been desperate to leave. Plum told herself that one more hurt didn't matter after all that had been heaped on her. But it did matter. She'd wanted Scrappy to *want* to stay. She needed to believe that *someone* wanted her.

When she returned to the couch, Jake had finished sketching his map. She reached out for it, but he held onto it, while giving her a stern look. "Plum, if I give you this, I want you to promise me something. I want you to agree to remember that you're a grown woman now, not the baby that was given away. And I want you to think about how young Flo must have been when you were born. A child herself."

Another wave of anger spiked in Plum. "By that same token, Jake, shouldn't we also remember that Flo's not that young girl anymore."

He gave his head a slow, questioning tilt. "Maybe not, but I've always thought there had to be some wound in Flo. She may not be that child-mother now, though I swear to you that she stopped growing a long time ago, for a reason I never grasped. Now I understand that losing you was that reason, Plum." That familiar steely look came over his face. "Do you promise to take that into account when you confront her?"

What a demand. Plum had to keep stoking that anger. She wasn't sure how much she would ever be able to forgive. Yet she also understood if she didn't agree, Jake would refuse to help her. Reluctantly, she nodded, unsure how she would make this work. She snatched the map from his hand an instant later, before he could change his mind.

* * *

As Plum drove through the darkened streets, her fear eclipsed her anger. Confrontation had never come easily to her, and this one was a doozy. "Look before you land," Crystal had always advised. Plum had never quite managed it, even with less at stake. Tonight, as she hovered mid-jump, while she had no idea where she might end up, she knew her landing spot could determine the direction of the rest of her life.

Applewood's residential areas didn't contain street lamps, owing to its dark sky laws. The lack of lights made the stars gleam extra brightly, but it didn't do much to help anyone find her way here on the ground. On some blocks, lots of homeowners left porch lights on, making those blocks easier to navigate. Where fewer homes were lit, Plum felt as if she'd stumbled into a black hole.

Plum really didn't know what she felt anymore. Crystal hadn't been an ideal mother, but she hadn't abused her kids. She gave them her best; her best was simply lacking. She didn't even overtly favor Sunni. It was that with her ego, it only made sense that she cared more for the child she'd borne, than the mutt she'd picked up at the pound.

Plum finally pulled up before Flo's address. At least, she thought this was the right place. No welcoming porch light here on the little ranch-style house. Even in the dark, Plum could see, from the weeds shooting through the gravel covering the front yard, it was as indifferently maintained as the bookstore had been. The lights were all off inside.

Before she could stop herself, she hastily marched to the door and rang the bell.

Nothing happened at first. Then she began to see lights going on inside the house and heard sounds within. Eventually, Flo flung the door open. Given her pillow hair and puffy eyes, she had been asleep.

Where to begin...? "Did I wake you?" Plum asked, feeling stupid for the ridiculous remark.

"Did you want to?" Flo asked in an acid tone.

Plum's heart beat so fast, she feared it might burst through her chest. "I found something tonight that I thought you'd want to see right away."

"Yeah? What's that?"

"My birth certificate."

Flo stood there in stunned silence. Then her eyes began to fill with tears. "My baby. My baby's finally come home to roost." Flo pulled Plum into her arms for a fierce embrace.

Wasn't it *chickens* that come home to roost? Plum thought, certain that she'd gotten that adage right, determined to distract herself with it so she didn't have to think about that hug.

Yet she knew. Her mother's arms wrapped around her felt better than she could ever have imagined.

CHAPTER NINETEEN

When she stepped across Flo's threshold, Plum heard the engine of a car passing behind her on the darkened street. One of Flo's neighbors heading home late? Or had Jake followed her there? He'd seemed worried about Flo, but if he had followed Plum, she hoped he had enough sensitivity not to intrude in this mother-daughter reunion.

The instant she stepped through that door, Plum felt an overwhelming impulse to flee. To rush back to her Jeep and speed away. But she had run so often lately. Maybe it was time to face something head-on.

Once they passed the warm exchange at the door, an awkward silence shrouded them both. Flo's request that Plum follow her to the kitchen proved to be nothing more than a jerky hand gesture.

Despite her discomfort, Plum's nosiness about Flo's circumstances caused her to gawk all the way through the house. While it looked cleaner than Plum expected, considering the state of the bookstore, it hadn't been updated in decades. The walls were papered in some fussy floral wallpaper that time had yellowed. The living room was carpeted in worn multi-colored shag. Plum felt no doubt that the awful chintz couch from the apartment over the bookstore had started its life here.

The time warp continued into the kitchen. Greeting Plum there were green Formica counters, whose surface had rubbed off in spots. The appliances were a mixture of gold and avocado. It actually reminded her of Crystal's kitchen. Maybe the mothers had compared decor ideas in their ongoing correspondence.

Flo appeared to have shrunken within the pink terrycloth robe wrapped around her. Gone was the woman who always acted so unconcerned with what anyone thought, replaced by one more tentative. It occurred to Plum that Flo probably wanted to flee, too.

Could they face this together?

With her back to the sink under the darkened window, Flo's voice sounded shaky when she asked, "Coffee or wine?"

"Got any ice cream?"

Flo's hooded eyes brightened. "Inspired choice!"

She yanked open the freezer compartment door of the side-by-side gold fridge. She had squeezed quite an impressive selection of Häagen Dazs pints in there—to the extent that Plum wondered whether Flo typically made ice cream her primary food choice. Plum was really more of a Ben and Jerry's-girl, but when the world-as-you-know-it has come to an end, there are more basic needs than Cherry Garcia.

It struck Plum that Flo's impressive ice cream selection represented a decent chunk of change. And that seemed strangely at odds with the condition of the house. Flo didn't lack the money to live better, she simply didn't choose to. Jake was right—Flo had gotten stuck somewhere. Like Plum had.

With her back to Plum, while she gathered together spoons and ice cream containers, Flo tentatively asked how Plum happened to come upon the bombshell she dropped at the door. Plum had already told her about the empty envelopes Crystal had left behind, which Flo pretended to have no knowledge of. Now, Plum limited her updating to what she found in the box containing Flo's correspondence and Plum's original birth certificate. Flo's choppy, sleep-tossed hair bobbed as she nodded her understanding.

Plum wasn't sure what she felt anymore. Not the anger that had consumed her earlier, although not the warmth of Flo's welcome, either. Maybe she was numb. It didn't take a lot of imagination to realize this mother was as screwed up as the one lying in that care facility back in California. Who would have thought one deck could contain so many jokers?

They stood on opposite sides of a tan tiled island that contained an avocado electric cooktop. Flo passed across a container of Vanilla Swiss Almond with a tarnished silver spoon stuck in it. "I hardly know what to say," she said in a tremulous voice, and then fell silent.

A wave of compassion rippled through Plum, prompting her to make things easier. "How about if I start?" she said. "Father unknown?" She threw that out as a question, hoping Flo would hear the humor she'd injected into it, not judgment. "Why did you hide that?"

Flo issued one of her familiar grunts. "Don't you believe everything you read. I'm surer about that than anything in my life." A sigh that seemed to have come from deep inside escaped from her. "I wish I could forget the exact circumstance of your conception, but—" She broke off abruptly. "You were sired by Gil and Hannah Russell's baby boy, Billy Dean."

Brian had said something about him. "He died, didn't he?"

Flo nodded. "Not even drunken princes can come out ahead when they take on light poles at ninety miles an hour. Isn't it funny how we both fell for the spoiled rich boys in our high schools? Fortunately, Brian has become a better man than Billy Dean probably would have."

With an exasperation that was becoming too familiar, Plum said, "Actually, the guy I fell for was decidedly middle class. Someone whose dad is known as Pudgy Paul Rowle, who sells car insurance out of an Indiana storefront." Did everyone here equate one date with a lifetime commitment? Plum stopped pushing that line when she remembered that long before she took up with Noah, she had fallen for Brian, who at the time was the spoiled rich boy in her high school.

Flo didn't seem to notice. She stared off into the distance. "I was over the moon when Billy Dean asked me out. I wasn't allowed to date yet. I was a sophomore, but only fourteen, since I'd skipped a grade earlier."

Fourteen? Plum remembered what Jake had said about Flo having been a child when she gave birth.

"I lied to my parents and got a friend to cover for me. Billy Dean was a senior and seemed so sophisticated. I couldn't believe he actually liked me." Flo snorted. "I didn't know that nailing awkward younger girls was a game the popular senior boys played. They actually gave themselves points for it."

She felt her own throat tighten, though she said nothing. That heartless boy had sired her? Plum found she couldn't weave that thread through the jumbled tapestry of her life.

"When I got pregnant, Billy Dean denied it ever happened, as did his parents. My own parents threw me out."

"Jeez," Plum muttered. Plum couldn't think of anything she and Sunni could have done that would have made Crystal turn against them.

"Oh, they did okay by me financially. They owned the building that the bookstore is in. They gave me that, and installed me in the rooms upstairs. They bought the bookstore from the prior owner. It covered the entire space in those days, including where Bonnie's restaurant is now. That was how I made my living. I ran it, starting right after I announced my pregnancy. Alone, at first, and then, with you. They made me leave high school—I didn't get my GED for years. They never even came to see you." Flo stared out again. This time, anger clouded her eyes. "Both Billy Dean and his parents denied you were his. I was a kid—I didn't know anything about establishing paternity. It wasn't as if we could Google things in those days."

Plum nodded. She could only barely take in what it had been like for Flo.

"My leaving his name off the birth certificate—that was a minor act of rebellion. If he didn't want us, we didn't want him. Feeling as beat up as I was, it was one of the few courageous acts I performed back then."

"What an awful story," Plum said in a hushed voice. "You made one mistake that any girl might have—"

Flo cut in with, "The only mistake I made was in agreeing to go out with him. As for the sex, there wasn't any consent involved." Her rosebud lips curled in disgust.

"He *raped* you."

Flo shrugged. "If that's what you call being physically overpowered by a boy. Nobody else saw it that way, of course, including the police. The Russells have always owned the department." She turned away, tossing her spoon into the sink and putting her own container of ice cream back into the freezer. "I stayed in the apartment over the bookstore, even after I turned it into two storefront spaces. When my father died—he was the second to go—they left me everything, even though they hadn't seen me since I was fourteen. My parents had amassed quite a bit of cash and property by then. I left the apartment and took over their house. Dancing on their graves."

Flo snapped out that last remark. Yet she hadn't really danced on their graves. She moved into their rundown house and didn't bother to make it her own. Their grimness of their lives was all Flo took on.

Plum walked around the island and slipped an arm around Flo's shoulders and guided her to an old-fashioned chrome-and-Formica table on the far side of the room.

Flo hadn't seemed all that interested in the ice cream—that surprised Plum, since she seemed to be the Häagen Dazs queen. Maybe she reserved it for less stressful times. Plum pulled open the refrigerator door and found an open bottle of Chardonnay. She looked through a couple of cabinets until she came across a mismatched selection of wine glasses. She poured the liquid nearly to the top of one and carried it to the table. When she placed it down before Flo, Plum caught her dabbing her eyes with a tissue that she hastily stuffed into her robe pocket.

Plum went back to the island, cocking her hip against it. She wrestled a chocolate-covered nut from her ice cream, which she nibbled slowly. "I didn't see any adoption papers in that box."

"And you won't," Flo said. "That was another courageous act I took to protect you. Like I said, the Russells denied you were Billy Dean's—right up until he died. Then, at some point during Hannah's grief, she realized you were all she had left of her son. After that she was determined to take possession of you. That told me they had always known their precious brat raped me, and they hadn't cared."

Never would Plum have expected any of this, especially that she was a child of rape. Yet didn't that fit?

"They demanded custody of you. But that was also when Crystal and Ben happened to be driving cross-country. They stopped in Applewood by chance. Crystal had run out of books, and you know how much she loved to read. Since High Desert Books was our town's only bookstore, it was inevitable that they would find me."

Plum had always regarded Crystal's love of reading as a paradox that never fit with her manic makeup. Settling into a book was often the only thing that calmed her.

"Gil had stormed out of the bookstore, after demanding that I turn you over to them. 'Before the paperwork comes through,' he'd said, as if their winning custody of a child away from her mother was a foregone conclusion." Flo shrugged. "Crystal and I got to talking. She had suffered a miscarriage, and she felt devastated."

Plum hadn't known about any miscarriage. Crystal had never mentioned it. Maybe it had hurt her too much to ever talk about. Plum struggled to keep breathing.

Flo remained lost in her story. "I was heartbroken by the idea of Gil and Hannah raising you. I knew they would destroy you the way they had Billy Dean. And knowing how Gil had always been able to use his wealth to manipulate the system, I also thought they'd succeed in gaining custody. Crystal came up with the idea of my handing you over to them, and it seemed like the perfect solution. She assured me that she and Ben would convince the LA authorities that you were theirs. I swear to you that I didn't know she was bipolar, I just thought she was lively and fun. And Ben...well, you remember. There was such a charm about him, and he could settle Crystal with ease."

Plum smiled. "Yeah, he sure had charm in spades."

"To me, at fifteen, they seemed much older and worldly, although now I know they were only in their early twenties at the time. I had a flash of insight that if there were no adoption records, if you were covered by a second birth certificate listing them as your parents, the Russells would never find you. I always insisted to Hannah and Gil that I'd given you up for adoption, though I refused to share particulars." Flo sighed. "They tried to follow the trail, many times. I would hear occasionally when they hired another private investigator to find you. When they did, I'd contact Crystal and tell her we had to lay low...you know, stop the letters and calls for a while. Later, we'd start up again. She promised me she would always keep in-touch, so I would never have to wonder about my daughter." Flo tilted her head to the side. "I realize now she might have fibbed at times about your circumstances, but she always did what she said she would."

Plum understood for the first time what it must have been like for Crystal. She had never stopped thinking of Plum as Flo's daughter. Plum felt grateful now that Crystal had taken that responsibility so seriously.

Plum also remembered her brief exchange with Hannah when she first came to town, when the older woman thought she looked familiar. It made Plum shiver to think about *who* Hannah must have been thinking about.

That memory raised another question. "Did Hannah always buy her books from you?"

Flo said she hadn't. "That started a few years after you went away. She does most of her shopping in Phoenix or Scottsdale, a two-to-three hours' drive from here. Always has. And I assumed she also bought any books she wanted there. Then, a few years after you went to live with Crystal and Ben, she started dropping into the bookstore. I always figured she thought if we became friends, I'd slip and tell her something."

Plum felt more generous toward her. She thought Hannah might have been merely trying to keep in-touch with the only connection she had to her grandchild. Plum had no doubts that her life with Crystal and Sunni, such as it was, had been better than the life she would have known with the Russells, with their arrogant sense of entitlement. But she also believed they suffered greatly over the loss of their son and granddaughter.

Flo pulled the crumpled tissue from her robe pocket again and noisily blew her nose. When she was done, she placed her hand on the table. It looked small and defenseless.

"Plum, can you forgive me?" A tear trickled down Flo's cheek.

"For choosing the best alternative you had to save my life? There's nothing to forgive, Flo," Plum said. She meant it completely. The torrent of emotions she'd carried within her when she arrived there had vanished.

Plum realized she'd lost too much of herself in those years with Noah. She'd come to care too much what he and the people who mattered to him thought of her. She'd let the essence of herself drift away until, on that awful day when she caught him cheating, she was nothing more than the worst kind of victim.

No longer. Plum felt a new flame burning brightly in her. One that she hoped would help her to stand up to people better than she ever had before.

"What now?" Flo asked.

"Now it's time for Flo Gallagher and daughter to come out." Once again, despite the power of her words, Plum felt that familiar urge to run.

Flo slouched in her chair, seeming to shrink even more. "I'm not sure I have the strength to deal with all of it again."

"I have enough for both of us." Plum hoped that was true anyway. "And I know exactly how to go about it."

CHAPTER TWENTY

Plum brought the Jeep to a stop in a sprawling supermarket parking lot. This wasn't the small neighborhood market she'd used when she first moved into the rooms above the bookstore. She'd heard there was a larger all-night market located in one of the newer parts of Applewood, with its twisty cul-de-sacs of Southwestern custom homes, and tonight she found it. Back in Santa Monica, she frequently shopped in the middle-of-the-night after getting off work, and there, the markets were often crowded. Here, she couldn't see why this market bothered to stay open. The parking lot was virtually empty.

That was how it went with national stores. Their corporate headquarters often instituted chain-wide conditions, even if local norms didn't support them. What would happen to this place if Budget-Mart came in? Budget-Marts sell groceries, too. Would it be a case of chain gobbling chain? Why not? Plum thought. That had become the American way.

With a sense of wistfulness, Plum wished there could be pockets where the steamroller of progress didn't move so relentlessly forward.

Rather than stepping out after she cut the engine, Plum leaned forward, resting her forehead on the steering wheel. She felt dizzy. Physically dizzy, emotionally, mentally—all the way through. Were there a fixed number of changes a person could take in a short period of time? Plum felt maxed out. Then again, maybe after months of living on nothing except for snack foods, the ice cream had been too rich.

And yet, as unsettled as her insides felt, Plum also experienced a consuming need to get back to real food. She felt the urge to cook again, with a yearning so strong, it shocked her. That was why she had to shop tonight—she couldn't put it off a moment longer.

Maybe that meant she was finally emerging from a dark tunnel into the light.

There was only one cashier on duty in the market. Slouched in boredom, it looked as if the hip she pressed against the wall of her checkout cubicle alone kept her upright. Fortunately, the other nighttime employees made better use of their hours by filling shelves. This market was better stocked than her favorite store at home usually had been at this hour. Plum started at one end and combed through the aisles carefully, snatching everything a dedicated foodie needed to keep herself well-fed: gourmet cheeses, proscuitto, paté, along with fresh pastas, olive oil, herbs, and much more, not to mention meats, artisan bread, and wines—and she hadn't gotten to the produce section yet. Before she'd gone even halfway through the store, the cart resembled a moving mountain.

In most of the aisles, she hadn't come across another shopper. Then, in the produce section, while reaching for a basket of raspberries, she accidentally backed into someone else's cart.

What are the odds? Plum wondered, that she and the only other person in the store should come to occupy the same few inches. Once she saw who she had crashed into, she felt less surprised. Jake pushed that cart. His expression looked unusually sheepish.

"Let's see, Jake, did you merely trail me to Flo's, and is our running into each other here a coincidence, or are you following me everywhere now?"

Jake offered up a feeble shrug. "Guilty to following you everywhere." He shuffled his scuffed boots. "I wasn't sure if you'd find Flo's place in the dark. And then I thought…you know, if maybe I heard shouting, that I could step in and help." He swallowed hard. "How did it go?"

Plum grinned broadly. "Amazingly great."

He exhaled so hard, he might have been holding his breath for hours. "I'm glad, kiddo." His forehead contracted. "She's okay? And you, you're okay, too."

"Yeah, we're both good." Dizzy, but good. Maybe dizzy *was* good.

Jake hadn't put much into his cart. Just a loaf of French bread and some cold cuts. While they talked, he added a few fresh fruits. Plum didn't imagine he ate much at home. There was an unfamiliarity to the way he stocked his cart, as if he didn't often do this.

Plum and Jake rolled their carts toward the check-stand together. When they drew close, Jake said, "Plum, I'd suggest we go somewhere together now for an early breakfast, so we could talk, but there isn't a place open here yet. Small towns have their downsides."

Given that her cart overflowed with food she wanted to cook, Plum said, "Why don't you come back to my place. I'll make you a breakfast you won't soon forget."

Jake asked in a pseudo-casual tone, "Why don't we call Brian Coburn to see if he wants to join us?"

Plum stopped and stared at him. "Seriously, Jake? Does everyone know Brian and I had dinner together tonight?" Plum glanced at her watch. It read 5:00 am. "Well, last night. All the nosy pokes in this town don't even know me."

"They know Brian, and your dating him is what represents big news in these parts." Jake pulled out his phone and speed-dialed a number. In a few moments, it was decided that Brian would join them. Plum wasn't sure whether she felt giddy by the thought of seeing Brian again, or even dizzier than before.

At the check-stand, when Plum reached into her tote bag for her wallet, she spotted her cell phone. She hadn't touched it since the night she left California, when she'd popped the battery out after seeing all of those messages from Noah. She hesitated for a moment now, before removing the SIM card. She slipped the phone back in her purse. Then she placed the SIM card down on the floor and violently crushed it beneath the heel of her shoe.

Jake choked. "Plum, are you crazy?"

"No, but I think I used to be."

* * *

Plum put away her groceries, struggling to find space for everything in the small kitchen, while Jake brought Brian up-to-date on Plum's discovery that Flo was her birth mother.

At first, Brian made a humming noise. Then he asked, "How did that come about?"

With her back to Brian, Plum only heard his voice. Even without facial expressions to guide her, Plum heard no surprise.

"You knew," she said. He was Flo's lawyer, after all. "That's why you questioned me about why I bought her business." Plum turned to him. "Did you think I planned to spring something on her?"

Brian hesitated, but if Plum thought an expression would tell her more, she was wrong. Brian kept his features blank. "It's my job to protect Flo," he said at last.

Had his concern for Flo actually prompted Brian's showing up at the bookstore door at night, instead of reconnecting with Plum? She knew she should feel glad that Flo had Brian in her corner. She wondered, though, when she would come first with anyone.

Plum moved on to cooking their breakfasts. Thankfully, the challenges of working on a nearly non-functional stove meant that claimed all her attention. Until Scrappy, the cat, appeared at the closed kitchen window. Plum's heart felt close to bursting when she realized her furry friend had come back. She quickly left her place before the stove and raised the window.

"Hey, is that the cat people around here have been feeding?" Brian asked, while he and Jake set the table.

People in Applewood really have nothing to talk about. Scrappy sure had gotten around before attaching herself to Plum. She was nearly as well known in Applewood as Plum seemed to be. While the cat stepped back into the apartment, Jake told Brian that, after refusing to partner up permanently with anyone else, the cat had finally chosen Plum to be her human companion.

"How did she get up to this window?" Brian asked.

"She seems to have figured out how to climb from the alley Dumpster, to the roof outside this window," Jake said. "Clever, huh?"

Plum would have described it as hopscotch, but that would have required explaining what it meant. Despite her joy that Scrappy had returned, Plum scowled at the little fur-ball, while pouring the cream she'd bought into Scrappy's bowl. She didn't need anyone else highlighting her most offensive traits.

Brian said, "Plum, we need to set up a time when we can talk, so I can update you on that business of finalizing your bookstore purchase agreement."

"What's wrong with now?" she said once she was back at the stove. "You can say anything you have to say in front of Jake. I don't have any secrets." None that she'd admit to anyway. Plum explained to Jake how she wanted to delay registering deeds, yet that Brian and Flo wanted her purchase legally protected. "Did you come up with a way of doing what I want?"

Brian's nodded. "But now that you know Flo's your birth mother, I'm not sure she'll still want to go ahead with selling you the properties."

"Come on, Brian. You promised. Put your monkey where your mouth is."

Brian laughed so hard he almost spit out his coffee. "Plum, I'm sure she'll want to give you everything. Or let you operate as if it's your own, and leave it all to you in her will. I can't speak for Flo, of course, but I'm pretty sure this changes everything."

Plum turned away from the stove and stared at Brian.

"Surely you see that. She got as close to giving it all to you as she could when you thought she was a stranger. You asked me if property values were so low here that you could buy all this for ten grand, remember?"

Jake choked. "Ten thousand? That's all you're paying? Do you know what my property cost me?"

Plum placed their breakfasts before them. Pecan waffles with cinnamon-raspberry syrup for Brian, and a scrambled egg wrap with hollandaise sauce for Jake, with a little of both for herself. Though the men dove in, Plum didn't.

"No, I have to do it this way. Brian, you and Flo promised."

Jake raved about his breakfast dish. "Plum, this might be the best breakfast I've ever eaten."

Brian put down his fork and stared across the table at her. "Is it possible that you're not over that guy in Santa Monica? Is that why you can't face him?"

He was asking, Plum sensed, not as Flo's lawyer, but as the guy who had curled her toes when he kissed her the night before. Plum met his gaze, though she said nothing.

After an awkward standoff, Jake said, "It's a fair question, Plum."

"Jake, not you, too," Plum cried, hurt.

Brian refused to be diverted. "Plum, you haven't answered me. Are you sure you're over him?"

Plum desperately wanted to tell him that her hesitation over sharing her new ownership of Flo's properties with the world had nothing to do with harboring feelings for Noah. It was a matter of not feeling ready to confront him again. She wanted to tell Brian that she had an idea. An idea for not only getting a bit of her own back from Noah, and one that might also help save the future of this town. Yet she couldn't bring herself to say anything about that. Plum's plans didn't always work. They *usually* didn't. They usually weren't in the same universe as a working plan that anyone else would devise.

She struggled to hide it when she said, "Brian, I have to ask you to trust me on this."

He kept that stern gaze trained on her. No wicked grin this time.

Plum hoped she hadn't blown the best thing she'd been offered in years. She bit down so hard on her lip, it surprised her that she didn't taste blood.

CHAPTER TWENTY-ONE

Plum caught a couple of hours' sleep after Brian and Jake left. She probably would have slept longer, only *someone* stuck a little pink feline nose into her face, demanding to be fed again. Plum wasn't ready to get up. She felt headachy and low. Crystal would have described it as lower than a stack of black cats.

She thought she should have felt elated. An important piece of her life's puzzle had come together last night. Gaining an understanding that Flo was her birth mother and finding answers to the questions that had always lurked around the periphery of her mind should have made her feel great. She *was* happy to have made that discovery. It was the time she'd spent with Brian and Jake that had made her this bummed, Plum realized, and the unsettling way she and Brian had left things, refusing as he did to believe that she was finished with Noah.

Forming relationships with both Jake and Brian were among the best parts of her time in Applewood. Reconnecting with Brian was the most exciting thing that had happened to her in...well, maybe ever. And Jake? For the first time since she'd lost Ben, someone finally promised to fill that dad-loss hole in her heart. Yet she fit with them like pickles and gin. People never seemed to like her as much once they got to know her and realized what a goof she was. Look at Noah. What other than her oddball qualities could have driven him to Claire?

It was always just a matter of time until Plum screwed up whatever good came into her life. A shrink would probably tell her that she didn't feel she deserved it. Big surprise. Understanding never did anything to prevent Plum from sabotaging herself.

Plum didn't eat any more after waking up, though she did brew another pot of coffee and quickly downed a couple of cups in the hopes of driving her headache away. She knew it would take more than caffeine to fix the greater offense of being hopelessly lame.

While slumped at the kitchen table over a cracked mug, listening to Scrappy happily crunching kibble from her new bowl, it occurred to Plum to wonder whether there was an oddball gene. She had always thought her quirkiness had come from Crystal and the erratic life they'd shared. But Sunni, who came through the same upbringing, didn't have it. That Plum might have inherited her oddness from Flo made more sense. You could hardly describe Flo as functional. Plum couldn't even factor in a cruel boy she would never know. It made Plum feel a smidge better to think that maybe her weirdness wasn't her fault.

When she could delay it no longer, Plum dragged herself down to the bookstore. Her plans for the place were all in the homestretch now. She'd scheduled her grand reopening for Friday, three days from now.

Just because she hadn't officially re-opened High Desert Books didn't mean she didn't have business. Given the speed with which gossip spread in Applewood, it seemed everyone there had heard about Plum taking over the bookstore. Every day lots of folks stopped to meet her, and since many also wanted to buy books, Plum saw no reason not to sell them, even if she wasn't officially open. She suspected some of them were thrilled to have an alternative to dealing with Flo. No question, in her own way, Flo topped Plum in the offbeat department.

Plum had also started choosing new stock. That was trickier than redecorating. For all the reading she did, Plum was never familiar with any bestseller lists, preferring to make her own book choices. That made it harder to decide what to order. How could she know what her customers would like? Other than Crystal, she had rarely discussed books with anyone. Now, as she read through reviews of forthcoming books in industry publications, Plum discovered she felt a little tingle when a title appealed to her. She put every book to the tingle test and only ordered those titles that moved her that way.

When the telephone rang, Plum felt the day's first surge of excitement. She thought it would be Flo, as eager as Plum to continue the connection they'd made the night before. But it was Becky. As much as she liked Becky, Plum felt a stab of disappointment that her caller wasn't Flo. She decided she was being unreasonable. The night's revelations had to be as emotionally exhausting for Flo as they were for Plum. She was older, too—although not by that much. How strange was it to have a mother who was only fifteen years older. Flo was probably still asleep.

"Hey, girlfriend," Becky said. "You keep putting off that interview you've promised me. Today or tomorrow are the last days if you want news of your opening to make it into Thursday's edition."

Plum had kept delaying the interview. She never remembered seeing Noah read the *Applewood Gazette*, not the paper edition anyway. But she wouldn't be surprised to learn he read the online versions of the newspapers in all the places he was trying to close deals for Budget-Mart. And as Brian had said, how many people could there be named Plum Tardy? She hadn't wanted him to learn where she was until she was ready to break that news. Still, if she wanted to out the Flo-and-Plum relationship, it had to be now.

They set up a time to meet that afternoon.

In addition to locals dropping in to meet Plum and buy books, some even offered to watch the bookstore for her. That way she could run errands and not miss sales. The door opened now, and Mindy, the strawberry blonde woman who had volunteered to watch the store for Plum came in, pushing a stroller. Mindy was the mother of a baby girl, Joy.

"We're here as promised, Plum," Mindy said with good cheer. "We can give you three or four hours. Will that be enough?"

"Plenty. I can't thank you enough, Mindy." Plum gave Mindy a quick hug, but it was with a suppressed sigh that she ran a gentle hand over Joy's fine hair.

She'd always heard how nosy small town people were. That was sure true—news in Applewood spread faster than the speed of light. Yet lots of people were uncommonly generous, too. The small town naysayers didn't acknowledge that.

"Oh, please. You're doing me a favor by giving me something fun to do."

Plum promised not to be away too long and sailed out the door. She stopped first at a print shop. The man behind the counter told her the banners she'd ordered announcing her grand reopening weren't ready yet, though they would be in a little while. Plum said she'd return later.

From there, she walked to the Western wear shop she'd been admiring since she first arrived in Applewood. Dammit, she was going to buy cowboy boots! Assuming she could walk in them.

The stocky middle-aged owner was busy at the counter when Plum entered. It looked as if she'd recently received a shipment because boot boxes were stacked on the floor all around the counter.

Still, the owner took a moment to look past those boxes and said, "I hear someone is having a party this Friday." She came around the counter to greet Plum.

"Will you be there?"

"Wouldn't miss it."

Though Plum had dropped into the boot store many times, she hadn't yet introduced herself. She did that now.

"Plum?" The storekeeper gave her curly black hair a little shake. "People sure give their kids fun names today."

Some more than others. Plum had forgotten to ask Flo which of her mothers she needed to thank for her name, though she suspected a fifteen-year-old might regard it as cool.

"I'm Sarah." After a bit more small talk, Sarah returned to the counter to finishing processing her delivery. "If I can help you with anything, give a shout."

Plum felt a wistful envy of Sarah for her ordinary name. She thought for sure someone with that name would never make a false step.

Plum took her time looking through the boots on display, including the new styles Sarah kept putting out after she checked them into her computer. Plum almost swallowed her tongue when she looked at the prices. Hundreds of dollars—she'd never spent that much on shoes, though she knew many women who did, starting with Sunni. But even though she was convinced the money in the satchel was what Noah had saved from ripping her off, it still felt as if she were spending found money. That made it easier. In the end, she came back to her first choice, a pair of dark blue boots with powder blue insets. They would look perfect with Crystal's navy suit with the pale blue piping. She'd wear that for the party.

Sarah measured Plum's feet, and thankfully, had the boots Plum had come to love in her size.

"They feel funny," Plum announced when she began walking in them.

Sarah nodded. "First time wearing cowboy boots, huh? They fit differently, that's for sure. You have to get used to the sensation of your heel being loose, and the firmer feeling over your instep. But they're more comfortable than you'd think."

That was true. Plum liked them so much she feared she'd go broke buying additional pairs. She resisted it this time, though, before she left, she bought another pair of jeans and a couple of Western shirts, along with a pale blue tank top to wear with the suit. She counted out a small stack of hundred dollar bills—for which she received very little change—and promised to see Sarah on Friday when she left.

Plum had never been one for retail therapy, but after her Victoria's Secret excursion on the road, and now this shopping spree, she came to the conclusion she might have been a bit hasty in dismissing it. Her spirits, which had dragged so low when she awoke, had now brightened. Plum felt herself bouncing as if to some lighthearted music.

Until the oddest feeling came over her… It began on the back of her neck, that twitchy feeling that someone was watching her. She resisted the urge to turn around for as long as she could because it seemed too paranoid. When she finally did glance back over her shoulder, while the sidewalk behind her was filled with a fair number of people, none showed any interest in her.

Did she need any more proof of how weird she could be?

* * *

Plum stopped at the print shop again, and this time, her banners were ready. She was really laden down with packages when she made her way back to the bookstore.

Becky was waiting there when Plum stepped through the bookstore door. With Mindy busy with a customer, she took Becky upstairs, where they could talk quietly. Well, apart from the sound of a cat batting around a ball that contained a bell. Plum waited until they had mugs of tea before them at the kitchen table before dropping her bombshell.

Becky's eyes widened in surprise. "Flo? Flo's your birth mother. *Our* Flo?" She had a small notebook before her, as well as a digital recorder. She didn't use either.

Plum gave her head a firm nod to indicate that was precisely what she meant.

"Did you know that when you came here? Was that *why* you came?"

"Becky, can we go off the record here?"

Becky directed a slow exhale up her own face, ruffling her bangs with the force of her breath. "Plum, I write a column that says, 'Hey, look at the cool new stores we have here,' for a small town paper. This isn't exactly investigative journalism for *The Washington Post.*"

Plum continued to stare pointedly at Becky.

"Okay, off the record."

Plum nodded with satisfaction. Then she began to tell the story...the situation with Crystal, the need to empty the house, all the envelopes from this address, and finally, the contents of the box that supposedly contained Plum's birth certificate.

"My California birth certificate is a total fraud. Crystal got her friends to swear they were present at a birth that actually took place in another state, to an entirely different woman. Well, girl."

She ended her talk by describing some aspects of her childhood, and how she should have known she wasn't Crystal's child, but didn't. Plum only held back a few facts that she didn't consider germane to the story.

Despite the extent of Plum's honesty, Becky looked skeptical. "Really? Flo handed over a baby to strangers, rather than putting her up for adoption, when the adoption route is legal, whereas, if she got caught giving a baby away she probably would have wound up in jail. Juvie anyway." Becky frowned. "Any idea why?"

Plum repeated Flo's rationale, that if she went through the legal route, the Russells would have been able to trace it, and gain custody of her daughter. "Besides, she was a sheltered fifteen-year-old kid. She couldn't have known what was legal, and what was not."

Still obviously skeptical, Becky pursed her lips. She glanced around Plum's little kitchen. "Do you have a computer here?"

Plum said she didn't. "Walked out without it. Turns out you don't need them. Cell phones, either."

"Speak for yourself. I need both of mine attached to my internal organs." Becky reached into her briefcase and pulled out her phone.

"What are you looking for?" Plum asked.

"A photo of your presumed sire." Becky stopped searching and stared at something on the phone, then at Plum. "You do look like Billy Dean Russell. Both he and Flo. And Hannah—I should have seen that resemblance." She gave her head a shake. "Not much of Gil in you. You lucked out there. He is a handsome man, if you can get past the personality. Still, I don't see his facial firmness working as well on a woman. But Hannah and Billy Dean—that's why you're so pretty."

Why did people always say that when Plum knew it wasn't true?

Becky gave her head a tilt. "Why did you want this off the record?"

Plum sighed. "I wanted you to have some background, but as for the article, it's all too complicated. Does anyone really need that? The envelopes, the years of letters between Crystal and Flo that I didn't know anything about." Plum bit her lip. "And doesn't it make me look like an idiot? I show up here after my fiancé dumps me, walk into a stranger's bookstore, and buy it without knowing the owner gave birth to me. I feel like a fool."

Becky laughed. "The complexity is what makes it interesting. And what makes you feel foolish is called 'human interest.' That's what makes it news." Excitement now burned in Becky's deep brown eyes.

Plum frowned at her. "That's what makes it news? When I asked to go off the record, weren't you the one who told me this was just for some little column in a small town newspaper?"

Becky shrugged. "You got me. But I was a hotshot reporter once for the *San Diego Chronicle,* and I know news when I see it."

"Why did you leave?"

Becky shrugged. "The police beat got to me. I thought I needed a change. A real change, more than just shifting to a different desk in the newsroom would provide." She sighed. "Mostly, I'm not sorry. I've built a good life here. But…well, let's say it's not what I thought I'd be doing when I graduated from journalism school."

Plum nodded knowingly. Her life had taken a few surprising bends, too. Plum's life was all bends.

Becky's penetrating gaze bore into Plum. "How are things going with you and Flo?"

"If you asked me last night, I would have said great. I'm telling you, Bec, we had the best talk. Now, today, she's gone silent. Is it just me, or is that strange?"

Becky shrugged. "That's Flo. She goes to ground sometime. Closes the bookstore, holds up in that house of hers, not answering the door or the phone." Becky snorted loudly. "You know what she did for a while when bluetooth headsets first came out? She would wear one and pretend to be deep in conversation with someone, so she could avoid interacting with her customers. It took us all a while to realize she was never talking to anyone. Who does that?"

Plum didn't say anything. She'd once considered the same idea when she had to go to a dinner party given by one of Noah's terminally boring friends. Maybe it really was all in the genes.

Becky tapped her fingertips against the table. "Flo is obviously a damaged woman. Having a baby at fifteen—"

"Are we still off the record?"

When Becky nodded, Plum told her about Flo's account of being raped.

"Date-raped, huh? The devil's spawn didn't fall far from that tree."

Plum thought that adage sounded like something she would say. "Do you believe it, Becky?"

"I never met the boy, but from everything I've heard, it fits." Becky sighed. "Look, Plum, can we go back on the record here? Oh, not about the rape—that's Flo's story, and I'm not sure raking it up now would do anyone any good. Besides, it would never make it into print here in Applewood. As to your relationship with Flo and how you learned it...will you trust me to tell that story? I promise you won't sound stupid."

Plum hesitated, before finally agreeing with a nod.

Becky didn't accept that agreement immediately. "Are you sure? You really want this to go out to everyone, including Hannah and Gil?"

"That's the plan. He'll see it, right? Gil, I mean."

Becky gave her head a tilt. "There were days when he had to approve every comma. Believe me, I've been called on the carpet, sometimes along with the copy editor, for a little knuckle-slapping on some minute point." Anger flared in her eyes. "And I was always right in those situations. Dammit, I know what I'm doing."

Plum could see how big a price Becky had paid for her life here.

"Lately, though, there have been a few occasions when I've wondered if he even saw some stories. You know, things he would have objected to at one time. He doesn't seem well anymore. If you want a relationship with him, Plum—and why you would I can't imagine—but if you do, I wouldn't put it off."

Plum nodded. "If I do, it's gotta be on my terms." She had never before thought that about a powerful man, but she found she meant it now. "Can you make sure he hears about this?"

Becky choked. "In this town, with the way people talk? There's no doubt that Gil and Hannah will learn it. That's definitely what you want?"

"I know what you mean. That word of our news will run like sausage in busted casing. And maybe we won't be able to handle the outcome, right? But...yup, that's what I want."

She wished she felt half as strong as she probably sounded.

CHAPTER TWENTY-TWO

At four-thirty, with her errands done and Mindy and Joy gone, Plum decided to call it a day.

She had another date with Brian tonight. *If* he showed up. He hadn't been that enthralled with her during their early morning breakfast, convinced as he was that she was still hung-up on Noah. Would he have called if he intended to cancel?

Speaking of calls, she hadn't had one from Flo yet. Could her birth mother *still* be asleep at this hour? Unlikely. Plum thought this was a case of Flo being Flo. She read Flo as one of those people who justified any behavior because of the hurts she'd suffered, without giving a thought to how many new hurts she inflicted on others in the process. She tried to remember all that Flo had given up to make her own life better, using that to moderate the annoyance brewing within her.

Plum kept telling herself that it was Flo's turn now, that Plum shouldn't be the one to make the next move. She stood before the bookstore phone, resting on the counter, stewing. Finally, Plum grabbed it and dialed a number Jake had since given her.

"I warn you, Plum." Jake had said. "Flo doesn't always answer."

Then Plum would leave a message. A message that would make Flo want to reach out.

The phone rang and rang. Until the telephone company's canned message began, telling her Flo's voicemail box was full and couldn't take any more messages.

Plum slammed the phone down. "Of all the passive-aggressive..." After a calming sigh, she reached into a drawer under the counter, where she'd taken to storing her Jeep's keys. Plum took a moment to toss the keys lightly into the air, while thinking. Sure, not ever listening to messages, that was passive-aggressive. But not calling? That could be something else. What if Flo had an accident? Before she could reconsider, Plum locked the door, and dashed out the back to her Jeep.

The drive to Flo's house only took minutes. In daylight, with its trim paint peeling and far more weeds popping through the gravel than Plum had noticed in the dark, the small ranch looked even more rundown. Plum marched up to the door again and rang the bell. She waited. Nothing. Plum pressed her ear to the door, but couldn't hear anything beyond it. That might not be significant. Flo could be sitting absolutely still. Or she could be hurt.

Plum found a gate at the side of the house. Locked, of course. It wasn't a tall fence, though, and she scaled it easily. She'd look through the windows to assure herself that Flo wasn't lying in there unconscious. To Plum's surprise, the curtains or blinds on every single window were shut tight.

Plum sighed. "Damn, Flo. You're not supposed to go to ground to avoid me."

* * *

Back at the bookstore, Plum raced up to the apartment to get ready for her date with Brian. After her shower, she squeezed her wet hair tightly in a towel to strengthen her curls, letting it dry naturally. Then she perused the playground of Crystal's wardrobe for something extra special to wear, spreading out outfits across the bed—to Scrappy's annoyance, since she was sleeping there. Plum wished Becky and Ginger were here to advise her. On her own, she didn't have the fashion sense of a duck. Now, since she had all these clothes at her disposal, she also thought it might be time for the duck to develop a little flair.

She finally decided on a longish challis skirt, coupled with a Gypsy-styled blouse that fell off one shoulder. Adding a few smudges of makeup and giving her reddish hair a toss, her look was complete.

Once again, when she caught sight of herself in the mirror, it stunned Plum to see how good she looked. People were always saying she was attractive—was it possible that she was better looking than she'd always believed? Maybe Crystal's wardrobe contained magical powers. Would those garments make any other woman look as great?

She heard the tinny sound of the bell she'd added to the front door, so she could hear even while upstairs when the door opened. Once again, the fear that Brian might be too mad to come rose up in her.

Brian short-circuited it by shouting, "Where's my girl?"

His girl! "Be right down," Plum called, taking one more second to steal another look at herself in the mirror. Damn! She liked what she saw.

Despite promising to meet him downstairs quickly, she took a few moments to straighten the apartment. Though it was only their second date, they had waited twenty years for it. Anything could happen.

If she had any doubts about how well she'd come together that night, one glance at Brian's face, at the foot of the stairs, dispelled it. His wicked grin softened into something more thunderstruck, while a soft "Wow!" drifted out on a sigh.

Without saying a word, Plum came into his arms, lifting her face for a kiss. Rather than the quick kiss she expected, he pressed his lips hard against hers, revealing a deeper hunger. In an instant, while she opened her mouth to welcome him, her desire matching his.

Brian moved his lips to the side of her neck and left a trail of kisses there, punctuated by the touch of his flickering tongue, down her neck and across her naked shoulder. Plum admitted to herself that she'd chosen that off-the-shoulder blouse purely in the hope that Brian would put it to that use. The shock his lips and tongue sent through her was even more electric than she expected.

When his hand closed over her braless breast, bringing her nipple to a feverish point, she couldn't hold back her groan.

"Do you really want dinner?" he asked in a breathless whisper.

"All I want is you."

As one, clasped in each other's arms, their lips desperately locked, they started up the stairs. When Plum stumbled moving backwards, Brian scooped her up into his arms and carried her the rest of the way. *Is there any woman who doesn't want to be carried off to bed?* Plum figured that since Rhett carried Scarlet up that sweeping staircase in *Gone with the Wind,* every woman has dreamed of it. Plum's staircase wasn't nearly as grand, but Brian handled it beautifully.

Still carrying her effortlessly in his arms, he swept into the bedroom. He placed her down gently beside the bed, and they fell onto it together. They removed each other's clothes with an urgent neediness. At the sight of her in her Victoria's Secret undies, Brian almost choked. "God, you're beautiful," he said on a shallow breath. "I always knew you would be."

In that moment, Plum felt more desirable than ever.

When he mounted her, she felt a gasp of delight within her. As they rocked together in that age-old dance, with excitement building to dizzying heights, Plum grabbed the finest ass on God's green earth and helped him to drive even harder within her.

When the fireworks finally went off, Plum swore she saw colors in the ceiling over them. It took all she had not to shout, "So that's how it's supposed to be done!"

CHAPTER TWENTY-THREE

The second time was more leisurely, but no less passionate. The third time went deliciously slow as well, with time to make discoveries. By the end of it, Plum had never felt more exhausted, or more satisfied. She actually reached her lifetime apex of satisfaction, she felt sure. Better than this, it couldn't get.

Then, they luxuriated together between the tangled sheets. Laughing over silly jokes and messages they wrote on each other's backs with their fingertips.

Finally, after hours of play, Brian asked, "Plum, are you hungry for anything other than sex?"

"Like food, you mean? Ravenous."

Brian rose from the bed with unselfconscious ease, and calmly looked around her bedroom until he found where he had flung his watch. He chuckled when he said, "I doubt the restaurant kept our dinner reservation. We'd be more than three hours late." He began dressing.

"I'll make us something. I did buy out the grocery store last night."

Plum rose and unexpectedly found herself mirroring Brian's unselfconsciousness. That was a first. She usually rushed to cover. Maybe this time she saw her body as it had been reflected in his eyes. A way she'd never seen it herself. She finally took her sexy new nightgown from the dresser, especially glad now that she had bought it.

Before she could slip it on, Brian pulled her into his arms. "We're going to have to make our reservations later if all of our evenings start like this."

There were going to be more such evenings? Plum felt so giddy with joy, it was hard not to cheer.

Catching sight of her bruised lips and tousled hair in the corner mirror, Plum started to rake her fingers through her curls, but Brian stopped her by nibbling her fingers.

"Leave it. It's sexy," he said. "I like it."

She still felt sexy while pulling her flashy nightgown, with its plunging neckline, over her head. She even allowed her hips to sway when she led him to the kitchen.

"Woman, you're playing with fire," Brian said in a gruff voice.

Plum turned and fell into his arms, laughing.

In the kitchen, she looked through her cabinets and refrigerator. She settled on BLTs made with artisan bread, topped with chipotle mayonnaise, hash browns with red peppers, and a salad with shallot vinaigrette. Plum really felt hungry. Brian let Scrappy out through the window, since she seemed to want to come and go via the roof now.

Plum took pleasure from watching Brian dig into his sandwich. As they ate, they chatted and laughed. There was such a warm, domestic quality about it that made Plum feel surprisingly settled, considering it was their first time together.

Brian offered to go home, but Plum urged him to stay. Plum fell asleep bathed in the warmth of knowing a hot man lay beside her.

She couldn't say how long she'd been asleep, only that it was pitch dark when her eyes suddenly popped open. Rather than the joy that had filled her before falling asleep, anxiety now gnawed through her. And unexpected thoughts filled her mind.

What in hell am I doing here?

This wasn't her life. This wasn't even hopscotch—it was insanity. Wounded as she had been, it wasn't surprising that she hadn't known what to do after she discovered Noah and Claire together. Maybe that even explained driving to the one town whose name she could glom onto.

What about the rest of it? After little more than mere moments there, she'd bought a business, in an industry she knew nothing about. Surely, it took more than a love of reading to run a bookstore.

What the hell have I done?

Now she was lying next to a naked man she'd allowed to ravage her. Just because he used to be cute boy she remembered from high school. Maybe she simply had exceeded the amount of change a mind and body could take. More than the heart could take, too. Maybe it wasn't so hard to understand why Flo had made herself scarce. Flo probably surpassed her limit, too.

Plum felt a deep visceral longing to go back to... To what? To a house in Santa Monica soon to be owned by the bank? To unemployment? To a life alone? To a comatose mother, who had merely seen herself as a caretaker of someone else's child? She had no life left there.

In her desperation to cling to something, Plum found herself longing to return to the little apartment she'd had before she even met Noah, which was certainly someone else's now.

No, there was nothing for her there, but nothing here was really hers, either. None of it was real. Grasping new things as she had— that wasn't how you built a life. It was just *pretending* to build one.

So Brian really was her rebound guy, she decided with a sad realization. And the life she thought she'd found here—it was her rebound life. It wasn't real.

And sadly, the fantasy she'd been clinging to had crumbled into dust.

Now, what was she going to do about it?

CHAPTER TWENTY-FOUR

After Plum's startling revelations, it was hard to recapture the magic of the night before. She tried. When they awoke, she didn't resist when Brian took her into his arms while still in bed. But then, she leaped to her feet, wrapping her robe around her until it resembled a straitjacket.

From the bed, Brian stretched out his hand to her. "Hey, come back."

"You'll thank me for showering," Plum said over her shoulder, while rushing toward the bathroom.

The mood was shattered. She knew it.

Apparently, Brian did as well. How could he not? The awkwardness filling the space between them had become so thick, Plum suspected it couldn't be cut with a chain saw.

While she searched her kitchen cabinets for something to make for breakfast, Brian stood behind her. Silently.

"Plum," he said at last.

She wanted to turn to him. She wanted to blurt it all out. To say something like: *look, all I want is to curl up in a ball. I need some time. I lost an entire life in a flash. I created another one just as fast. My body and mind are suffering from ricochet fever. And I've never felt strong enough to be sure about new choices.*

She couldn't say it. Anytime she revealed too much about herself, people pulled away. Or they laughed at and chided her, like Sunni with her "Little Plum" crap. She couldn't take that from Brian.

She did need some time to sort everything out. She needed, she felt suddenly—a mom. Someone to hold her and guide her during times like this. Someone who would love her just as she was. Her throat tightened. But anger also rose inside of her. With two moms in the running, didn't it fit that there wasn't even one in sight?

"Plum."

She finally turned to him.

Brian still stood there, holding out a business card. "Remember when I said I'd try to find a jeweler who'd pay you top dollar for your engagement ring?"

"Vaguely."

"This guy will give you a good price." After a moment, he added, "That is, if you still want to sell it."

So he still believed that she couldn't get over Noah. What did she expect, when she didn't tell him the truth? Before Brian left, he took Plum into his arms again, though he limited himself to planting a kiss on the top of her head. After he walked down the stairs and out of the store, she felt as if they had broken up, even if nothing had been said. He had to think that, too.

What the hell was she doing?

* * *

In that extreme state of disconnect, she went downstairs and began following through on last minute details of her grand reopening event.

Despite the intensity of the revelation that had come to her during the night, she no longer felt as certain that the life-choices she'd made here were mistakes. Not that she believed her choices to be wise, either. The only thing she was sure of now was that she was sure of nothing at all. Not where she belonged, not who she belonged with. Not even which mother she should be clinging to, assuming that was even an option. She'd have to proceed with everything related to the bookstore until she figured things out. As to Brian, it seemed unfair to keep toying with his heart. Or even her own.

She spread out on the counter the banners she'd had made, deciding where to hang them. She was also scheduled to host the No on Budget-Mart meeting in the bookstore the next night. It felt strange to be involved, while emotionally disconnected.

When it came to hanging the banners, this time, instead of stacking tables onto each other, Plum checked with neighboring merchants and borrowed a ladder. She hung one banner outside, over the door, and another over the door inside, with the final smaller one, on the wall over the entrance to the backroom. She had to admit they looked pretty good in the spiffied-up store. But the magic had gone out of what she'd accomplished there.

She should be thinking of how to get out of the play-life she'd created, but then decided it made more sense to focus first on how she'd get out of purchasing the bookstore. She still hadn't paid for it. If she never did, would Flo really force her daughter to buy a business she didn't want?

But...what if Plum actually did want it, and all of this anxiety was only some fear of having moved forward too fast? If she left Applewood, where would she go? Assuming just vanishing wasn't an option, curling up into a ball sounded better than ever. She never expected life on the fly to be this hard.

While in the funk that bit of sucky wisdom brought about, the door opened and Diggy Long entered. Diggy, the short, muscle-bound blockhead who'd hassled her earlier.

"Hey, you're still here," he said.

That she didn't belong there must have been even clearer to him.

She couldn't say why, but this guy brought out the curmudgeon in her. "Don't give me any grief, Diggy. I'm not in the mood." Plum made a snarly face to drive the point home.

"Plum, I think it'd be great if we could be friends, but I unnerstan if you don't want to. Sometimes I come on too hard. Now, I'm here to make it up to you." He cracked his knuckles.

How? By hitting her?

"Hey, did you ever give Flo that piece of paper I left with you? The one with those names and phone numbers I said she should call?"

He meant the paper with Claire Denton's number. Hers and Javier Silva's, the LA commercial real estate broker. "Uh...yeah. For sure."

That is, by "giving it to Flo," she meant ripping the paper into tiny shreds and tossing it all into the trash. Plum found that you could often transform a lie into a rationalization with the right translation.

"Hmmm...funny...she still hasn't checked in with me." After an infinitesimal pause, he added, "I guess I gotta talk to Flo directly. But how? She doesn't answer her phone, doesn't answer her door."

There's a lot of that going around. Instead of confessing that she also couldn't reach Flo, Plum passed along Flo's threat to kick him in the ass.

He chuckled. "Flo was one tough little chick."

She was still tough-seeming, though only on the surface Plum saw now. Flo's hard shell hid a weak core. Yet that didn't mean her tough shell wouldn't kick him.

"Maybe I gotta tell you more. You see, Plum, Flo took the money that was supposed to go to me, or at least, half to me, half to her. No small sum, either. Forty K."

Forty thousand? There had been forty thousand in Noah's satchel. Was it possible that Noah hadn't saved that money, but had it to pay bribes on behalf of Budget-Mart? Where would he have gotten it? Plum wished Flo would surface if only to ask her again about Diggy's claims.

"I don't want you to think I'm greedy or nothing. I need the money for my ma. She's got that...whatchacallit...Alltimer's Disease. Half the time she don't know me. Last week, she told me which girls she wanted to invite to her Sweet Sixteen. I gotta put her into some kinda place, but I can't afford it."

Having sunken too much of her income in Crystal's care, that reached Plum, even though she suspected Diggy was lying about his mother. Diggy wanted that money for himself.

"Diggy, where did this money come from? This money you, or you and Flo, were supposed to get?"

A wall slid down over his pinched features. That was something he didn't intend to tell her. "Aw, you don't need to worry about that, Plum." He began backing toward the door. "Have Flo get in touch with me, huh?" He turned and quickly made his escape.

Was the amount of her satchel money significant?

How much of a mess was Plum really in?

* * *

Plum finally sent through her first electronic book order. She hoped her eccentric choices paid off. Primarily because, if she bailed, she didn't want to stick Flo with unsalable merchandise. A fog of confusion closed tightly around her.

The front door suddenly flew open and Ginger Maddy, dressed in her Applewood PD uniform, burst though. She rushed to Plum's side behind the counter, her pretty, friendly face now tight with distress.

"Oh, Plum, I'm so confused. I don't know what to do."

"Join the club," Plum muttered.

Ginger seemed not to have heard. She rushed ahead with, "I've been given an order by my chief. If it's an order I have to follow it, right? But this order, I absolutely *can't* follow. It'll hurt so many people, especially Becky, you, and Jake. And Bec and me—we're like sisters from another mother, you know? I can't do this to her, yet how can I refuse to obey a direct order?"

Ginger's distress got to Plum. No matter what happened, she still cared for Ginger and the other friends she'd made in Applewood. She had to try to make things better for her. "Slow down, Ginger. Tell me what this is all about."

Ginger took a deep breath. "I've been ordered to help shut down the No on Budget-Mart meeting here tomorrow night. The department is going to make a show of force."

"How? They can't shut down a legal gathering in a private business. How can they even think they can get away with that?"

Ginger shrugged. "Gil Russell and Chief Timley are combing through the town charter, trying to find some justification. I'm betting they'll come up with something. It's not like Gil doesn't have judges in his pocket, too." Her face crinkled up again, and one small tear slithered over her toffee-colored cheek. "This wasn't why I became a cop."

Plum's fog of confusion cleared instantly. Whether she remained in Applewood or not, she believed this town had a right to maintain the character most of its people wanted. How dare the fat cats think they could steamroll over that. Instead of retreating into her usual intimidation when it came to powerful men, she found herself eager to rumble with Gil Russell. Maybe it was the knowledge that they shared a relationship, which Gil knew nothing about, that gave her a sense that she held the power.

After giving Ginger a comforting handclasp, Plum hastily dialed Jake's number, and quickly related the danger to their cause.

Jake rushed through the door of High Desert Books only minutes later. He also gave Ginger a friendly pat on her arm. "Ginger, this is really good of you to share this with us, but we can't let you risk your job any further. You leave this with us now. We'll take care of it. You go ahead with whatever the chief orders, and don't be surprised by anything."

Ginger nodded gratefully. Without another word, she turned and left, looking furtively over her shoulder as she scurried away.

"Jake, what are we going to do?" Plum noticed she said *we* not *you*. The outcome of this struggle mattered more to her, it seemed, than she knew.

Jake stared out into the distance. "Plum, you're about to see one of the downsides to small town life." He flashed her a short smile. "This abuse of power can't be allowed."

"You know what this means, don't you? That someone on your committee ratted you out."

He nodded. "There's always someone who wants to be on the winning side, whichever that proves to be. I can't waste my time trying to figure out who it might be. We have to deal with this now and move on."

Jake began placing calls to other committee members, but Plum didn't pay attention to his plans.

To Plum it meant something more important. It meant this town wasn't the quirky Utopia she thought it was. That people there were the same there as everywhere else. She wouldn't have thought it possible, but her level of disenchantment with Applewood deepened even further.

CHAPTER TWENTY-FIVE

A florist made a delivery at High Desert Books the next day. It wasn't the first floral delivery of the week—Jake had sent a colorful spray of flowers the day before to celebrate High Desert Books' grand reopening.

This delivery absolutely took Plum's breath away. It was a delicate orchid, in a rich purple. The card read, "A perfect plum for a more perfect Plum," and it had been simply signed, "Brian."

After issuing a soft sigh, Plum noticed the deliveryman still stood beside the counter.

"It's called the Plum Orchid," he said. "Our customer insisted that we get this for you. He wanted it to go out yesterday, but we had to special order it. You can't imagine what it cost him."

The florist's deliveryman finally left, leaving the door open behind him. Plum stood in awe of this breathtaking flower that Brian considered less perfect than her. Was that before or after she went all awkward on him?

Steps behind her startled Plum. Since the deliveryman had left the door open, the bell didn't sound when someone entered.

"Like it?" a voice asked. The orchid's sender. Brian. "I asked the florist to call me after they dropped it off. Do you like it?" he asked again.

"You gotta ask? It's...perfect." Much more than she was.

Brian approached the counter. While his ruggedly handsome face looked closed off, the words sounded vulnerable. "I thought things were pretty good between us. Didn't you?"

"Heavenly," Plum said in all honesty.

"Until they became strained. What happened? Did you feel the pull of the old guy, and that made it impossible to take on the new guy?"

"Not that. Believe me, not that. I wish you'd accept it."

"What then?"

Plum desperately wished they weren't having this conversation, but neither could she pretend the awkwardness that came over her hadn't existed. She risked saying some of it. "It was more a matter of my not having my old life anymore, while I didn't yet have a new life. I felt adrift."

Brian gestured to the bookstore around them. "You did kind of throw this together rather hastily. Didn't you imagine it would take a little time to grow into it?"

Plum gave her head a toss. "There you go again, Brian. Making it sound stupid."

He laughed, but cut it short after only an instant. "I can wait a while, Plum. Not too long, but a little while. Should I? Is there something here to wait for?"

Before she even considered the question, she answered it with an emphatic nod. Only afterwards did she wonder if she was still stringing him along.

Before they could take their conversation any further, other merchants and residents began streaming into the bookstore for the No on Budget-Mart meeting. After Ginger's startling warning about the police chief's determination to shut the meeting down, Jake contacted everyone involved and rescheduled it for hours earlier. So that nobody unassociated with the movement crashed the meeting, Plum hung signs on the window, such as, "Really Closed," and, "Leave now, and come back later," to temporarily stop the flow of customers who dropped in despite the usual *closed* sign.

She'd shoved all the bookshelves and furnishings to the side and filled much of the space with chairs Jake had rented for the occasion, taking care not to place them too close to the door. They wanted the element of surprise on their side. It was essential that the bookstore's interior not be too visible from outside.

She and Becky also stole a moment alone. "Okay, kiddo," Becky said. "Operation outing Flo and Plum has gone to press. I think you'll be happy with the story I wrote. Now remember, I can't promise that Gil will read it, but I absolutely guarantee that someone will question him and Hannah about it."

Plum felt a little shiver of fear over what she'd unleashed. Gil presented such a threatening presence. She stoked her anger over his and Hannah's treatment of Flo to keep her sense of power strong.

Plum met lots of new people as they flowed in. Some she already knew, such as the man who loaned her a ladder, and Sarah, the woman who'd sold her cowboy boots. To Plum's surprise, Bonnie, the café owner from next door, and her son, Davy, also came through the door, with a young girl Plum hadn't met yet, her daughter, Anne. That Bonnie's face remained frozen in a permanent scowl made Plum wonder whether she was there under protest. Davy acted more receptive.

Plum kept watching for Flo, not expecting her to come, since she hadn't yet shown any interest in this fight, but still hoping. She confirmed with Jake that Flo had been invited.

"I always send her our emails, Plum, but I never expect her to show up. What's the matter? Things not so good between you two now?"

Plum shrugged. "She kinda went AWOL." She described Flo's disappearing act, and Plum's attempts to reach her.

Jake gave his head a slow shake. "That's Flo, all right. Two steps forward, and one back."

"Four steps back. Eight," Plum announced emphatically. She immediately wished she hadn't said it. How many backward steps had she taken with Brian? She felt relieved when someone called Jake away.

Finally, the meeting began. Plum had expected great enthusiasm for the fight to flow from the crowd. She expected outrage over Gil Russell's intention to use the force of law unfairly against them. Instead, what she mostly heard was whining. If it had ever been greater, the group's resolve had now worn down.

Plum tried to keep out of it, yet after one particularly wimpy remark, she snorted. Louder than she intended.

"Plum, do you have a suggestion for us?" A lift of Jake's eyebrow begged her to jump in.

She had to lend him a hand. "Well…maybe. Look, the tourist business isn't in question. It's the local trade we have to fight for, right? What does Budget-Mart offer people here that we can't?"

At first people just stared at her, some with expressions accusing her of treason. Because she hadn't stuck to the well-trod script? Then others started to speak.

"Cheaper prices," someone said. "But we can't compete with their buying power."

"Maybe we can," Plum said, her own enthusiasm rising. "Some of the businesses here are in related industries. Like restaurants and bars. How about if those business combine their orders to get a volume discount they could share, and pass onto their customers?"

She heard some murmurs, though she couldn't tell whether or not they agreed.

"We aren't all made of money," Bonnie snapped. "Even with combined buying power, we still might not be able to lower our prices."

"Believe me, I know." Plum said. Even if Dylan, her old boss, had put her down, she actually had a good sense of pricing structure in the restaurant business. "The discounts on books are awful. There's no way I can compete with Budget-Mart's book pricing." She really couldn't believe how bad book margins were. If she left there without buying the bookstore, she vowed to never again buy another book in a chain or online bookstore, supermarket, or drugstore. It would be strictly independent brick-and-mortar stores from then on. "There are other ways to try to compensate for that." Of course, that didn't mean she'd be the person doing it. "Let's move on. What else do Budget-Marts do well?"

"Why don't you ask what we do well?" one man shouted aggressively, as if he thought she had sided with the enemy.

"Fair point," Plum said. "What do we do better than the big box chain stores?"

"Offer better customer service," that man said, with more open-minded excitement now. It sounded as if spirits were rising finally, at least in some of them.

"Okay. How about if we offer more of it? How many of you make deliveries to local customers?"

No hands went up.

"What if we add that to our services? Another thing those big box stores offer is one-stop shopping. What would you say to the idea of allowing our customers to call in orders to many local stores, and pick up all their merchandise in one location?" Plum thought she saw interest in more of those faces now. "Look, we have to think in new ways to lure customers in. You know that old saying: you can lead a horse to the water trough, but you can't put him in it."

For some reason, she sensed she had lost them again.

Jake jumped in. "Plum may express things differently, but she has the kind of ideas and fresh approach we need."

"Her ideas are great," Sarah, the owner of the Western store, said. Several others agreed as well.

Jake beamed at her with more pride than she'd seen on any man's face since Ben was alive. "What else, Plum?"

Totally warming to the subject now, Plum said, "It occurred to me that we need a new media outlet. A way of spreading beliefs that counter the Russell propaganda."

Jake shook his head. "I don't know, Plum. We don't have local TV here, and starting a new newspaper would be impossibly expensive."

"Not if it were an online paper," Plum said. "If we all combined mailing lists, we could reach a good part of the town's population."

Davy piped up with, "I might be able to get an online newspaper going. Some of the guys in my computer class could probably help. Maybe we could use it as our class project."

Judging by Bonnie's flash of outrage, Plum figured Davy had been cut out of the will. Was Bonnie the one who'd ratted them out? Maybe Jake was right not to pursue it. Whichever way it went, they'd all have to live together afterwards. Well, everyone but Plum, most likely.

With time passing, they brought the meeting to a close, hastily passed out assignments, even forming new sub-committees. While Plum made most of the suggestions, she successfully avoided volunteering for any of the work. She didn't want to let anyone down, especially those who had become her friends. They'd all hate her enough for leaving.

Jake looked at his watch. "Okay, people. Time to get serious now."

Virtually everyone went swiftly into motion. Plum finally felt hit by a wave of the kind of excitement she hadn't witnessed earlier. The confrontation with Gil Russell and the police chief was why they had come to the meeting. Loads of them hastily folded up the chairs and stowed them on the carriers the rental company had provided, and they wheeled them to the back of the store. Jake went to the counter for his iPad, which he had left there when he came in. Earlier that day someone on the committee had installed some electronics outside the front door. Jake checked the settings now with a satisfied smile.

All at once, several people pulled out guns Plum hadn't noticed before. Then even more of them did the same. Plum stood there staring, aghast.

Jake laughed at her reaction. "What's the matter, Plum? Didn't you know you were in the Wild West? Don't people in LA carry guns?"

"We have the good taste to only shoot at each other from our cars," she said with a sniff.

Once everyone took their positions, someone doused the lights.

Plum stood beside Jake in the center of the store. "No gun for you? You look more like a cowboy than most of these other guys." She indicated a man in a collared polo shirt, who looked as if he'd stepped off a golf course.

Jake said, with a smile and a shrug, "I'm more of a hippie-cowboy. I do sell supplements, after all."

Plum chuckled, before falling silent. They waited for what felt like an eternity. Plum began to wonder whether Ginger had gotten it wrong, or if Gil Russell and the police chief came to their senses. Finally, some figures approached. Two men stood before the door, while others remained in the background. Plum surmised that was Gil Russell and Chief Timley at the door, while the police officers they'd brought along held back.

Someone yanked at the front door—the rattle echoed through the store crowded with silent people.

"Locked," someone said. The voice came through distinctly, thanks to the microphone installed there earlier. Plum presumed that was Chief Timley speaking, since it wasn't Gil's voice. She'd heard Gil when he came in to pick up Hannah's books. "There's no one here. Let's go." Timley sounded like someone who would rather be anywhere else. But he'd agreed to this lunacy.

"Break the glass," his partner in crime said decisively. "She must be upstairs. We need to talk to her. Since she's new in town, she needs to understand the kind of people she's aligning herself with."

Ooh! Grandpa is a thug.

"No, Gil. That's too much. I'm not breaking into a private establishment. I am the chief of police, after all."

Good of him to remember that, however late.

All at once inside the bookstore, volunteer armed guards walked toward the door in a show of force. Plum wasn't sure how visible they'd be in the darkened storefront, especially since it wasn't much brighter on the street side of the door. When the chief inhaled sharply, she surmised the citizen militia from the No on Budget-Mart committee was on display. She also thought she heard fear in that breath. Maybe Timley alone had the sense to realize how tense this situation had become, how the threat of violence could escalate. Gil continued rattling the door.

Plum and Jake walked up to it. "Gentlemen, I've recorded your remarks," Plum said. "Officers from the Department of Public Safety are on their way here to pick up that recording." Arizona's state police force. Plum's threat was only partially true. Their words had been recorded, though she lied about the state police. The committee felt they should handle this conflict on their own. But that should have been a serious threat to a small town police chief.

Though the glass door was between them, they spoke as if they were face-to-face.

"Nothing has happened here yet," Timley said. "We're all friends and neighbors. Things don't have to get ugly."

He turned and gave the cops standing behind him a signal to back away. Including Ginger, hovering at the rear, who looked as if she wanted to sink through the spaces in the wooden sidewalk. Plum avoided looking at Ginger. She couldn't risk anything showing on her face that would compromise her friend's job.

The chief held his hands out to show he wasn't holding a weapon. Nearly everyone else backed away. Gil alone refused to budge, until Timley grabbed the sleeve of his jacket and pulled him back.

To the last second, Gil continued to glare at Plum. She had formed a powerful enemy in him, and that sent a shiver of fear through her. Still, Plum had a chit she had yet to play—Gil's late son had to be a chink in his armor. Whether she stayed in Applewood or not, she vowed to wound her sire's sire.

CHAPTER TWENTY-SIX

High Desert Books' grand reopening finally arrived. Plum awoke that Friday morning, to see Scrappy curled up on the pillow beside hers. As much as Plum had come to care for the cat, Scrappy was a comedown from finding Brian there.

"At least you settled on the place where you belong, Scrap. I wish I knew as much."

Every time she considered formalizing her arrangement with Flo, the more like lunacy it seemed. And yet, the memory of her old life contained all the substance of a dream hours after awakening. She felt like a puddle evaporating in the dry desert air.

When she stepped into the kitchen, to Plum's complete astonishment, she saw Flo seated at the table. For once, she only vaguely noticed the beautiful Plum Orchid she'd moved there, which usually commanded her attention.

Without any preamble, Flo blurted, "I truly can't tell you how much I've come to dislike being in this apartment."

Flo's reddened eyes were so swollen, they'd narrowed to slits. Despite the anger rising up in Plum like bile, she couldn't bring herself to spit out any of the nasty vitriol rolling through her thoughts.

Flo tentatively stole a glance at Plum. "Do you hate me?"

As if the cat understood that Flo needed some consoling, Scrappy jumped onto her lap. Flo absently began to stroke her.

"I'm confused, Flo. I thought…we'd come together in understanding. Then you disappeared. I feared something happened to you. I called you, I went to your house—I scaled your freakin' fence—I asked everyone where you could be. Did I imagine how we left things?"

"There's something you should know about me, honey: I'm a mess." Flo's chin quivered. "I screw up everything in my life as quick as I can because it's just a matter of time until it happens anyway."

So it really is all in the genes.

Flo took a deep breath, then said, "I haven't been worth a damn since I lost my baby."

That remark unexpectedly pierced Plum to her core, stripping away months of denial, mountains of pain and loneliness. The truth she kept trying to block out by slamming the door on it. "I'm a mess, too." She hesitated, before finally admitting, "I haven't been worth a damn since *I* lost *my* baby." An ache that started in her heart radiated out through her whole body.

"...Baby...? When?"

"Four months, fifteen days, and..." Plum glanced at the clock built into the top of the old stove. "...around seventeen and a half hours ago...give or take, you know, twelve minutes." She took a big gulp of air to hold back the tears. "It wasn't an actual baby. I had a miscarriage. I tried to pretend it didn't matter. Now I know it eviscerated me. The joy went out of me, out of everything. Life, work, my relationship...everything." She pinched her eyes closed.

Plum wondered how she could have been so blind to the way it had damaged her. Because it had been nothing more than the potential of hope, she thought she hadn't lost anything other than a possibility. Instead, she saw now that something she'd always longed for was gone and could never be recovered. How could that help but devastate her? That was when all the enjoyment went out of cooking, when it and everything in her life had become a chore. Things went downhill between her and Noah then, too. She'd never let herself grieve. Unlike Flo, who'd never stopped grieving.

"I've never told anyone." Plum took a deep, shaky breath, and slowly let it out.

"Anyone but Noah, you mean."

"Not even Noah." She shrugged. "Right after that, he started talking about how much kids tie you down, and what a burden they are. I didn't know where that came from. We'd both always said we wanted them. Anyway, knowing I wouldn't be able to handle it if he looked too relieved, I chickened out on telling him."

"He knew," Flo said with brusque certainty. "He'd learned about the miscarriage, and he wanted to prevent you from telling him, so he wouldn't have to support you."

Given how erratically her brain sometimes worked, Plum suddenly remembered a conversation she'd had with Diggy Long, and a curious question came to her. "Flo, have you ever met Noah?"

Flo looked confused. "Your Noah? No, how could I have?" She cleared her throat. "When you were little, I used to travel to California sometimes, when you were in school plays and such. Just to catch sight of you."

"Why? I was never more than the spear carrier."

"Oh, honey, you always carried a mean spear." Flo smiled at her with beaming, unconditional approval, though it faded fast into a look of despair. "After a while, though, I guess...I just fell into a rut here."

Plum immediately flashed on why Flo stopped traveling to California to catch glimpses of her. She imagined what it would have been like for her if her own baby had been born, and then, after only a short time together, she'd had to send her daughter away. With a visceral connection that formed in her gut, Plum grasped that it got too hard for Flo to limit their connection to catching pitiful little sightings of Plum. A lump the size of an aircraft carrier formed in her throat.

Flo shook off her funk, literally, by giving her messy hair a shake. "Just because I haven't met Noah doesn't mean I haven't known guys like him."

Plum sank into another chair at the table. "He couldn't have known about the miscarriage. He wasn't home when it happened. I raced to my gynecologist's office. I never told anyone. I mean—not anyone, until now. Sunni would have gushed about how great it was, like I'd dodged a bullet. I didn't really have many female friends anymore. Noah never seemed to like them, and I let the friendships drift away during our years together."

Flo's lips twisted in derision, though she didn't comment.

Plum caught it anyway. "Yeah. Dumb, huh?" She shrugged. "But about the miscarriage...nobody at work knew, either. As much as I was hurting, I didn't even miss work that night." That she didn't even allow herself that time off pierced her heart again. "Good old stoic Plum, the most loyal schmuck ever." She remembered something Jake had said to her when they first met. How everyone deserves to live big and boldly, to claim a sizable place in the sun. Plum knew the sliver of sunlight she was living in had to be too small to measure.

"I still say he knew," Flo repeated. "That's the only thing that makes sense. What kind of man isn't there for the woman he loves when she loses his baby?"

"I sure know how to pick 'em." Plum rose and began making coffee. Then, without asking, she took food from the cabinets and fridge. That awful time of not taking pleasure from cooking had somehow passed. That was something, even if it wasn't even a fraction of what she wanted for herself. "I've always favored the good-looking ones who don't even have the depth of paint on the wall."

"It must be in the genes. Look what I picked."

Plum placed a mug of black coffee before Flo. "Billy Dean can't have been your only one."

Flo made a gravelly sound in her throat. "You'd be surprised."

Plum *was* surprised. "Really? You never had another guy?" She poured pancake batter into a pan.

Flo shrugged. "Not many. Spread out over all the years I've been around, it feels like that part of my life has been nonexistent."

Flo rose and set the table. After some time at that feeble excuse for a stove, Plum was starting to get the hang of working with it. She placed a stack of pecan and cinnamon pancakes on a platter between them. She added a pitcher of warm buttery syrup.

"You know, Flo, the shrinks would say it's because we have low self-esteem that we keep picking losers. Because we don't believe we're worth the really great guys."

Another noise came from Flo's throat. "There's a news flash."

Plum slathered her pancakes with lots of syrup. When all the flavors met together on her taste buds, she enjoyed a moment of pure ecstasy. Plum hoped she hadn't groaned aloud—she did that sometimes, when she made something really special. Still, it occurred to her that she'd eaten so many gooey foods since she arrived there. Too bad the comfort they promised hadn't spread to the rest her life.

"This is probably a matter of shutting the burned door after the horse is scorched, but you have to know the most wonderful man would do anything for you. Why, I can't imagine, given the way you treat him."

Flo assumed a look of confused innocence.

"Don't give me that. You have to know Jake's absolutely besotted. You could do worse, you know. Worse? Hah! It's hard to imagine how you could possibly do better." Plum stuffed a forkful of pancakes between her lips and hastily chewed. "And, hey, look at it this way: If you married him, you'd keep the same initials. Flo Gallagher—Flo Green. You wouldn't even have to change the monogram on your tea towels."

"And you know I'm all about those gracious little touches."

Mother and daughter shared a laugh.

"Plum, I've never had what it takes to make relationships work, not with anyone. Not with men, not women friends. As soon as things start going well, I can't seem to stop myself from driving right off the cliff. I always screw things up. Look what I did with you."

"You *can* help it. You choose to go over that cliff. You're rejecting them before they can reject you. Doesn't it even occur to you that maybe they won't?" How much of a hypocrite did saying that make Plum? Hadn't she driven off the cliff in her relationship with Brian?

Flo busied herself eating, too. She didn't respond, but she didn't deny it, either.

After a while, Flo said, "Brian tells me you're not so sure you want to stay here anymore."

"I didn't tell him that." Not in words anyway.

"He guessed." After a tremulous sigh, Flo asked, "Do you really have to go?"

Plum shrugged. There was so much she could have said. How she felt rootless. How she'd faced too many changes too fast. How losing a baby wounds a woman so deeply, she doesn't know how to move on—Flo already knew too much about that one.

Instead, what she said was, "I've never known how to walk a straight line. My whole life has been a matter of playing hopscotch. A jump here, a jump there, forward and back, no rhyme, no reason. I can't make decisions. I flip-flop back-and-forth too many times to count. And now that I would give anything to learn how to walk a more straightforward, determined path like everyone else, I'm not sure I even know *how* to learn."

Flo moved the Plum Orchid's pot closer to her, while seeming to study the unusual flower. "I'd say you have lots of reasons to try. But what do I know?"

CHAPTER TWENTY-SEVEN

Plum changed into her party outfit, before she and Flo went downstairs to get ready for the bookstore's grand reopening. She felt more stupid than usual for hosting a party for a business that she hadn't actually bought and which she might be ready to abandon. Might—she couldn't even say that for sure. Pretty lame. How was she going to apologize to the people who came to celebrate with her if she did happen to drive off the cliff?

With a suppressed sigh, she decided to shelve that question for another day. Too bad she now had shelved questions stacked to the ceiling.

One good thing Plum could say about this miserable day was that she'd gotten her wish for a mom. A perfect hopscotching mom for a hopscotching daughter. Sure, Plum knew Flo would go to ground again. Now that she understood Flo's need to hide, she supposed she could roll with it. Most importantly, that she had shared her harshest secret with Flo made the burden of carrying it lighter.

And, hey, for once, Plum actually felt good about her appearance. She loved the flirty quality of the navy suit's flared skirt. It made her long to twirl and twirl, like some demented four-year-old or a really inept ballerina, to keep making the skirt swirl out. And the cowboy boots were the best. She couldn't wait to buy more.

She and Flo set up the folding tables she'd borrowed from neighboring stores to hold the party food, and covered them with the tablecloths she'd bought in the days leading up to the event. Even though her own interest in cooking had returned, she'd hired Bonnie to do the catering—a gift for someone who probably wouldn't appreciate it. Plum knew all about that. She hadn't been too appreciative of the gifts she'd been given lately, either.

To Plum's surprise, when Bonnie arrived carrying steamer trays, along with her son and daughter, excitement brightened her forgettable features in a way Plum thought made them look more special. Before Bonnie and the kids returned to Cup o' Joe for the food itself, she happily shared some of the creative touches she'd added to the catering choices Plum had made. Maybe all Bonnie needed to get out of her funk was for someone to believe in her. Plum wondered if there was a lesson there for her.

Plum and Flo continued setting up the book displays Plum had planned for the occasion, some with new books, and others with a few of the more interesting rare books she found in the boxes Flo had accumulated upstairs.

Flo sighed softly. "You did such an amazing job transforming this old bookstore, honey. I wish I had your creativity and talent. I would never have been able to think of any of this."

Did Flo really regret that she didn't know how to wash walls with old paint? Plum glanced around and wondered why she did any of it. Ideas that had seemed so inspired at the time, now looked more questionable than ever. She found the streaks of turquoise over the russet base on the counter particularly gaudy.

"What you really mean is that I'm not remotely like anyone else. You may not want to say it, but we both know I'm odd." Maybe she should have used the turquoise paint to draw a big loser "L" on her forehead. Plum felt sure everyone saw it there anyway.

"Not odd, creative, quirky. You come at things in the most unusual ways," Flo went on.

"Quirky" was a euphemism for someone who rejected a nice neutral beige in favor of a mountain of old paint colors that nobody else would have used.

"Hopscotch!" Plum exploded. "I told you, it's hopscotch. I'm always out-of-step. I can't see the world like other people." To her surprise, tears streaked down her cheeks. She roughly wiped them away with the back of her hand. "I would give *anything* to be more like everyone else. Everything I've ever had or ever will have," Plum said with fierce intensity.

Flo stared at her with an open mouth. "What is it you think everyone else—"

Jake picked that moment to burst through the door. Flo sent

Plum a quick look, an unspoken way of saying they'd continue this conversation later, though now wasn't the time. Plum couldn't see why this particular truth ever needed to be explored again.

Jake didn't seem to notice he'd interrupted something. His color was bright with excitement. He carried another bouquet of flowers. Plum had placed the arrangement he'd sent earlier in the week on the counter. While she hunted in the backroom for a vase for today's bouquet, she set Jake to work opening the wines Bonnie had placed on the drinks table. While Jake worked the corkscrew, Plum playfully arranged today's bouquet—alphabetically by flower colors—and placed it on the food table.

Jake planted a kiss on her forehead, which felt so warm and fatherly, she almost burst into tears again. "Plum, sweetheart, I'm proud of you. I hope you know what a welcome addition you've made to this town."

Inside, Plum squirmed. How long had she waited for someone like Jake to enter her life? How would he feel when she walked out of it?

Though it was a little shy of the party's official starting time, it wasn't surprising that her friends showed up early to share in this event. Becky came through the door first.

"It's party time!" she shouted, waving a bottle of champagne, which she insisted that Plum not add to the drinks table, but bring upstairs for her own private celebration later.

Though her friends had seen the bookstore's progress, Plum led Becky on a tour now, explaining why she made the choices she had. *What a hypocrite.*

Brian showed up next. After a brief awkward moment, he opened his arms to her, and Plum came into them. There was nothing wrong with a friend-on-friend hug. Only the hug immediately became something more, for Plum anyway. Being that close to him made Plum's heart flutter. Breathless now, she quickly came out of the hug.

Jake had poured a glass of sparkling water for Brian and wine for the rest of them. Once they all had their drinks, he held up his glass in a toast. "To the future of High Desert Books, and to Plum and Flo finding each other." He raised his glass out to first Flo, and then Plum. "Salute!"

After a cheer, everyone took a drink. The bell on the door clanged again. Plum turned to greet her guest.

It was Hannah. Looking pale and stunned, she stopped in the open doorway, and stared at Plum. "Is it true?" she asked in a shocked whisper. Her gaze drifted to Becky. "Rebecca? Is it true, what you wrote?"

She meant the article that Plum asked Becky to write. The truth about Plum being Flo's daughter, and therefore, Hannah's granddaughter. Plum felt a shiver of panic at what she'd set in motion. Could she maintain her resolve before the Russell powerhouses?

Becky nodded. "From what I've seen, there's no reason to doubt it, Hannah."

Hannah began to choke and sob all at once, there in the doorway. Brian placed his glass on the table and rushed to her side. He helped her to move forward, until she had paused a few steps before Plum.

"Oh, my dear," Hannah said, the words floating out on a sigh. "It *is* true. I can see it." She drew closer and cupped her hands around Plum's face. "You are the image of my darling Billy."

From where she stood behind the counter, Flo snapped, "And me."

Slowly straightening her shoulders, Hannah turned toward Flo. "Yes, Florence, you're right. Plum looks so much like both of you." She swallowed hard. "Despite the unfortunate circumstance of her conception, you should be proud of this beautiful child you created with my poor boy, however it came about."

Flo made a little sound. Not her usual grunt, but more like the suppressed sound of someone taking a punch.

Plum wanted to strike out at Hannah. What she said was wrong on so many levels. How awful of her to have denied the rape for years, when she obviously knew what her son did to Flo. Plum's loyalty to her birth mother soared within her. She felt renewed gratitude that Flo had sent her away so Hannah wouldn't get to rear her. And yet, she couldn't bring herself to wound Hannah, as she wished to. Hannah looked vulnerable when she finally owned up to what should have been admitted long ago.

With Hannah's skin still so pale that Plum feared she would faint, she didn't protest when Hannah clasped her hands. Gil picked that moment to stride through the door his wife had left open.

"Hannah? What are you doing?" Gil said. "You can't buy into this preposterous story without proof." He glared at Plum. "Without DNA testing, you won't see one cent of my money."

His money? That was the first thing he had to say to me after learning about our connection?

"Dude, I don't want your money."

"I'm not your 'dude,' young lady," he said.

"Gil, what's wrong with you," Hannah said, still holding on to Plum's hand. "If you can't see your son in this beautiful girl, you're blind."

Gil fumed in silence, though his stony eyes studied Plum's features. And as for Plum, despite the vow she made when he tried to shut down the No on Budget-Mart meeting, she could see his vulnerability, too. Even if he and Hannah had made their son into a privileged brat, and no matter how badly they treated Flo, they were still hurting. Plum couldn't bring herself to wound him, either.

"She doesn't need your money, Gil," Flo spat. "I can take care of her."

Plum threw Flo an exasperated expression. "I don't need anyone's money. I've been taking care of myself for a long time."

Gil snorted. "If she is ours, she gets her sense of self-reliance from me."

Plum threw up her hands, turning away from all of them.

From there it descended into pure chaos. Her friends began arguing with her grandparents on her behalf.

"Gil, you'd be lucky if you and Plum shared the same blood," Jake said. "But don't kid yourself—you're not one-tenth the person she is."

Others shouted their own remarks, and true to type, Gil came back at them, separating himself from Plum, even as his gaze, with its hopeful expression, remained glued to her face.

While everyone else argued about her, Plum felt like an observer, not the person at the center of it. All at once, the kaleidoscope of life shifted, offering up another view. Just as instantly as she had rejected what life had offered her here, Plum now felt like a fool for doubting what she had found: great friends, a mother, a man worth having. If she felt adrift because she didn't have roots, it meant that she hadn't chosen to sink them into the ground here yet. If she wanted to be part of this place, she had to stay and commit to it. Commit to making it what it should be. Commit to the people who'd already given her so much.

Wait! Am I really flip-flopping again? She felt her cheeks sear with the heat of embarrassment for her own goofiness. Why, oh-why couldn't she stride straight forward like everyone else? How could she continue to be this strange?

No, she wasn't being honest—that wasn't the only thing she felt grateful for. She might still feel hopelessly out-of-step, but the clouds of confusion about her future had cleared completely. She was home, and she felt so deeply appreciative that she'd finally grasped how much it meant to her, this place where she longed to build her future. She would stay in Applewood, all right, Plum suddenly knew with certainty.

In the midst of all the shouting and posturing, Ginger, dressed in uniform, came into the bookstore, along with a male police officer whom Plum didn't know. That surprised Plum, since Ginger said she would be on-duty at this hour and wouldn't be able to drop by until later.

Ginger stood there, seeming stunned by the bedlam that had overtaken that peaceful bookstore, with arguments crossing other arguments. After a moment, she took a whistle from her belt and blew into it strongly enough to produce a loud shriek. The shouting stopped instantly, and everyone turned to her.

"Now that I have your attention…" Her ginger-colored features crinkled in distress. "Plum, I'm sorry to have to do this. We're here to arrest you for grand theft. You're being sent back to California."

CHAPTER TWENTY-EIGHT

Just when she'd decided to stay there, they were making her leave? The silence Ginger had created with her announcement held firm. Plum finally broke it by sputtering, "What…?"

"You've been accused of stealing forty thousand dollars."

Ginger's male colleague added, "And an upscale piece of luggage."

"No!" Plum said. "That was *my* money."

Ginger shrugged helplessly.

"Gil, do something!" Hannah cried.

Gil cleared his throat and said with a self-possessed air, "Officer Maddy, there has to be some way to deal with this. We'll pay whatever is necessary to make it go away."

Flo came around the counter and announced, "No, I'll pay. She's my daughter—I should be responsible for her."

Plum was starting to feel like the rope must in a tug of war. She held her hands up in the stop position to both Hannah and Gil, and then to Flo. "I'm telling you this is a mistake. It's my own money. I took a small fraction of what my ex owed me. He cheated me out of much more." She turned back to the police officers. "I can't believe Noah sicced the dogs on me." To the male police officer she said, "No offense intended." She gave her curly hair a shake. "And how in the world did he find me?" She thought she'd done such a good job of hiding her trail.

"No offense taken," the officer said. He pulled out some legal papers from where he'd tucked them into his belt and ran his gaze over them. "The person who sicced the dogs on you is one Claire Denton." He read on silently. "Look here. It says the theft happened at the home of Noah Rowle and Plum Tardy. That's you," he added, as if he were telling her something she didn't know.

Meanwhile, partygoers were now drifting into the bookstore.

Some found a nearby spot from which to watch the show, while others chose to rubberneck from the catering tables.

"Claire? That can't be right. The money was in Noah's satchel. I should know what that piece of luggage looked like—I paid for that set of suitcases when he wanted them, but couldn't afford that much."

"Oh, yeah," Ginger said. "We need to take possession of the suitcase, too."

While the town folk continued to stream into the bookstore, most gawking openly, those already there shot photos and videos with their cell phones, or texted other people about what most of them seemed to regard as good theater.

"Ginger, this is highly irregular," Brian said. "When was the last time you heard of someone being extradited to another state for such a small theft?" He insisted on seeing the paperwork her partner held.

Ginger shrugged. "It's Plum's bad luck that this Claire-girl's uncle is a judge in Los Angeles, who happens to fish with some judge-buddy here in Arizona. You can't fight that kind of connection. Plum is going to have to go along and settle this thing there."

"Okay, Plum. I'll return to California with you and represent you," Brian said.

"Gil, do something," Hannah shrieked again.

"Brian, with all due respect, my granddaughter needs better representation than some small town yokel can provide," Gil said.

Some respect, old man.

"Hannah and I will fly along with her, and we'll hire the best defense attorney in Los Angles to represent her."

"Excuse me, Gil," Brian said with a sniff. "I may choose to practice in the same small town where you run what some would call your yokel media enterprise, but I am a USC-educated attorney."

Maybe they could charter a whole plane. Then everyone could go.

Gil bristled like a rooster challenged for dominance of the hen house. Plum took hold of Brian's arm and tugged him behind the counter, the only spot not flooded with gawking guests.

"Brian, I appreciate your wanting to help, more than I can tell you." Plum desperately hated having to leave him. Now she couldn't believe she'd ever considered it. "But you need to stay here, and let Gil and Hannah accompany me there."

Brian's sexy lips twisted into a decidedly un-sexy angry line. "Are you asking so you can meet up with this Noah?"

When was he going to forget about Noah? She had. She really had.

Plum gave her head a hard shake. "You have no idea how wrong you are on that. I wish you'd believe me. Besides, I'm not thinking of me, I'm thinking of the future of this town." She drew closer to him and hissed, "Listen, I'll keep the king out of the castle, so you can let democracy reign." Besides, she couldn't let him see her at what was sure to be her lowest point.

His confusion cleared at the reference to a remark he'd once made to her.

"You can use this time to settle the whole Budget-Mart mess, but only if you stay."

Brian looked stricken, like someone being tortured. "It doesn't matter. Nothing matters except for you. I can't let you go through this legal matter with only Gil to protect you."

"It has to be Gil. Please, Brian. If we're to have any kind of a future together, I need you to trust that I know what I'm doing." She *hoped* she knew what she was doing. Did she? Plum's plans rarely worked, though this time she felt so sure.

That wicked grin returned. "Are we going to have a future together?"

"I want us to, more than anything." The words sounded inadequate. She wished she could convey to him *how* fervently she wanted it.

Brian confirmed his agreement with a reluctant nod. "Even more than I hate to let you go, I really don't want to see you turn your legal affairs over to Gil. If he pays for your lawyer, he's going to call the shots. He could easily commit you to some plea deal that would ruin your future. Sometimes, with the best of intentions, he makes the worst choices."

"Yeah, I get that—Grandpa is a control-freak. Don't worry. I won't necessarily keep their attorney. I'll have Sunni find me someone she trusts." Assuming Sunni would have anything to do with Plum after she took off without a word.

Ginger tapped the crystal of her watch. "Time, Plum."

Plum nodded and took a step toward the waiting officers. Then, suddenly, thoughts began to tumble through her mind, and new connections came together.

"Ooh! I can't go," she announced, realizing there was something she still had to do, *if* she was to pull this off.

CHAPTER TWENTY-NINE

"Plum!" Ginger said, more sternly now to Plum's insistence that she couldn't leave.

Plum backed away from where the officers stood beside the counter. "I have to get you the money. And the luggage."

"We'll find the bag," the male officer said.

"You don't know where I keep it hidden. Ginger, I'll be right back."

The male officer turned to Ginger. "Officer Maddy, we can't—" he began.

"Oh, unwad your shorts, George. She's not going to escape across the rooftops." Ginger lifted one eyebrow as she turned her scrutiny on Plum. "You're not, are you?"

"No!" Though Scrappy had shown her how.

Jake stepped forward. "Officers, if it'll make you feel better, I'll accompany her upstairs."

Flo stood beside him. "Me too."

Together, the three of them formed a conga-line headed up the staircase. Even as they moved up the steps, Plum continued to make mental connections.

As soon as they reached the apartment, Plum said. "Flo, have you ever taken any money from Claire Denton?"

Flo frowned. "Plum, how is it you know Claire?"

"Noah's partner in infidelity and the Budget-Mart deal? That was Claire. Small world, huh?"

"As tight as last year's jeans." Flo seemed to swallow a snort. "Now I'm extra glad I threw her out. Nope, I never took a penny, though she intimated I could pick up a tidy sum for nothing more than merely listening to her. I told her to get her skinny ass out of my bookstore and never to return."

How funny that Flo had met Claire, but not Noah. According to the travel plans he'd shared with Plum, he came here often. Why would he go to Applewood if not to sweet-talk Flo, Diggy, and any other holdouts into selling? Before she could follow that thread, however, more connections snapped into place. Plum was starting to form a bigger picture of what must have happened. She reached into the kitchen cabinet where she had stuffed the satchel with the remaining cash.

Scrappy jumped onto the kitchen table and sniffed at the plum-colored orchid.

"Oh, God. My cat and my orchid—what will happen to them?"

"We'll all feed the cat," Jake said. "I told you everyone in the neighborhood did until you adopted her."

"She adopted me," Plum said. "None of you took good enough care of her, or she wouldn't have chosen me to live with."

Flo cleared her throat. "I'll move back in here and take care of the cat, the orchid, and the bookstore."

Plum turned to her birth mother. "You hate it here."

"True, but I'll do it for you." Her eyes glazed.

Seizing an unexpected chance, Plum shifted gears. "Jake, since you know the cat, too, maybe you could stop by and help Flo with it."

Jake's eyes brightened at the idea. "Sure thing, Plum."

"Hey, I can feed—" Flo started to say.

Plum spoke over her. "And you know what this awful old stove is like. Maybe you can bring some take-out occasionally."

"Great idea, Plum," Jake said. "Don't worry, Flo, I'll see to it you're fed."

Flo gave Plum an *I know what you're pulling*-look, but surprisingly, she didn't object. From the barest trace of a smile, which she struggled to hide, Plum suspected Flo liked the idea more than she'd admit.

Instead, Flo said, "I wish you didn't have to go. How can I be sure you'll come back?"

"Believe." Plum came into Flo's arms and hugged her tightly.

"How can I? You implied that you probably wouldn't stay here," Flo muttered into her hair.

Plum came out of the hug, throwing her arms up in frustration. "I flip-flop, okay? Accept it—I have." No, she really hadn't. "Like I told you, I play hopscotch. But I swear to you, I will come back."

"Plum, *now*, you hear me?" Ginger shouted from the foot of the stairs.

"If…you know…the cops and the courts let me," Plum added. She gulped hard. But that couldn't happen. It couldn't, right?

After giving the cat a quick kiss on the head and a hug for each Flo and Jake, Plum grabbed the satchel and her tote bag, and started down the stairs. Retrieving the satchel wasn't all what she needed to do, however—the most important part of it still lay ahead of her. In the crowded bookstore, rather than follow the cops to the door, she hastily ducked behind the counter, where Brian still stood.

Ginger frowned. "No, Plum. No more delays."

Plum held up her index finger to indicate, *One minute*. "Brian, I need you to do something for me."

"Anything."

"I need you to execute the terms of my contract with Flo as soon as you can. Like yesterday, if you can manage it." She whirled around to her birth mother. "Flo, I also need to pay you."

"You don't, Plum, honey." Flo said. "Whatever I have is yours. You should know that. You don't have to give me anything."

Hannah came to the counter. "We'll pay whatever Plum owes."

Would these people ever stop trying to give her money? Where were they when she was back in Santa Monica going broke?

Ginger took a step toward the counter, still tapping her watch crystal.

Brian moved closer to Plum and said, "Plum, do you really need to deal with this now?"

Plum raised her eyes to the ceiling and shrieked, "How is it possible that I am the least naïve person here?" She sighed heavily. "Flo, I *do* need to pay for it." She looked at Hannah. "*I* do." She turned to Brian. "That's the only way things will work."

Plum went to the cash register and rang up a sale for ten thousand dollars. Where the point of sale program allowed for notation, Plum typed in, "For the purchase of the business High Desert Books, the building in which it is housed, and for the property noted in the contract," and she added the plot identification number of that land, which she now knew from memory.

It was the number that first jumped out at her when she saw it in the contract, after Flo added it to the bookstore-purchase agreement, that night when they got tipsy together. Some of the maps over Noah's desk back in the house in Santa Monica had broken out blocks of land by their plot IDs. Plum had spent so long staring at those blocks of land, their numbers had been burned into her brain. Still, because she was buzzed, she hadn't been absolutely certain of that number. But in that drunken moment she did know one thing: if she was right about the plot ID, she saw a way to stick it to Noah and Claire, and by extension, Budget-Mart.

Plum reached into the satchel and began pulling out packets of cash.

"Plum!" Ginger shouted. "You can't use *that* money. We have to confiscate it. Now!"

"Plum, you really don't have to pay me anything," Flo repeated. "I don't want your money."

Brian put a hand on Flo's arm to stop her. "She does have to pay for it, Flo. By going ahead with this contract, she's buying herself a bargaining chip."

Finally, *someone* got it. Flo and Hannah still looked confused. Gil frowned. Brian alone smiled in understanding.

"If I can actually pay for anything," Plum muttered. "In for some penne, in for some pounds." She groaned helplessly. She reached into her tote bag, which was slung over her shoulder, and took her debit card from her wallet. Would it work? She had linked that debit card to her savings account. Would the bank's safeguards kick in to prevent her from spending more than a quarter of her savings? Taking a deep breath, she pulled the card through the card swiper beside the cash register.

She held her breath. After the longest moment in her life, the purchase went through.

"Brian, forget about that clause I told you I wanted. You need to have those deeds recorded right away. In my name."

"Plum, it's Friday afternoon," he said.

She shot him a look.

"Right. I'll make some calls," he vowed.

With a satisfied nod, Plum came out from behind the counter and held out her wrists to the police officers for cuffing. Then with a nod to Hannah and Gil, Plum said, "Westward ho, folks."

Taking a deep breath, while her colleague handcuffed Plum, Ginger said, "Plum Tardy, you have the right to remain silent..."

After everything she had set in motion, remaining silent was probably the only option Plum had left.

CHAPTER THIRTY

To her eternal shame, Plum knew that she couldn't stride straight ahead on any plan if her life depended on it. Whether she was quirky, as Flo had suggested, or offbeat, she wasn't like other people no matter how hard she tried to be. She played hopscotch, and couldn't seem to stop. But *never* did she think she'd ever make a move *this* goofy.

Arrested and jailed!

After walking in on Noah and Claire, and leaving California with her ego beaten into complete defeat, Plum had secretly harbored the hope that one day she would return there in style. She could not have said precisely what that meant. Nothing as grand as being given the key to the city, or a street named in her honor, certainly. Maybe it would have been enough if her formerly nearest and dearest universally came to hold the view that in hopping off to spontaneously start a new life, she hadn't screwed up as royally as usual. Now she had a feeling that moving into a room with bars and wearing a jumpsuit, which even she knew to be fashion-challenged, didn't quite make the "in style" cut.

To everyone who complains that airlines today treat travelers like cattle—Plum said, "Hah! Try it in handcuffs and leg-irons." For one thing, opening peanuts with restrained hands qualified as cruel and unusual punishment. And for someone who had spent her life trying not to stand out so people didn't realize how hopelessly out-of-step she was, she didn't have a clue until now what it was to stand out.

On a flight with no movie, a prisoner automatically becomes the entertainment. One passenger after another asked her escorts, "What did she do?" Did they think that, by being confined, she had lost her ability to speak? At times Plum longed to bolt toward the emergency exit in the hopes the California police officers guarding her now would shoot her.

She wouldn't have thought it possible, but even greater indignities awaited her upon booking. A fire hose of delousing solution, to prevent Plum and her supposed lice from bursting into flames, she imagined, drowned most of her dignity. In case she retained a bit of it, a stranger searched her various body cavities, more thoroughly than either lovers or her gynecologist ever had.

Now, having been jailed for much of a day, and noting the delousing solution could have doubled as paint remover, Plum scratched her dried-out skin while waiting for Sunni in a shabby conference room where prisoners met with their lawyers. While tracing with her finger some of the lettering carved into the scratched metal table, she realized with some surprise that she didn't feel anxious about the chewing out Sunni was sure to dispense. Maybe she even felt some justifiable bring-it-on anger.

Plum hadn't noticed it before, but she wasn't exactly the same person who had bolted away from the scene in that bedroom in Santa Monica with a level of humiliation that was all but fatal. Oh, she still hated being goofy. But why should her behavior seem that repulsive to the people who claimed to care for her? How could Noah and Sunni have simultaneously insisted they loved her yet demand she change everything about herself? How can you love someone and not *like* anything about that person?

Besides, it wasn't as though they were so damn perfect, no matter what they thought. Why was it okay for them to flaunt their most distinctive traits, while demanding that Plum stifle hers?

Maybe she'd loved living in Applewood, because without their constraining presence, she had managed to blossom there. Was that anger the reason she was able to confront Gil now, when not that long ago, she should have withered before his frigid stare?

Would she be able to stand up to anyone else? She supposed she would find out soon enough. Sunni waited on the other side of the glass-paneled door, while a guard unlocked it.

Plum expected Sunni to dump her ire the instant she came through the door, but the control Sunni had cultivated throughout her life served her well. Instead, her only actions were to tug down the jacket of her trim beige suit, and to adjust the strap of the brown leather briefcase that hung from her shoulder. While staring at the concrete wall over Plum's head, rather than making eye contact, Sunni tapped against the floor a classy taupe pump that had probably cost enough to feed a Third World family for a year, but which Plum didn't believe made one-tenth of the personal statement of her cowboy boots. Plum really hoped the warden didn't help herself to the boots that she'd been forced to turn in during her booking.

In a chilly voice, Sunni said, "I've arranged for a defense attorney for you. Someone from the firm—he's the best. He'll be along in a little while, but I came earlier so we can talk." The only sign of the fury Sunni had to be holding inside were the red spots that burned though her pale cheeks.

Finally, the explosion that Plum expected detonated. "What were you thinking, Plum? Or I should say, *Were* you thinking?" She snorted unattractively. "This is typical of you and mom. Flaunting your craziness, no matter how it affects anyone else." Sunni flung herself into the chair across from Plum, which sent her ritzy briefcase crashing to the floor. She repeated, "What were you thinking?"

Plum drew herself up as much as a short person can while seated. "Tell me this, Sunni: did you even know I was missing? Before Noah called, that is."

Sunni bit her lip, making her look unsure. "Noah never called me. He texted a couple of times, asking me to meet with him, but I ignored his messages."

"Okay…then, Roy called you, right? He promised he would, right after I laid a big brick of cash on him."

"Paying him before he followed through—that was your mistake. Roy didn't call me, either."

"So you didn't know I was gone? Did you ever think about me, or think about calling to see how I was? Or even how my emptying Crystal's house was coming along?"

Sunni stared at Plum, before finally shaking her head no.

Plum felt sudden anger rise up inside of her. "If you give that a little thought, you might be able to figure out why I took off alone. Here, you see, I was always alone."

She hadn't expected to say that, but as soon as she heard her own words, she realized how true her statement was. It felt as if someone had hauled off and aimed a kick at her heart.

Sunni stared at the wall above Plum's head again. With a sigh, she said, "Maybe we have more to talk about than I thought."

* * *

Plum hadn't gotten far in her story, just up to the point of describing Claire as riding the Noah pony.

"And you didn't feel you could come to me?" Sunni asked. "How many times have I told you Noah wasn't worth it, that he was just sucking you dry? When the inevitable happened, you should have turned up on my doorstep, not some strangers' in another state."

"Maybe I didn't because I didn't want my nose rubbed in my own stupidity. But I guess there's no avoiding that." Plum stared pointedly at Sunni.

To Plum's surprise, Sunni looked away. "I'm in therapy."

"...huh?" Plum said.

"Therapy—where you tell some stranger what a mess you've made of your life, and have to pay for the privilege."

"I repeat—huh?" Plum asked, sarcastically now. "I can't believe Sunshine Meadows would—"

"Sunshine Meadows!" Sunni said. "Do you know how much I've always hated that ridiculous name? It sounds like a housing tract or an old folks home."

Plum Tardy wisely kept silent on the subject of names.

"I haven't had a date in two years. Never mind about sex," Sunni burst out with, all at once. "You don't have any trouble finding men. You've probably already got another one lined up in Arizona."

Funny, Plum never saw herself that way. Though since she had already slept with the former hottie of Venice High, she generously bit her tongue, rather than flaunt her conquest. Besides, in her goofiness, she may have already wrecked it.

"I didn't think Noah was worth all the effort you poured into that relationship, but...well, maybe I was also envious that you had someone."

Feeling unexpectedly like the successful sister now, instead of the screw-up, Plum said, "Noah's probably up for grabs again. Someone like Claire normally must shoot a lot higher."

"Not me. I'm aiming for adequate."

That sounded so unlike Sunni, Plum burst out laughing. After a moment, the little sister she remembered, before Sunni turned into Ms. Perfection, Esq., joined in.

Eventually, they got around to Plum's discovery about her birth history.

Sunni nodded. "Gil Russell called me, as you asked him to, and explained everything. Great guy, incidentally."

Plum didn't choose to be diverted into arguing how great Gil might be. Yet given how often she found herself biting her tongue, she hoped she hadn't already cut clear through it.

"Gil's gonna want to pick my lawyer," Plum said.

Sunni waved that objection away with a toss of her hand. "I convinced him that you can't do any better than Roger Hamish, the one I hired for you. Don't worry—he's quite happy we snagged him. He's also agreed to pay your legal bills."

It sounded as if Sunni had Gil eating out of her hand. She was the granddaughter Gil would have picked for himself. Was anyone ever happy with what they got?

"And speaking of bills...after Gil called, I searched through every inch of Mom's house and found some correspondence to match those empty envelopes and a few pages of financial records. Your birth mother—"

"She would want you to call her Flo."

"Will she still want me in your life, now that I'm not really your sister?"

Another blow. "You'll always be my sister. *I* want you in my life."

Sunni lowered her head and dabbed at her nose with her knuckle, suddenly sounding as if she had the sniffles. "Anyway, it seems Flo sent Mom money during all those years when we were growing up. She even paid for your college expenses—you wouldn't have had to work the way you did in college and cooking school. I can't believe Mom kept that money for herself. I'm so ashamed of her." Sunni gave her straight, highlighted hair a shake. "Are you terribly angry?"

Plum said she wasn't, and she meant it. She supposed Crystal thought she should be paid for raising Flo's child. At least now, Plum wouldn't have to feel guilty when she left.

Eventually, their surroundings reminded Plum that they had more than personal concerns to discuss. "Sunni, don't you want to ask me if I did it? Stole the forty grand, I mean."

"No! And neither will Roger. No lawyer ever asks his client about guilt." Sunni went on to explain the legal rationale. "If he knows a client did whatever she stands accused of, he can't put that client on the stand to deny it without suborning perjury."

Plum dismissed Sunni's reasoning. "I did it," she said. "I thought I was taking money Noah owed me. It didn't occur to me until now that I've had some time to think about it that he probably only bought the same set of luggage that Claire had because he wanted to impress her." Plum shared the way that Noah had cheated her financially. "I really thought I was taking what he owed me, which he had accumulated by not making house payments, I swear to you."

"I believe you. It's so…you, Plum," Sunni said with a sigh.

"Can you do me a favor, Sunni? Make sure Noah can't get in to visit me." She told her sister about her miscarriage, and Flo's belief that Noah knew about it and made sure she wouldn't tell him.

Sunni's features contracted in sorrow. "Oh, Plum!"

Plum rushed past her sympathy. "You were right about him. I could do much better." Once again she chose not to tell Sunni that maybe she already had. "Anyway, you can see why I'm not ready for that particular confrontation right now. Besides, I don't trust him as far as I can throw up."

Sunni smiled. "I'll take care of it."

"Now, I'd love to see Claire," Plum went on. "Well, not *love* it—actually, the way I feel is about as far from love as you can get. But I'm sure if I can see her, we can settle this whole business without the bother of a trial." Plum giggled. "Incidentally, I'm calling it The Case of the Vanishing Hartmann Satchel. Doesn't that sound like something Crystal and I would have read?"

Sunni stared at her, aghast. "Plum, you can't see Claire alone. Not ever without your lawyer and hers present. She's the accusing witness."

No! Plum had counted on a one-on-one with Claire. The entire rest of her life required that.

The door rattled. Plum looked up to see an attractive, albeit somewhat beefy, blonde man in his forties chatting amicably with the guard who had unlocked that door for Sunni.

"That's Roger, your lawyer," Sunni said. "Not a word about taking the money. Please! Promise me."

"Sunni, if I can't talk directly with Claire—"

"*Nothing* about it, Plum."

Roger, who looked like he had played college football, flashed Plum an unexpected pair of dimples when he extended his hand. He was really pretty cute.

Plum thought she must have introduced herself, but she honestly couldn't remember it. The only thoughts filling her head were that if she couldn't clear things up directly with Claire—she was so screwed.

CHAPTER THIRTY-ONE

Plum had a bail hearing in the morning. As Roger predicted, bail was denied. For such a minor offense, that was unusual, especially with her well-heeled grandparents ready to pony up whatever amount the judge might set. Claire's excellent connections had come through for her once more.

Later, after being returned to the jail, she and her cellmate went to the prison library to pick up some reading material. It wasn't much of a library in Plum's opinion, not even as good as the bookstore she'd left behind. With its utilitarian gray metal shelving and the old-fashioned card catalog, it certainly didn't have the flair Plum had brought to High Desert Books. It did contain an overflowing section devoted to legal books—necessary in there, she supposed. Books were shelved in sections like every other library or bookstore. Nothing like the imaginative arrangement she'd brought to Flo's bookstore. She started to feel better about the choices she'd made in revamping that bookstore and hoped she got to see it again.

Plum learned she'd be working in the prison library, which made for a better than average fit. If she squinted hard at the gray shelving, and overlooked the fact that all the customers were dressed the same, she could almost pretend that she'd never left High Desert Books. Besides, it could have been worse—they could have assigned her to kitchen duty. Given how fragile her renewed love of cooking was, she didn't think it could survive turning out a thousand portions a day of slop.

Her cellmate was the infamous Nora Cabot, the Pasadena socialite accusing of trying to kill her Hollywood producer boyfriend. Roger considered it unseemly for someone like Plum, charged with a relatively small theft, to be housed with a woman believed to be an attempted murderer. But Nora and Plum had bonded over their mutual *he done me wrong*-stories, so she begged him not to break them up.

Nora admitted that she wasn't much of a reader, yet there also wasn't a lot to do in prison. Plum found a couple of humorous novels that they could take turns reading aloud to each other, and hopefully, share a few laughs, which they both sorely needed. They hadn't gotten around to talking about guilt. Roger warned Plum repeatedly not to discuss her case with anyone, because prisoners sell each other out all the time. But the unspoken understanding that emerged between Plum and Nora was that they both had committed the acts of which they stood accused.

Now, they were in the cafeteria, seated across from each other at a table they alone shared. Nora still looked too impossibly beautiful to have spent weeks in that place. Her glossy black hair, cultivated through years of high-priced salon patronage, had managed to resist the effects of using cheap shampoo without good conditioners. And her delicate patrician features seemed remarkably untouched by whatever she might have experienced there.

A raucous burst of coarse laughter cut through the buzz of conversational noise filling the cafeteria. Plum followed the sound to a crowded table in the center of the room, packed with burly, tough-looking women.

"Don't even look at them," Nora warned in a whisper. "They'll make you pay for staring."

Plum hastily looked down at the compartments on her food tray. "This is like high school, huh?"

Nora nodded. "Except in high school the mean girls only cut you with nasty remarks. Here, you actually bleed."

Ooh! Way too real. A shiver of panic shot through Plum.

She looked instead at the brownish-green block filling one of the compartments in her plastic meal tray, "What is this?" Plum asked, gingerly touching it with a fork. "Is this a Brillo pad one of the kitchen workers misplaced?"

"Are you kidding? That's zucchini bread, my girl. One of the better desserts you'll find in here."

Plum tentatively took a tiny bite of one corner. "Ewww. You should taste my zucchini bread. I make it with marzipan and cinnamon. Incredibly moist and obscenely good. I'll bake it for you when we get out of here."

Nora bent her head forward, sending her hair over her face, which blocked it from Plum's view. After a moment, she looked up, with teary eyes. "Plum, don't you realize that we're probably not going to get out of here, not soon anyway. For you, it shouldn't be more than a few years, but for me…"

A few *years?* No! Denial alone had held Plum together. Now that Nora had stripped it away, the weight of truth came down on the shoulders like a sack of bricks. Her life couldn't take this turn. Even if hopscotch had defined her existence, she couldn't make this move. It wasn't fair. She was the victim, dammit. The one who had been cheated in every possible way, the one who had simply tried to get back a little of what was owed to her. Was she really going to be punished for that?

Plum viciously stabbed the Brillo pad-zucchini bread with her fork, and then again and again, until that compartment came to be filled with dry, brownish-green crumbs.

She felt like screaming in outrage. But Plum knew if she started, she wouldn't be able to stop.

* * *

Plum's blithe denial of their situation, and the necessity of having to set her straight, must have saddened Nora. She'd started crying after returning to their cell. Plum figured weeping wasn't the ideal way to build up a tough rep for the joint's mean girl clique. She started telling Nora funny stories of some of the goofier choices she'd made in her crazy life. Finally, she managed to lift Nora's mood, enough to stop the flow of tears anyway.

Afterwards, Plum felt all used up. There was nobody she could turn to, nobody to lift her spirits. She felt certain everyone on the outside—even those who cared for her—would believe anyone who had stolen a bag of money deserved to be behind bars. They wouldn't understand how it came about.

But this was Tuesday. While she'd endured the day, now that the clock had reached the evening hours, it promised something better.

A way that she hoped would help her to restore herself.

Within fixed periods of time, prisoners were permitted to make calls from a bank of pay telephones. One of the worst parts of prison life was having to ask for everything, and frequently, being denied. After finally learning to stand up for herself, would she have to give that up and resume doormat status once more?

Fortunately, she was given a chance to make a call. When the guard came for her, Plum grabbed her phone cards. Sunni had left her with a few phone cards for making calls and some rolls of quarters that she could use in the vending machines.

"All these years in corporate, and I've never had to give a client coins," Sunni had groused at the time.

"Sunni, you should thank Plum for broadening your horizons," Roger said with a droll grin.

So he thought Sunni's horizons needed broadening, too. Plum believed that as well. Maybe they could both have done without this particular educational opportunity.

Plum didn't have to wait long for the phone. When it was her turn, she hastily dialed a number from memory. With a soft sigh, she sank against the concrete wall, settling in to listen to the outgoing voicemail message once it began to play.

"You've reached the law office of Brian Coburn. My staff and I are either away from the office, or on another line..."

Of course he was away from the office. On Tuesday nights, he attended a Narcotics Anonymous meeting, where he sponsored a couple of newbie addicts beginning their recovery. He never missed that one.

"...At the sound of the beep, leave as detailed a message as you wish," Brian's voice went on to say.

Plum didn't leave any message. She'd called at that time specifically because she knew Brian wouldn't be there to answer her call. She hung up just after the beep sounded. And then, she immediately dialed Brian's number once more.

"Hey, give someone else a chance, why doncha?" a woman shouted from farther back in line.

Plum knew she shouldn't hog the phone. It wasn't simply rude, it was foolhardy, considering what Nora told her about the games the girls in stir play. She couldn't help herself. The mere sound of Brian's voice made her heart sing. She needed to hear him. She needed it even more than breathing free air, or eating decent food, both of which she desperately craved. But she couldn't risk calling when he was likely to answer. She couldn't risk hearing him say that he never wanted to see her again. And now that he'd had time to think more about the goofball woman he'd been foolish enough to get involved with, why wouldn't he?

CHAPTER THIRTY-TWO

The next morning, a few women cornered Plum during the exercise period out in the yard to "explain" how things worked in prison. Of course, their "explanation" was more a matter of nearly dislocating Plum's shoulder with a hard shove. She wanted to blame Nora's warning of the day before for bringing it on. But Plum suspected that whether Nora had told her or not, that "explanation" was part of Prison Orientation 101.

While trying to recapture the wind that shove had knocked out of her, Plum glanced right and left in search of a guard. There wasn't one in sight. Naturally. That provided Plum's first lesson in how guarding worked in jail. When you're doing something you don't want the guards to see, they descend on you in a flock; when you need them badly, there isn't one to be found.

With no help available, and before those women could dislocate her other shoulder, Plum promptly offered up her lawyer-sister's help on their appeals. Plum couldn't possibly know whether those women had appealable convictions; she didn't even know what they were in for. With that, she learned another prison lesson: virtually every prisoner believes she can get out on appeal, with the right lawyer.

The shoving quickly turned into a chance for the toughest of those women—the obvious ring-leader—to offer her cigarettes. Since Plum had never smoked, she nearly refused. Until it occurred to her if prisoners kept trying to "educate" her on the ways of the joint, some, who'd exhausted all their appellate chances, might prefer a smoke to free legal help. After only a few more days, she had signed up dozens of clients for Sunni, and Plum was on her way to opening a behind bars cigarette shop.

Plum quickly took on a smug belief that she had found a way to counter the potential violence in the joint. Until she met Tattoo

Girl. That was Plum's private name for the quick-to-hit girl who looked young enough for juvie, but who easily took on hardened criminals with her jab-and-weave boxing style. Given that she'd covered most of her skin in decorative ink, Plum thought Tattoo Girl made a perfect name for her. Far better than DeeDee, which Plum had since heard the girl called.

The first time they'd clashed came during a rare moment when Plum found herself alone in the shower. Savoring the unexpected privacy, she gave herself over to the moment, completely letting her guard down. Big mistake. An instant later, she found she wasn't alone, after all. Beside her stood a small, fisted girl, who couldn't have weighed ninety pounds in a hurricane, but who possessed unexpected wiry strength. Before Plum even registered the pain of being hit, she found herself crumpled on the cold tile floor.

"What the hell?" Plum had cried involuntarily.

That time TG said nothing, she just knitted her thick brows in a fierce scowl. Plum especially found that sour expression sent her way when she worked in the prison library. Tattoo Girl used her time there by strolling through the shelving, without ever even glancing at the titles, but always using the occasion to glare at Plum. Within days, it got so whenever she found herself in a vulnerable place, her nemesis was there to give her a few slugs. Before long, Plum hurt all over.

Plum tried reminding herself of one of Crystal's favorite sayings from when she and Sunni were little. "Sticks and gnomes may break my bones, but..." She never actually let herself finish the adage. Given the poundings that small, tough girl kept giving her, she didn't think name-calling mattered at all.

Finally, one day, when Plum went into the backroom at the library to retrieve boxes of used books someone had donated, Plum heard the door to the room being quietly closed, and she realized that Tattoo Girl had cornered her again. She tried to position herself for a fight; somehow she over-corrected and ended up falling to the floor anyway. "Lunch before you leap," Crystal had always said. And because Plum hadn't remembered that adage, she wound up knocked down once more, hurting. Her hips couldn't take much more bruising, and if she kept banging her head against walls, she was going to lose the few marbles she had.

"Quit it, okay?" Plum shouted, while rubbing her scalp, knowing how lame that sounded.

For the first time, the girl said, in a low, scratchy voice, "I heard about you."

And somehow whatever she thought she knew translated into a need to punch Plum? Plum was about to offer up another consultation with Sunni, yet she couldn't do that to her sister. If Plum couldn't handle this nasty girl, Sunni, with her prissy corporate lawyer-ways, would never manage it.

She decided to make her own deal. "If you quit hitting me, I'll..."

Once again, as she so often did, Plum had started speaking without an end in sight for that sentence. In here, what did she have to offer anyone beyond legal services and a few smokes? Suddenly, her mind's-eye flashed on the girl's strange library behavior, the way she moved through the shelves, yet never stopped to look at a book. That instantly translated into an understanding.

"If you stop hitting me," Plum began again. "I'll teach you to read."

The instant shock in DeeDee's angry, sherry-toned eyes told Plum she'd hit her mark. "Who says I want to," Tattoo Girl shot back. And then immediately followed it up with, "Who says I don't know how to?"

"Which is it?"

Hard eyes held hers for several beats. Then that scratchy voice said, "Nobody ever thought I could learn. They never wanted to try."

"I do," Plum said, and not only, she discovered, so the girl would stop punching her. She found she wanted to share something she loved.

That was what it took to turn an enemy into a friend. Thereafter, whenever Plum and DeeDee could get together, including the lunch they always shared with Nora, they worked on reading. Plum had divined it exactly right. DeeDee had heard Plum owned a bookstore, and now with her working in the prison library, she simply envied

Plum her ability to do what DeeDee could not. Read. Actually, DeeDee could read, though at a low level. Plum made it her mission to bring her new friend up to speed. She hoped they wouldn't both have years to devote to it.

* * *

Three weeks after Plum's arrest, time continued to move at a snail's pace. Both fear and boredom remained her constant companions. Every day presented a relentless struggle against the depths of depression. Prisoners, Plum had learned, love court appearances. They get to leave the confines of prison, and even sometimes, wear street clothes. Plum thought she'd have the chance to leave, to breathe a bit of free air, for the preliminary hearing, but Roger passed on it.

"It shows the prosecution our hand," he'd told her.

He had filed several motions with the court on her behalf, though none that required Plum to be present. Roger came to see Plum when he had something to report. Sunni visited unexpectedly often. Yet time still dragged.

One day, a stout female guard stopped by their table at lunch. "Tardy, you have a visitor. Says she's your grandmother. She's getting processed now."

Hannah was there alone? She and Gil had come together a few times. Gil invariably offered Plum pointlessly inappropriate advice for surviving in jail, something he knew absolutely nothing about it. Most of it amounted to, "Keep your chin high and let them know you're an Applewood Russell." Sure, that was all it would take to keep her safe. She'd never told him that her own solutions worked much better. The fact was that she and Gil were strangers, trapped in an untenable situation. What did they have to say to each other? Unlike Gil, Hannah rarely spoke at all. She locked her gaze on Plum's face and stared hopelessly for as long as they were there. It hurt Plum to know how important she'd become to them.

DeeDee looked up from one of the children's books Plum had found in the prison library for her to read. "Your gramma's here? I'm glad I stopped...you know... I wouldn't want her to see you bruised." Her throaty voice squeaked with embarrassment, and a blush rose up her tattooed neck.

Though DeeDee brought her gaze back to her book, Plum continued to stare at her thoughtfully.

In the gloom of the reality Nora had forced on her about how much time she'd likely serve, Plum had an idea. One that offered the only slimmest ray of hope. It would require that she manipulate Hannah, callously using Hannah's feelings for her. Could she do it? Plum knew her plan would never work with Gil, who always thought he knew better than anyone else about any situation. Yet it might with Hannah. Guilt traveled up her throat like bile, though she forced it back down. Could a woman in the slammer afford the luxury of feelings for someone else?

Her plan also required that she violate the strongest rule Roger and Sunni laid down for her. But they wouldn't be the ones spending years behind bars if she was convicted.

Was this playing hopscotch yet again?

After a whole life lived this way, what choice did she have?

"DeeDee," Plum said at last. "I think I'm gonna need one last pummeling."

* * *

DeeDee had balked at the idea of punching Plum again, even after Plum explained why she needed another beating.

Even Nora argued against it. "Plum, the bruises won't show immediately."

But Plum had seen her own image in the mirror often enough before DeeDee's blows had grown into bruises. The reddened skin made it equally evident that she had been in a fight.

Naturally, of course, precisely when they couldn't afford a guard to appear, one did—thus, proving Plum's guard-theory. Nora smoothly went into distracting her, while DeeDee and Plum hustled into the shower. To maximize effectiveness, DeeDee threw a few good punches at her face. And though Plum positioned herself to take the blows, she slipped again, banging her hips once more against the hard tile floor. By the time the guard led her toward the visitors' center, Plum didn't have to fake limping.

She did have to force herself to take slow, deep breaths to stave off the impending panic attack that hovered in her chest. Anxiety and guilt threatened to gag her.

Unlike the attorney conference room, where Plum continued to meet with Sunni and Roger, in the visitors' room, inmates were separated from their visitors by thick sheets of Plexiglass. They had to speak through phone receivers. Whenever Plum had seen such arrangements on TV shows, she had always regarded it as touching when characters placed their hands on opposite sides of the glass. Now, when she found herself in that position, it reinforced how isolated she was. That she really had lost her freedom, to the extent that she couldn't even touch someone else's skin. Not the skin of anyone not incarcerated anyway.

Plum wasn't sure whether her reddened blows would be visible enough from a distance and through the scratched Plexiglass. Proof came even before she took her seat. While still several yards away from the station assigned to her, where Hannah waited on the other side, Plum saw her grandmother's eyes widen, and her fingers pressed to her mouth in shock.

Hannah yanked the receiver on her side. "Plum, honey, what happened to you?"

Plum shrugged, wincing when she moved. "Things happen in here. I've been lucky to have avoided it until now." "Lucky" meant making Sunni into a sacrificial-lawyer, but Hannah didn't need to know that.

"We have to do something. Gil will call the warden. Or perhaps Sunshine can—"

Plum shook her head no. "It's like getting picked on in school. If your parents complain, that makes it worse."

Hannah bit her lip.

"At least I lucked out with a good cellmate."

"Yes, I heard. Nora Cabot! How fortuitous. You belong with a well-bred young woman from a good family," Hannah said. "Of course, it's absolutely ridiculous to think of her shooting that producer."

Plum didn't disabuse Hannah of that notion.

Do it! Plum ordered herself.

Instead, she bit her lip, while listening as Hannah chattered on about all the folks back in Applewood, who kept calling in good wishes.

"You know, things between Gil and Jake Gold haven't been good for a long time, and I'm afraid that has spilled over to me. Now, that seems behind us. Jake and Florence call all the time to check on you. They want you to know that your orchid and your cat are thriving."

The orchid and the cat she might never return to if Nora's prediction was right.

Do it!

"Brian Coburn checks on you, too." Hannah's happy smile almost erased the fatigue that ravaged her attractive face. "Gil isn't Brian's biggest fan, but that's because they lock horns. Such a male-thing, you know."

No, it was a Budget-Mart-thing. And a Gil-thing.

"I think you and Brian would be adorable together. I can't put my finger on why, but Brian reminds me somehow of your dear father, my darling boy. "

Plum thought the substance abuse problem they'd shared might have given her a clue.

"Brian gave me the most curious message to pass along to you."

Plum held her breath. "What's that, Hannah?"

"He said 'All's right in the castle.' Do you understand that?"

Do it! Not trusting herself to speak, Plum shook her head no.

With their allotted time running low, Hannah pressed her hand to the glass. Once again, the sight of it stabbed Plum in the heart. Despite her wish not to, Plum placed her hand opposite Hannah's. Was she really going to let this chance go?

Just as a sniffling Hannah was in the process of hanging up her phone receiver, Plum shouted directly at the glass, "Hannah, wait!"

Other inmates stared at her, and an annoyed guard ordered her to use the phone. "Be quick now," the guard added.

Frowning in confusion, Hannah lifted her receiver to her ear again.

"Maybe there is a way you can help me avoid future beatings. Will you do something for me?" Plum asked in a breathless voice.

"If I can, darling."

Plum finally spat it out. "I need you to contact Claire Denton. Tell her we have to meet. Alone." She waited to see if Hannah understood why such a meeting wasn't legally Kosher. "Tell her that I can see to it that she'll get exactly what she wants out of this arrangement if she meets with me. Then maybe, I can get released and be safe again."

"Are you sure, Plum? Your attorney seems quite capable of handling things."

"Positive," Plum said, though she knew she was nowhere near sure.

And what if Claire reported Hannah? Could Hannah also be charged with a crime? Could Plum really take that chance with someone who had treated her with kindness?

"I'll see what I can do," Hannah said, though she sounded hesitant.

Let it go with that. Plum couldn't let it go. She went in for the close, saying, "And, Hannah, don't tell Gil, okay? I don't want to disappoint him if I can't fix things." She lowered her eyes. "I want to make him proud of me."

Finally raising her eyelids, she saw her last remark came closer to sealing the deal.

"I'll try," Hannah said, showing more hope than she had since she first learned her long-lost granddaughter was about to become a jailbird.

Great! If it was such a good idea, why did it make Plum feel like crap?

* * *

Plum wasn't back in her cell for that long, when the guard returned to tell her she had another visitor.

"Another grandparent," the guard said. "Are they working shifts?"

Did that mean Gil was there now? "Grandparents" had taken on new dimensions. Considering that Crystal's parents were dead, and Ben's hadn't left Florida in over a decade, who else could it be?

Hannah must have ratted her out to Gil. Why else would he have come right after she left? Panic threatened to strangle Plum.

She also didn't want him to see the marks left by the blows DeeDee had thrown her way. Those were to manipulate Hannah into doing her bidding. Gil would bungle everything by going to the warden.

"Nora, I can't let him see…" Plum gestured to her face.

Nora reached for the makeup bag that she kept in her cell, even though she rarely used it, and took out a pricier tube of foundation than Plum's skin had ever seen. She gingerly patted it on the reddened areas. "Plum, I hope you know what you're doing," Nora said.

As if Plum ever did.

In the visitors' center, Gil stood on the other side of the window, as he always did, waiting for Plum to be seated before he sat. What a courteous old gentleman. Like he was visiting some five star restaurant, rather than a waiting room that reeked with the dueling scents of disinfectant and body odor. He wore a collared polo shirt today under a navy blazer, rather than his ever-present suit. Formality still oozed out his pores.

Plum's old fears of intimidating men flared up again. Though they both clutched their phones, she could only nod in response to the small talk he started with.

Then he got to it. "When I arrived at the entrance here, I ran into Hannah leaving. She hadn't told me she planned to visit you." Gil hesitated. "Did something happen?"

Did it ever! "No," Plum said, finally finding her voice. "Why do you ask?"

He frowned. "It's that Hannah looked…happy. Happier, you know, than she has since this all began."

He meant since Plum entered their lives and ruined them.

"I wondered whether you said something…"

So he didn't know. Hannah hadn't told him.

Plum didn't trust her voice. She just shook her head no and tried to look as innocent as possible.

With no warning, Gil suddenly covered his eyes with his hand, leaning hard on his elbow. If Plum didn't know better, she would have sworn a shudder went through the body of that rigid old man.

When he removed his hand, the whites of his eyes showed enough red for days without sleep. With a sigh, he said, "It's that Hannah isn't as strong as she seems."

Plum never believed that anything more than a lifetime of pampering held Hannah together.

"She barely handled losing Billy. For a long time, it was touch and go. If she lost you now, too…well, I'm not sure she'd survive."

The wrinkles on his stern face seemed to sag more right before her eyes. *And neither would you.*

What was she doing to them?

CHAPTER THIRTY-THREE

By the time Plum returned to her cell, she had slipped into a terrible funk, partly for the way she was treating people who were kind to her. When Gil discovered the way she had manipulated Hannah, would he pull his support? How much did Roger's firm charge? Could she possibly cover the cost of her defense with what she had left in her savings account?

Mostly, though, she felt stupid. Like someone who couldn't do anything right. Other people got cheated on by their significant others, and they didn't take off for parts unknown and start lives over there. They didn't grab bags of cash on their way out of the door. And, apart from Nora, who might have gotten a trifle heated with her boyfriend, they usually didn't end up in jail. The person *cheated on* usually wasn't facing a stretch in prison. Only Plum, who couldn't do anything normal on a bet.

She fell onto her bunk and slumped against the rough cinder block wall.

Nora, who seemed to have finally moved past her crying jag, looked at Plum with a scowl. "You look worse than me now, and I'm lower than whale dung. What gives?"

Plum shrugged. She couldn't bring herself to confess how awful using Hannah made her feel, especially since she was certain Nora wasn't as sentimental. If Nora made a play to get out of there, she wouldn't regret it as soon as she put it in motion.

Plum hesitated too long before answering. Finally, feeling stupid even for that, she said, "It's this place, you know?" A believable excuse for the despair she'd bet most inmates experienced most of the time.

"Do *I* know? It's all I think about, every minute of every day. How I hate it here, how I would do anything to win my freedom. Lie—I'd say anything about anyone if it would get me out that door.

Steal—tell me what to steal, and I'll do it."

She'd lie about anyone? Maybe Roger was right when he told Plum not to trust anyone. Still, if she couldn't talk to her cellmate about how she felt, she was more isolated than she'd ever been in her life.

Plum closed her eyes and fell back on the thin lumpy pillow on her hard little mattress, knowing that she hadn't entirely lied to Nora. As bad as she felt about using Hannah, as embarrassed as she was about being stupidly offbeat, she did also feel terrible about being stuck in there. The perpetual confinement made the walls close in on her. She understood that the loss of every freedom she'd ever taken for granted mattered more than anything, other than life itself.

The ceaseless noise rubbed her nerves raw. The constant din of buzzing voices. The shouting by those who probably felt as trapped as she did, but who found some outlet in voicing their angry rage. The noise never really died down, not even after lights out. During the day, it was deafening. Normally, sounds didn't bother Plum. She was used to a noisy environment—commercial kitchens aren't anything like cloistered convents, after all. Yet that evening she felt as if all those sounds were trapped inside her skull, making her head feel like it was about to explode.

When she couldn't stand it anymore, she called the guard and begged to be taken to the phone bank. Other than her hopeless calls to Brian's voicemail, Plum never called anyone. She didn't want to hear anyone say this was all her own fault—she heard enough of that trash talk in her own mind. Or worse, hear how much they pitied her because she couldn't help being hopelessly lame.

Tonight, to get out of a space that was surely growing tighter, she'd call the one person she trusted most not to do either of those things. Or so she hoped.

After being brought to the phone station, she waited in line until her turn came. Then, before she could change her mind, she hastily dialed Jake Gold's cell phone.

He answered on the first ring. "Plum, is this really you?"

She hesitated before asking, "How did you know?"

"Caller ID, of course. You're the only person I know in the LA Twin Towers prison. I figured you hadn't been trading my number with strangers for cigarettes." He chuckled. "How are you, honey?"

After her desperate need to reach out to someone, she found she couldn't confide in him, after all. She produced a laugh of her own. "It's an experience, I'll tell you that. But I'm handling it okay."

She must not have been as convincing as she thought because now it was Jake who grew silent.

"Really," Plum added.

"Uh-huh." Jake sighed. "Everyone here misses you so much. For someone who hadn't been a part of our community for too long, you sure made your presence felt. Ginger feels terrible that she was the one who had to arrest you."

"She shouldn't. Please make sure she understands that I don't blame her at all. This is all my fault. If only I hadn't…" She broke off in a sigh. "How's Flo?"

Jake's enthusiasm rose notches. "Plum, you wouldn't believe the change in her. She's been outgoing with the customers, hand-selling books, and really taking pride in the appearance of the bookstore. She told me she's determined to do things just as you would until you come back."

Could she really keep that going until Plum served out her sentence? What would her incarceration do to Flo, someone who'd already suffered too much? Still, imagining a newly gregarious Flo holding court in the bookstore made Plum smile.

"And how about the two of you together? Are you bringing her dinners like you promised?"

This time Jake's sigh sounded happy. "Yeah, I think maybe things are happening for us."

"That's why she's sociable now—she's falling in love." Would Plum finally have another dad, now that she wasn't around to enjoy him?

"No, sweetheart, I don't kid myself. She's like this for you. Because she has a chance of getting her little girl back. Because of that hope, she can let me into her life."

That made Plum feel a little better.

"Plum, Brian misses you, too. Something awful. He struggles with the idea of going to you, but he's trying to honor your wishes. And those calls you made—you really got him with that."

"How did he know?"

"Caller ID, remember? Apparently, you're the only one he knows there, too."

"Lame, huh? I...I just wanted to hear his voice on his outgoing message. I only call when I know he's gone."

"I bet he'd like to hear your voice as well," Jake said.

"Jake, you don't burden a new relationship with a criminal prosecution."

Jake made a noncommittal sound. "Plum, he's not at his office tonight."

"You're sure?"

"Positive. Said he had a meeting elsewhere. Why don't you call him again? And this time, leave a message."

She wouldn't leave a message. The mere possibility of hearing his voice again tonight, when she didn't expect it, stripped some of the ugly off this awful day. Plum brought her conversation with Jake to a close, feeling more hopeful than she had before she called him. And when he asked her to call him again, she promised she would.

This time she returned to the back of the line after hanging up. But the line moved faster than usual. Before she knew it, she was at the head of it again.

Using a phone card once more, she dialed Brian's office number. It answered on the first ring. The voicemail usually gave it three or four rings before playing the message.

Tonight, the voicemail didn't answer—Brian did. "Don't hang up," he said.

"...Brian? Jake told me you weren't there."

"I know. He knew I was working late, and he thought that we... He called me right away to tell me what he did. He thought he was helping, Plum. Don't be mad at him for tricking you."

Plum wasn't sure what she felt. Mixed feelings stirred within her like a hive of swarming bees.

"I need to be there, with you," Brian said with feeling.

Oh, how she wanted that. "No, you need to be in Applewood. Without Gil, you have the chance to change things for the better there."

"We already voted to strengthen the zoning. Didn't Hannah give you my message?"

"She did, and it thrilled me. But you need to keep the other council-folks in line, prevent them from calling for a new vote and changing it back. You told me their track record of countering Gil wasn't that impressive."

Brian breathed heavily into the phone, though he said nothing. He had to be remembering that he had told her that.

"And I think maybe...I need to find my own way through this." Brian had once told her how he had to work his way up after hitting bottom in his addiction. In a different way, Plum thought, this was her bottom.

"What if you *can't* find your way through it, Plum?"

That was the question. She wished she had an answer.

CHAPTER THIRTY-FOUR

More weeks passed, and Plum's life in the Big House settled into a predictable routine. She did get to make one court appearance with Roger. She'd been so excited about it—even though it meant wearing a conservative dress Sunni had bought for her—because she assumed she'd get a chance to talk to the judge. Too bad the judge never acknowledged her presence, and it was over in a heartbeat. Sunni continued to visit frequently, seemingly trying to be a better sister. Her grandparents dropped in every few days, always together now. And Sunni kept plying her with phone cards, allowing Plum to connect to the Applewood lifeline, making calls to Jake and Flo, and even on rare occasions, Brian. Hannah never said another word about her request, and neither did Plum.

Plum continued working in the prison library. At least the job got her out of her cell, and gave her a break from Nora's moods. Plum didn't know why she hadn't noticed it at first, but Nora's feelings rode the same roller coaster that Crystal's had. Actually, Nora's swings were more extreme; she not only suffered from manic episodes, but also deep depressions that produced crying jags. It wore Plum down. Thankfully, all those years with Crystal had taught Plum how to tiptoe through the emotional minefield. She knew when to agree and when to laugh along with Nora, and also when doing those exact things would set off an explosion. It made her wonder if Nora's producer boyfriend hadn't been bright enough to figure that out, or if he just liked playing with dynamite.

Plum's ex, Noah, remained a distant irritant. Sunni reported that he kept insisting he had to see Plum. He even came to the jail a couple of times, only to be turned away.

"Why don't you just see him and get it over with?" Sunni had asked.

"He's slow—he doesn't learn too fast. He'd be here every day needing to hear it again." And lording over his jailhouse ex—Plum still wasn't ready for that. "Why don't you assume for once that I know what I'm doing?" Plum demanded.

"Two words," Sunni said. "Track record."

"One word—therapy."

The sisters had laughed together. Plum couldn't believe it, but her incarceration was actually breaking down barriers and bringing them closer.

That wasn't to say that she and Sunni didn't have their tiffs, too.

"Plum, would you stop offering up my services for convicts' appeals?" Sunni had demanded in exasperation on more than one occasion. "I'm not a criminal lawyer, and there's a limit to how much *pro bono* work I can do. Besides, they're always guilty."

"All the more reason you should consider a few jailhouse consultations worth it to keep me safe. If they're guilty, it probably means they have no brakes."

Fully exasperated, Sunni had said, "Plum, you're guilty, and you have no brakes."

Plum had sighed. The lines between guilt and innocence had blurred for her, since she'd taken up residence there.

* * *

Gossip about the jail administration was the lifeblood of the inmate population. Since DeeDee cleaned the guards' offices, she often picked up dirt she could pass along. Plum would have sworn that she'd never care what anyone in prison officialdom said or did, yet after seven weeks in stir, she found herself as hungry for tittle-tattle as everyone else.

Today, when DeeDee pushed her cleaning cart into the library, before the end of Plum's shift, she sidled up to where Plum sat behind the checkout desk, and hissed, "The guards are all in atwitter about you. They want to know how many lawyers you have. How many *do* you have?"

"You know. There's Sunni and Roger and sometimes a paralegal who works for Roger."

DeeDee grinned, and said in her oddly scratchy voice. "Not so.

They're about to come for you now. You have another one, some new chick." She stretched her inked arm across the checkout desk, while dusting.

Plum shrugged. "Maybe they've sent someone else from the office."

"From what I overheard, this chick thinks she's God's gift. She practically bitch-slapped the guards. Naturally, now, they're bowing at her feet." DeeDee ended with a nasty snicker.

"Still don't..." Then it hit her: God's gift...bitch-slapping the guards. There was only one person she knew who warranted those descriptions: Claire. "Oh, no," Plum's blood froze within her, leaving a block of ice where her heart used to be. She buried her face in her arms on the desk. "Why do I do these things?"

When a guard entered the library and headed toward them, DeeDee hastily continued pushing her dust cloth around. "Who?" she demanded under her breath.

Plum groaned. "Someone who falls into the most overworked category in my life: it seemed like a good idea at the time."

CHAPTER THIRTY-FIVE

It seemed like a good idea at the time—Plum often thought that one line summed up whole hunks of her life.

It had seemed like a good idea when she asked Hannah to contact Claire and put together a secret meeting. Now that Plum was being led down a prison corridor for precisely what she asked for, she realized it was one of the worst ideas she'd ever had. Worse even than jumping into her Jeep and driving to some unknown place and starting a new life on someone else's bag o' bucks.

How could she have believed there could be anything promising in the idea of coming face-to-face with Claire again? Plum had refused to see Noah, because she still felt too beaten by his treatment of her. Yet Claire was infinitely more arrogant. Had Plum forgotten how she'd stood in the doorway of her own bedroom, retching from the pain they had caused her? It didn't matter that now Plum realized she and Noah hadn't been that far from the end. It didn't even matter that she'd reconnected with Brian. All that mattered was that it was Claire's savage disregard for her that had set the craziest part of Plum's life in motion.

Despite her effort to avoid it, Plum's mind's-eye filled once again with the sight of Claire riding Noah. And with the casual confidence Claire had brought to her ironing board body and grapefruit breasts when she rose to dress.

If Plum hadn't been able to even breathe the same air as Claire then, how could she bear it now? Now that she wore a prison jumpsuit and washed her hair with such awful shampoo, it transformed her normally soft, shiny curls into a fright wig?

Plum wished she could turn and run back to her cell, but that was only a small part of what being jailed denied her. Instead, with her hands cuffed before her and her legs clamped in irons, she shuffled along toward the awful inevitability she herself had set in motion.

"You must have a lotta lawyers," the female guard said.

DeeDee had said that, too. It took Plum a moment to realize what that meant. She noticed she was headed for the meeting room where she always gathered with Sunni and Roger, rather than the visitors' room where she and Gil and Hannah met. So this would be *really* face-to-face. She wouldn't even have the meager protection that sheet of Plexiglass between them provided. How had Claire managed to score the attorney-client conference room if their meeting wasn't even legal? A moment ago Plum wouldn't have thought it possible, but now she felt even more out-classed.

When the guard flung the conference room door open, Claire stood on the far side of the scratched metal table. There, she struck a clothed version of a pose she had once assumed naked in Plum's old bedroom, with her hip cocked to one side, while she ran a hand through her long blonde hair. She wore another one of her mini pencil skirts, this one in taupe. She'd coupled it with a short, tight sweater in cocoa and amber, which pushed her breasts out the top, while simultaneously offering up a wide expanse of midriff.

Confidence wafted off her with gale force strength, pelting Plum right in her own self-doubts.

Once the guard left them alone together, a desperate need to say something to break Claire's confident spell overcame Plum. "This room is reserved for lawyers only," Plum said in a voice that sounded priggishly righteous even to her. As if she were the warden, not an inmate.

With her fingers drifting lazily through her silky hair, Claire said, "I am a lawyer. Well, I graduated from law school." She gave her head a tilt. "Close enough."

"Couldn't pass the bar exam, huh?" Plum didn't know where that remark came from, but she wasn't sorry she said it.

"Didn't want to," Claire said with a sniff. The small line that twitched between Claire's brows told Plum she'd hit a nerve. "Real estate suits me better than the law would have."

"But you're not *my* lawyer," Plum said with a sputter.

Claire shrugged. "I certainly didn't belong in the visitors' room. I'm sure it's filled with the most vile specimens." With a sweep of her gaze, she seemed to indicate that Plum *did* belong there. "I find that if I tell people what they expect to hear, they normally fall in with my plans. It wasn't hard to convince anyone I was your lawyer. I look like a successful woman, after all; why not a lawyer?"

Plum actually thought Claire looked pretty slutty for a professional woman. That didn't mean her self-assurance wouldn't pave the way for her. Plum had to take that idea on faith, though, since she'd never had enough confidence of her own to test the theory.

"You can have your boyfriend back," Claire said. "I'm through with him."

Claire slipped into a chair on her side of the table, while Plum remained standing. She felt as she had when she used to be called to the principal's office to discuss why, thanks to Crystal's eccentric efforts, she and Sunni could never adhere to the school's dress code.

"Yeah...that's okay. I've moved on to someone else."

Claire arched one eyebrow. "Good for you. I wouldn't have predicted that. Noah must be shocked, too. He always made it sound as if you idolized him."

Was that the way he saw it? The shame almost gagged Plum.

"You know, you could still take him back. It would give you the upper hand in the relationship. It wasn't his fault—he couldn't have resisted me. No man can."

Plum got the idea that Claire loved the idea of other women accepting her sloppy seconds.

"I can be quite appealing, you know," Claire added.

Plum took that on faith, too, never having seen the dazzling aspect of Claire's personality. She didn't bother answering.

Instead, she finally took the chair across from Claire and asked, "How did you know where to find me? In Applewood, I mean. "

"I *saw* you. Applewood, Arizona is one of the places I visit often, given the Budget-Mart deal."

Plum nodded. "Noah used to visit it, too. Along with the other places."

Claire laughed. "No, he didn't. I convinced him to leave the travel and making contact with the buyers to me. When he told you he was traveling for business, he was always at my place."

Plum couldn't hold back a shocked gasp. Even if she had moved on, learning another way that Noah had betrayed her gave the knife an unexpected twist. If they normally got together in Claire's place, what were they doing that day by cavorting in Plum's bed? How could Noah have been that heartless?

"What were you thinking by going there?" Claire asked.

It had occurred to Plum that she had gone to one of the places Noah or Claire was likely to visit. Yet she'd felt certain she'd spot them first. Even the little confidence she'd brought to that decision was misplaced. But then, she also hadn't expected to stay. She hadn't expected to *want* to stay.

"You were bopping down the street, looking all happy or something. Carrying a bag from some Western store—where you probably spent *my* money."

Plum remembered that day, when she thought someone was watching her. Why hadn't she paid attention to that feeling? Maybe they could have thrashed it out there, and she wouldn't have had to end up here.

"Where the hell did you get off taking my money and throwing it around?" Claire demanded.

Plum could have explained that she thought it was Noah's money, what he owed her—the true explanation she'd given everyone else. But Claire had given her the opening she'd hoped for.

"*Your* money? I don't think so." Plum had a lot of time to think about all the connections, and for once she was positive she had put it together right. "You see, I don't think you truly were an employee of Westside Homes and Offices and Noah's partner in this Budget-Mart deal. You were spying there for Javier Silva, right? Westside's competitor. I'm betting Silva's your actual employer." Plum actually figured Claire and Javier were probably a couple. She could be wrong about that, of course, but she liked the idea of Claire cheating on Noah with her real lover. "I'm guessing that forty K was Javier's money, bribe loot that you were supposed to use to win over Diggie Long and Florence Gallagher in Applewood, and more holdouts who refused to sell their land in other locales Budget-Mart wanted."

Instant anger flashed across Claire's face, in the form of narrowed eyes and an unattractively clenched jaw. That told Plum she'd hit another target.

Claire fumed in silence. Then she spat out, "Got it all figured out, do you? What a joke. Save the intrigue for others—you don't have the brain for it. Everyone laughs at you. Do you know that? Everyone at Westside Homes and Offices. From your clothes, to your sappy attitude—you're ridiculous. Noah laughs, too, when he isn't dissolving in embarrassment."

Claire also hit a bull-eye's with her remarks. Her words were sabers. With every slash, she cut Plum's pitiful self-esteem into bits too small to be put back together.

"You're a freak. An absolute freak. Everyone thinks that."

By throwing Plum's most dreaded fears back at her, Claire had eviscerated her completely. Plum wished her voice weren't shaking when she finally spoke. At least she said the right things.

"Maybe so," Plum said. "But I'm the freak who has what you want."

CHAPTER THIRTY-SIX

Claire glared at Plum across the scarred table in that attorney-prisoner conference room. "Yeah? What could you possibly have that I'd want?"

Plum's voice finally steadied. "I'm the new owner of the acreage that Budget-Mart wants in Applewood. The land previously owned by Florence Gallagher."

"No way."

"Way. Big way."

From the side pocket on her slim skirt, Claire pulled out her smartphone and began to search.

"Hey, you can't bring cell phones into prisons," Plum said.

"You're such a good girl. Do you always do what you're told? Hasn't anyone ever told you it's more fun to break the rules?"

Actually, Plum was usually so much into her own realm, she often didn't know there were rules. She'd only learned that prisoners couldn't have cell phones when she asked Sunni to buy her one. She'd also discovered that to make sure prisoners didn't get hold of them, visitors weren't allowed to bring them in.

"How did you get it past the guards?" Plum asked.

Claire shrugged absently while continuing to search. "I shot the redneck guard at the gate a look down my boobs, so he didn't notice what I put in my pocket."

"Is there anyone you don't trash?" While Plum had never actually longed to be more like Claire—the gap between them seemed too great to bridge—she did assume that it was better in every way to be Claire Denton than Plum Tardy. Now she understood that there were things about Claire that didn't measure up to her, starting with her sense of humanity. If Claire was capable of feeling anything for anyone, she sure kept that hidden.

"As I said, you're such a goodie-goodie—" Claire looked up

from her phone, startled. "You *do* own that land."

Plum remembered how she made Brian promise to transfer the deeds immediately on the day of the party, counting on needing that edge at some point. She hadn't known it would take all these weeks until it mattered.

"How...?"

"Flo Gallagher is my mother, my birth mother. I'm adopted."

Plum doubted that Claire was often caught flat-footed. Now, though, she couldn't hide that the implications of this news dumbfounded her. "That changes everything. Why didn't Noah make use of it?"

"Noah doesn't know. I never told him." She didn't mention that she didn't know herself until recently. That felt too freakish to admit.

Claire seemed to study Plum from a distance. "Maybe you aren't quite the fool I took you for."

Plum finally felt the balance of power shift. From her sigh, so did Claire.

"What do you want?" Claire asked, a shade less rudely now.

Plum smiled. "It's more a matter of what *you* might want. Do you want Javier Silva's firm to process the sale directly between me and Budget-Mart, with you collecting the commission...or would you like to buy it yourself, so you can sell it to them?"

Claire's eyes flickered to the corners of the shabby room, as if she were searching for someone she could ask, "Is this idiot for real?"

"You would sell that land to me?"

Plum nodded. "For whatever was in that satchel I took, for whatever's left, that is."

"Didn't you count it?"

Plum said she hadn't.

Claire rolled her eyes. "Why would you do this? You could demand over a million bucks for that land. Maybe several million if you remained firm enough. Those fools at Budget-Mart are convinced they can only put their store on that spot. Who wouldn't want that kind of money?"

"I'd love it. Only it'd be a little hard spending it in here." Plum gestured to the walls around them. "You do control the keys to this castle."

Claire smirked.

"I'd do anything to get out of here, including selling a plot of land potentially worth a fortune for a pittance. You have to promise me you can make the charges against me go away. The sale would have to be contingent on that."

Avarice gave Claire such an attractive glow, Plum felt positively anemic in comparison.

"Count on it."

"With my life on the line, I need to do more than count on it. I need it in writing. My lawyer, Sunni Meadows, will produce a sales contract for it. You better sign that—as is; no negotiations. And I'll expect to be out of here pretty damn fast."

Claire hesitated. "That Applewood land in exchange for whatever you haven't spent in my Hartmann bag?"

Plum nodded.

"I'll want my bag back," Claire added.

"Wouldn't think of keeping it." That much was true.

Claire thrust her hand across the table.

Ewww. Plum wasn't sure she could stand to touch the dreaded bitch. She beat down her revulsion. *Where there's a witch, there's a way.* Plum extended her own hand for a quick shake.

"Good deal," Claire said.

Well, only if Plum convinced Sunni to go ahead with her part of the operation.

CHAPTER THIRTY-SEVEN

Free air! Plum's time in stir had lasted for almost eight weeks. Now, she stood at the final door in the prison's complex exit system waiting to be released. Through the edge crack, a bit of a breeze blew in, carrying the freedom from outside. From the time Plum met with Claire, it had taken another four excruciatingly long days, but Plum was finally about to be released, with all charges dropped. She would never again take the ability to move freely for granted.

Her anxious desperation to flee nearly overwhelmed her. *The wheels of justice grind exceedingly slow,* Plum thought, quoting that old proverb to herself in the hopes it would help her to settle down. *And they miss a few now and then.* But not this time.

Plum's only regret was leaving her friends behind. She gave DeeDee her vending machine change and her phone cards, and gave Nora all the cigarettes she had collected. DeeDee would come up for parole in only six months. Since she'd mostly stopped hitting others, she had a good chance of scoring her release. Plum made her promise to come to Applewood, where a job and a bed would be waiting.

"And keep up with your reading," Plum ordered. Nora had promised to continue the lessons. It would be good for both of them. They were in tears when they hugged Plum good-bye.

It was even harder saying farewell to Nora. "I don't know when I'll be able to get back to see you, Nora, and I hate it—"

"Don't you ever come back," Nora had said with fierce intensity. "I want to know you're out there somewhere living free, living it up for both of us."

Plum's throat had tightened. "When you're released..." she didn't name when that would be. "...the Cellblock C girls are gonna party."

Leaving Nora...she still misted over thinking about it. As

challenging as Nora's emotions were, she had been a friend when Plum needed one.

In the cubicle at the final door, the guard, Cubby, waited for the release order. He was a plump black man, whose full belly pressed at the pickle-colored shirt the guards wore, and who always sported a perpetual smile, despite what he must have seen in there. Plum figured for a person to be able to keep his sense of humor while working his job, he either had to be deeply at peace, or demented. And Cubby wasn't demented. He held the receiver of the prison phone up to his ear.

"Plum, you sure look fine today," he said.

Plum flashed him a confident smile. She wore the outfit she'd had on when booked, the one she'd worn for her bookstore's grand reopening party: Crystal's navy suit with her two-toned blue cowboy boots. Sunni had offered to stop by her old house for something more practical, but Plum decided to go out the same way she went in. In her flashy new style. She made a vow to never again wear anything hopelessly sensible.

Cubby's face took on an uncharacteristic sternness. "Plum, I don't want to see you back here ever again, you understand?"

Giving her head an emphatic shake, Plum said, "No, sir, Cubby. Never. I swear."

Of course, given the way she lived her life... But what were the odds she'd end up in *this* jail?

The final order came through, and Cubby hit the release, allowing the door to swing open for her. Plum stepped out into sunlight that warmed her face. She would have dropped and kissed the dirty sidewalk, only she didn't want to risk scuffing her boots.

The honk of a car horn caught her attention. Sunni waved to her from the curb. She'd bought a new car during the time that Plum had been incarcerated. A red Volvo wagon. Plum regarded the choice as a tad schizophrenic, though it did accurately reflect Sunni's life in transition.

Plum jumped into the passenger seat. "Picking me up on a workday? I didn't expect that." She could have requested a cab or Uber before she left the prison, or called Gil, assuming he and

Hannah hadn't left town yet. Plum actually thought she'd appreciate stretching her legs on a walk in a space with no walls. But riding with her sister was pretty good, too.

"We're a full service law firm."

"Don't remind me. I owe you so much, Sunni."

She didn't mean just taking off from work, she also meant Sunni's dealings with Claire. Plum had expected Sunni to hit the roof when she spilled that she'd met with Claire, and that she needed Sunni to write what was sure to be a pretty odd contract. Well, given Plum-logic, what else could it be? Instead, Sunni had sighed and said, "Why didn't I expect this? At least it worked. It didn't net you another charge."

"Did Claire balk at the terms of the contract?"

Sunni choked. "You bet she did. But what choice did she have? She'd already recanted her charges against you and set your release in motion." From the driver's seat, Sunni briefly looked in Plum's direction. "You know, she might be wily and aggressive, but she's not that smart. She's neither as smart, nor as pretty as you are, Plum. And she's sure not as good."

Other than the good-part, which might mean that Plum was a sucker, she didn't buy it.

"Well, milady, where to?" Sunni started the engine.

"To the home, where Crystal is. I need to have a come-to-Plum talk with Roy."

"Do you want me to do it? I owe you for everything you did on Mom's house."

Plum said she didn't. "I'm the one who fed his delusion." Not to mention her own. "It's my place to let him down."

Sunni nodded. They drove for a while in silence. Plum glanced over at Sunni and noticed that she wore a pretty dress today, instead of one of her buttoned-down suits. Of course, it was black and had to be from one of her frou-frou designers. Still, progress.

When Plum commented on the change of style, Sunni joked, "Roger says I owe you for broadening my horizons."

Sunni and Roger did work together, and on Plum's case, so it was natural that they would talk. Still, there was something about the way Sunni said his name that made Plum wonder if there wasn't something more between them than merely being colleagues.

"Roger, huh?" Plum asked suggestively, knowing Sunni would pick up what she meant. They did share sister shorthand.

Sunni flushed prettily. "We're just friends. But…well, you don't think he's too old for me, do you?"

"Not in dog years."

Sunni laughed. "Oh, Plum, you say the strangest things."

Don't remind me. She meant that in so many ways, it was Sunni who was the old fart. With the changes she was making, though, the years between them might even out. Plum couldn't be happier for her. Maybe there was hope for Crystal's girls yet.

* * *

Plum sat at Crystal's bedside, holding her limp hand, the way she had before her whole life unraveled. Crystal remained as still as always. Pale, nearly as waxy as a corpse, lifeless in all but the most basic definition of life.

"I love you, Crystal. I will every day I have on this earth. You came across a baby who needed care, and you gave it freely and generously, never giving any inkling of your charity. You taught me everything I know about having fun. I forgot it for a while, though I'm getting back to it now. Sunni, too. You gave us such a shining example of what an adventure we could make of life."

Plum had to stop, take some deep breaths to keep from crying.

"I have to go now. I need to spend some time with my other mother. Getting to know her, and maybe helping her grow up." Despite herself, Plum sniffed. "I'll miss you. I have missed you all this time you've been gone from us."

After that, she silently clutched Crystal's hand, willing her back to the life she once knew, one last time.

Then she went to talk to Roy, to tell him the truth they both should have faced earlier.

They met in the garden outside of Crystal's room, where roses and hollyhocks bloomed around amber paths of stepping stones. Crystal would have loved it.

Plum told him about the new life she'd found, before adding, "I need to bow out now, Roy. Bow out in every way."

"I don't know how Cryssie and me can make it here without you."

Plum could have reminded him how much she'd done already, though what would be the point? Instead, she struggled to find the right words. "It's time, Roy. For Crystal, life was joyous. This isn't how she would want to live."

He lowered his head. "I can't let her go, Plum. Not yet. You know, I never thought Cryssie and me..." He covered his face with his hands. "We need this time."

He needed it, not Crystal; this was his love story. He would have to find his own truth, in his own time, Plum decided. Still, she couldn't support his denial anymore. Roy wished her well, yet only half-heartedly. An instant later, he was gone. Plum figured he'd tap Sunni next, but she knew Sunni was made of sterner stuff.

Plum still felt so emotional when she walked into the waiting room. She'd planned to ask the receptionist to call her a cab, since Sunni had gone back to the office. Only she saw Hannah waiting there. Sunni must have called her and Gil.

"Hannah. I thought you and Gil would have gone back to Applewood," Plum said. "You know, once the charges were dropped."

"We've been waiting for our granddaughter," Hannah said with great warmth. She pulled Plum to her for a hug. "Are we ready to go...back?"

Plum suspected that Hannah intended to say "home," though she probably decided not to presume.

"Not quite. I still have some things to do. If you need to go..."

"We wouldn't dream of leaving without you." Hannah beamed happily.

Gil was in the parking lot, behind the wheel of their rental car. Plum eyed the Buick sedan they'd chosen.

"We're going to need a bigger car. An SUV, maybe, towing a large trailer," Plum said. To her surprise, Gil agreed with a nod.

They both seemed happier. Gil even looked healthier, with

brighter skin and eyes. They had given her a lot. They'd spent megabucks on her legal bills, though Plum rationalized that she had saved them the major expense of a trial by making her end run around the legal system and going directly to Claire. Still, she had given them something, too. Plum vowed to do everything in her power to make this relationship work. And to never-ever try to trick Hannah again, even if it worked out this time. She'd also make sure Gil understood that the zoning changes Brian had convinced the Applewood Town Council to make, covering Diggy Long's land and what she had bought from Flo—the Budget-Mart land—would have to remain untouchable.

"Onward," she said, once she was seated in the backseat. She felt her gut clench when she gave them directions to a house in Santa Monica that had never really been her home.

CHAPTER THIRTY-EIGHT

Plum stood in the driveway of the Santa Monica house. When she left it this time, it wouldn't be fleeing from a shame that wasn't hers, it would be with the stuff she wanted for her new life.

Before arriving at the house, she'd directed Gil to drive to Fourth Street, where there was a box store she had used when she and Noah moved into this place. They'd bought as many cardboard boxes as they could fit in the Buick's trunk, along with lots of packing tape. The store's owner promised to have more boxes delivered when his teenage delivery guy came on duty a short while later. At the house, Plum unloaded the trunk herself, piling the flat boxes on the driveway's stone pavers. She hadn't let Gil help, despite his insistence. He might be looking healthier, but who knew what was going on in his ticker. If they were to share any kind of relationship, Plum felt certain they'd need enough time to develop it. She didn't want him kicking off here.

Once Gil and Hannah left to exchange the rental car, Plum stood in the driveway, delaying the inevitable. There was no doubt that Noah was inside the house. The silver Lexus SUV in the driveway told her that. The one he always left outside until he pulled it into the garage before going to bed. That it was there now must mean that he didn't have another cutie in there with him. Or that he didn't have to hide them anymore. Would it be awkward if he did? Plum found she didn't care enough to for that.

Plum didn't want to have to deal with him. She admitted to herself how much like Flo she was, fleeing from whatever threatened to be uncomfortable. This time, it couldn't be avoided. Maybe, she admitted, she and Flo both had some growing up to do. Maybe?

She opened the tote bag that hung from her shoulder. When she had been booked into jail, she'd surrendered all her possessions. Upon her release, a guard reviewed everything being returned, and she'd had to sign an inventory sheet. Plum felt so eager to leave, she hadn't paid much attention to it. She saw now that everything she'd had when she went in was still there, including a key ring, with keys to this house, her car—and even a defunct Westside restaurant—as well as a bookstore she'd hastily bought in Arizona.

Refusing to allow herself to stall any longer, she grabbed a couple of boxes and a roll of tape, and unlocked the front door.

Noah wasn't in sight, and she didn't feel like looking for him. Instead, she made up some boxes and took them to the den to begin packing her books. An unexpected wave of emotions hit her when she passed through the kitchen and into the den. There had been more good times in that house than she wanted to admit. When they first moved in especially, decorating their new home. She remembered some of the great meals she had cooked in that kitchen, which they'd shared by candlelight. Plum wasn't sure whether she wanted those good memories back.

Before she could decide how she felt about them, Noah stumbled in. Drunk. Still as good-looking as ever, but flushed and disoriented.

"Well, look what the cat dragged in," he said, slurring.

Reverting away from this confrontation, Plum instantly thought of cats. Specifically Scrappy, her cat in Applewood. Had Flo really taken care of her?

The man standing unsteadily before her demanded her attention. "Your bitch sister wouldn't let me see you in jail. I wanted to be there for you."

"That was me. She did that because I asked her to. *I* didn't want to see you."

"Then you're the bitch."

It made it easier that he saw her that way. Plum resumed her packing, while Noah started to stagger out.

With no warning, she suddenly said, "I had a miscarriage. We did."

He turned to her and nodded sadly. "Knew that."

That Flo had been right floored Plum. "How...?"

He shrugged. "I met that girl who works in your doctor's office at a bar one night. She assumed I knew, expressed her sympathy."

He hadn't pronounced *sympathy* right, but he didn't seem to notice. "When she realized I didn't know, she told me all about it."

Plum knew the girl he meant, her OB's young receptionist. In years past, Noah had come along with her to a couple of appointments there, after which they went to lunch. The flirty little receptionist had always come on to him, right in front of Plum. Plum had never complained to her doctor about that because it made her feel insignificant. This time she would tell her doctor about this breech of medical confidentiality. She wasn't so insignificant that she didn't deserve that. Nobody was.

"Why didn't you say anything, Noah?"

He started to blubber quietly. "I felt so bad. We'd always wanted to make a baby. Me, a daddy—I wanted a little one to look up to me, you know?" He sniffed hard. "Only I was interviewing for a new job then. I was dealing with too much to take on anything coming from you."

He was dealing with too much? Plum suffered such an awful loss it gutted her, but he had job interviews to deal with. Why hadn't she ever seen how right Sunni had been about this empty suit? How could she have valued herself so little?

Noah wandered off somewhere, relieving Plum from having to rehash any more of the time they'd shared. She continued packing, moving full boxes out to the driveway, bringing empty ones in. The days she'd spent redesigning High Desert Books, carrying around heavy cartons of books, had increased her muscular strength, and she found shifting around heavy cartons easier than she once would have. Besides, Santa Monica was at sea level; Jake had told her she'd feel stronger here. She did, she realized, in every way possible.

During one of her driveway trips, the box store teenager showed up and unloaded another stack of cartons. Plum kept filling them. After the den, she moved to the kitchen, packing up pots, knives, and serving pieces selectively, keeping only what she really enjoyed using and leaving the rest.

At one point, she came across her old set of dishes, the ones she'd first bought herself when she went out on her own. The dishes and bowls were square, rather than round, and they looked as if

Jackson Pollack had designed them by flinging gold and cream paint drops across tomato-red plates. Noah had never liked their shapes or colors, but Plum found that she still loved how unusual they were. She packed those.

She ended up in the bedroom closet. She noticed Noah's stack of expensive luggage was gone now. Had he sold the set? Who cared?

While she successfully avoided dredging up any memory of the last time she was in that room, she heard the front door slam.

"Is she here?" some woman screamed. "At the jail, they said she was released. Where else would she go?"

Claire?

Plum walked into the living room. Claire stood just inside the door. She wore another one of her skimpy, body-hugging outfits. In her hand, she clenched a few sheets of paper. Noah, who was slumped on one of the couches his designer-friend had chosen for the room, frowned in confusion. He didn't even seem to notice the revealing outfit. Plum guessed that whatever spark had existed between them had truly died.

When Claire spotted Plum, she shrieked, "You!" She shook the pages. "I knew signing this contract was a mistake, I just knew it." She whipped around to Noah. "Do you know what her lawyer did to me? She put in a clause that if, after that property passed to me, I didn't sell it to Budget-Mart within sixty days, ownership would revert again to *her*." With that she gestured to Plum. "How am I going to sell it to them? They have no interest in Applewood anymore, since her boyfriend rammed through a zoning change. That property can't be used now to build a big box store."

"Hey, you do get to keep the money." Plum wanted to demand the money back as well as the land, but given that it probably had come from Javier Silva, Sunni advised her to make the wise choice and leave it with Claire. Plum didn't want Silva's lawyer coming after her. She'd had enough of the legal system to last the rest of her life.

"Javier's demanding it back. He dropped me. Me! He fired me, too."

So they actually had been an item. Plum took some comfort from knowing she had orchestrated what must have been the only time in Claire's life when she got dumped.

Noah looked too confused to follow most of that. He didn't know about Plum's relationship to Flo, or that Plum now owned the property he'd also tried to wrangle for Budget-Mart. He did, however, perk up at one word.

"Boyfriend?" he demanded. He sent an accusatory look at Plum. As if he had that right.

"She who laughs first doesn't also get to laugh last," Plum said with sage wisdom.

Claire shrieked again and threw the contract she'd been holding onto the floor. Claire probably figured she'd contest it, but Sunni would follow up on returning that Applewood property to Plum. Sunni would follow up on Noah's fraudulent second mortgage, too. Neither one of them was any match for Sunni.

"Ooh! I hate you," Claire shouted on her way out the door.

Plum felt a serene sense of relish. It might be small and petty, but she had won. Plum thought she deserved a bit of satisfaction.

Plum went back to the bedroom closet, and finished boxing it up fast, packing all of her chef's things, though few of her old regular old clothes. She took none of the utilitarian undies or toiletries. Finally, she packed away her strongbox of important papers, including a fictitious birth certificate listing Crystal and Ben Tardy as her parents.

After carrying the last of the boxes to the driveway, Plum stopped and looked at the ocean in the distance. How could she have possibly thought she wouldn't miss this? For most of her life she'd walked in the mornings along the shore. For most of her life, she'd savored the feeling of moist air on her arms. How could she think she wouldn't miss it all dreadfully? But it was time to let new experiences into her life, to love some new sensations.

Maybe she would bring Flo here at some point and share with her all the things Plum had cared about. Or she and Brian might return together. They didn't have any great high school memories to share, though they could make new memories. But all of her old ones—the ones that were hers alone, Plum realized, were pretty good. She felt glad to have them back before she moved on.

The front door opened and Noah stepped out. He looked weepy again, as he had when he talked briefly about Plum's miscarriage. She reminded herself that drunks' emotions are always close to the surface, and usually exaggerated.

"What are your plans?" she asked, assuming he, like Claire, was out of the running on the Budget-Mart deal.

He leaned against the wall of the house for support. "I'm gonna head back to Indiana for a while. Work for Dad. It won't be forever, just till I get on my feet again."

Plum doubted that. She suspected he would spend the rest of his life working for "Pudgy Paul Rowle," as Noah's father encouraged his insurance clients to call him, hating it all the while. Believing he was really destined for bigger and better things. Never understanding why those things didn't come to him.

It wasn't Plum's concern anymore. She just nodded at him. She started walking towards the curb, to watch for Hannah's and Gil's return.

When she turned away, Noah seemed to get past the sadness that came over him. "You know, Plum," he said. "It would sure help me to get started if you returned your engagement ring."

She whirled around to him. *Huh?*

"You're the one who moved on." He snorted. "Boyfriend! That didn't take you long, did it? What do you say you give it back to me?"

Had he really forgotten that he cheated on me? That he'd stolen my equity in the house? He must consider me such a doormat.

Once again, Plum wore the ring on a chain around her neck, as she had when she'd surrendered it during booking. That it had been returned to her restored her faith in the integrity of the people who worked in the penal system. Unlike fiancés.

"I mean, I would still have married you."

Disbelief flooded her. "Seriously?"

He nodded.

Plum threw her head back and started laughing. She kept on laughing, loudly and freely. The tinkling laugh sounded happy even to her ears. She imagined that laughter being carried off on a breeze, along with the last of the pain she'd suffered there, leaving her with nothing more than memories of good times. Then again, maybe it was the complete absurdity of his suggestion that she found hilarious.

CHAPTER THIRTY-NINE

Twenty-three hours later, Plum steered a black Yukon pulling a trailer into Applewood. Gil sat in the passenger seat beside her, while Hannah dozed in the backseat.

Plum's excitement had been building for hours, and now that they were actually in Applewood, she felt outright giddy. If she had been alone on this trip, she would have driven straight through after packing up. But she decided her grandparents needed their sleep. For their sakes, she'd insisted on stopping for the night somewhere around the border between the two states.

When Gil showed up with the exchanged vehicle, he'd also brought a workman he had hired somewhere. That sturdy young man helped Plum to load those boxes in the trailer. After a few moments, Noah had returned to the house. Probably convinced Plum wouldn't give him the ring. She hadn't even bothered to introduce him to her grandparents, despite the suggestive looks Hannah kept giving her. What would be the point? Plum suspected that he'd always blame her for his failure to reach the top, because she refused to return that ring. She found she didn't care in the least.

After she and the helper loaded her boxes, they went on to Crystal's house. Sunni insisted she take the rest of Crystal's clothes, and all of her books. The contents of Crystal's wardrobe and library exceeded the space in the trailer. Sunni promised to have the remainder shipped to Plum in Arizona. Plum knew she'd keep some volumes for herself, though many would go on the shelves at High Desert Books. She would also sell her engagement ring. Despite what she'd get for the ring and what was left in her savings account, she knew, to carry out her plans, she would need more money.

In Applewood, Gil gave her directions to their house. How funny. They were her grandparents, and they now shared an actual relationship, yet she didn't know where they lived. Well, that fit a hopscotch life. Before they went inside, she promised to stop by the next day. She suspected she would often check on them from now on. Flo might not like it, but Plum found she wanted all of them in her life.

She drove back to High Desert Books, angling the SUV and the trailer in the alley out back. She'd unpack it as soon as she could, so she could return the car and trailer to the local office of the rental agency. She didn't want to gouge their credit card any more than she had to. Plum Tardy still paid her own way. Mostly. With help from those who loved her.

After parking, Plum stepped out and stretched her travel-weary back.

"Plum!" a woman shouted.

Plum turned in time to see Bonnie leap up from a lawn chair placed beside her coffee shop's back door. In her fingers she held a lit cigarette. Bonnie ran to her and gave her a one-armed hug, holding the butt off to the side.

"Plum, I'm glad you're back."

Plum gave her a fervent, two-armed hug in return.

"When you...left, the party pretty well broke up. Flo said, if it was up to her, she'd throw all the food out. But she figured that wouldn't be what you'd want. Instead, we brought it all to the homeless mission. Was that okay?"

"Exactly right." When she'd worked as a chef back in Los Angeles, she had always given leftover food to soup kitchens. How funny that Flo knew her that well.

Bonnie took a quick puff of her cigarette. "I'm back on these things again. Can you believe it? It's the stress of running my own business."

Plum gave her a speculative look. "What time do you get here for your morning prep? I'm a little tired now from all the driving. And you can't imagine how loud jail is. Impossible to sleep well." She bit her lip. "But I'd like to help you with it one of these mornings this week, if that's okay. Maybe we can talk some."

"Sure. Anytime. I get here around four." Bonnie's brow wrinkled. "What do we have—"

"Later, okay?" Plum said, before turning and walking toward High Desert Books' rear door.

*   *   *

Plum paused at the rear of the bookstore, admiring her handiwork. She'd allowed the doubts to creep in for a while. Now she saw she had truly transformed it into a stylish space that should prove inviting to customers. She actually found it more attractive than she expected.

Flo hadn't merely been a caretaker during Plum's incarceration. She'd added a touch of her own. She'd placed a few stools along the front of one side of the counter, as if inviting customers to linger and chat. It would have floored Plum, only she saw who filled one of those stools now. Jake had pulled his stool close enough to the counter to allow him to lean his elbows there. Flo also sat on a stool on her side, bent toward him, until their heads were only inches apart.

Flo hadn't limited her changes to the stools she'd added to the bookstore. Her hair was shorter now, and the choppy look was gone. Plum guessed that she'd finally gotten it professionally styled into something quite flattering. Even more flattering was the pinkish glow her cheeks had taken on. She might have started wearing makeup, though Plum suspected the glow had more to do with Jake's proximity.

Completing the changes were a plum-colored orchid that seemed to be thriving in the bookstore, and a stumpy-tailed cat who appeared content to make herself at home there as well.

A warm sense of belonging filled Plum. Of course, it might have taken considerably longer before the aging lovebirds noticed her. After a couple of minutes of gazing at the scene at the counter, Plum cleared her throat.

Jake jerked up. "Plum!" he called. "You're back." He rushed to her and threw his arms around her. "Hey, kiddo, we really missed you."

A purring cat greeted her next. Plum picked up Scrappy and nuzzled her face into the cat's full mane, before carrying her back to the counter. Flo remained behind the counter. The tentative expression that froze her features, making her look once again like the old Flo, twisted Plum's heart.

"You're here, honey," Flo said, too softly. "For good?"

"If you'll have me. Do you know anyplace where I can stay? I hear you have rooms upstairs."

Before Plum knew it, Flo was at her side, clutching her in a hug that would have done a mama bear proud and sobbing with joy.

Then they all gathered again on those stools at the counter, and Plum caught them up on everything that had happened since she'd left there. They'd known about the changes to the local zoning, of course, but not everything that went on at her end. Jake laughed so hard when she told them about how she dealt with Claire, he nearly fell off his stool.

"Plum, you handled that so well. Sure, I know your sister gave you good advice when she told you not to approach Claire. And that legal route would work for anyone else. But you have your own style, honey. That's the Plum-way."

She wished he didn't keep reminding her of that. It was just luck that she managed to make it work. Luck, and the fact that, as Sunni had surmised, Claire wasn't that bright. Plum vowed not to let success make her cocky. She was still the same goofball she'd always been.

After the conversation wound down, Jake seemed to sense that Plum and Flo wanted to be alone. He excused himself, insisting he had to return to his store.

Plum stopped him at the door. "Jake, wait. I'd love to take you and Flo out to dinner tonight to thank you for all you did for me here. What do you say?"

"I'm in." He sent such a hopeful look at Flo, it hurt Plum's heart. Mostly because it didn't quite hide his underlying fear that all the progress they'd made would suddenly evaporate.

Flo, what are you doing to this guy?

Surprisingly, Flo sounded even more animated when she said, "What a wonderful idea, Plum. I'd love it."

As soon as he left, though, Flo became unexpectedly silent.

One step forward, lots of steps back.

Flo lowered her head and scuffed her shoe on the floor. Despite the new hairdo, the old Flo was never far away.

"Something on your mind?" Plum asked.

Flo's head popped up. She took a deep breath before blurting, "I want to buy back a stake in High Desert Books. I want us to run it together. I'll give you all the money you paid for whatever percentage you're willing to give me. More than you paid. Anything you want." Another quick breath followed. "I lost interest in this place long ago. Yet now, with the changes you made it in..." She looked around, as if taking it in again. "And the chance to do it all with you has energized me."

With that, Flo seemed to run out of steam. Plum reached across the counter and grasped Flo's hand. "Good. I'm gonna need that money."

"So you agree, Plum?"

"No."

Flo's face fell. "I don't..."

Plum took a deep breath of her own. "I don't want to sell you a *part* of it, I want you to buy back all of High Desert Books."

"You're leaving again, aren't you?" Flo asked, her voice low and guttural.

With a shake of her head, Plum indicated she wasn't. "I'm not a bookseller, I'm a book reader." She glanced around the store. "The apartment upstairs gave me a place where I could lick my wounds when they were bad. And revamping this bookstore gave me a purpose after I lost everything. But I don't know how to run a bookstore, and I don't want to learn. This isn't the job of my future."

"Then what is?"

"Same as always—I'm a chef. I feed people. I forgot for a while how much I loved it, but like you, I'm energized again." Plum took a moment to savor how excited it made her feel, just like when she started. "If she'll let me, I'm going to buy Bonnie's place. She wants out, and I want in, so it should work out perfectly. I don't know how much she'll want. If I don't have enough, I may need your help."

Flo stared at Plum, slack-jawed.

Plum pointed at the wall separating the two storefronts. "I thought we could carve an arch over there, connecting our businesses. "What do you say?"

Flo nodded vigorously. "That's the best idea I've ever heard! Are you going to keep the name, Cup o' Joe?"

"Nah. I'll be serving lots more than coffee. Well, Bonnie does, too, but I'll expand it even more." Plum's excitement built as she went on with, "I'm thinking breakfast, lunch, and eventually, dinner. Great menus, too. I plan to call it High Desert Grub. You like?"

"I love it. I'm in, all the way." Flo laughed happily. "Plum you never fail to surprise me. First the way you wangled your way out of jail with Claire, and now this. I never know what you'll do."

Nobody did. Not even Plum. Her own unpredictability dampened her excitement. "That's because I'm such a hopscotch-playing fool. I told you that." She sighed. "I would give anything in the world to be like everyone else."

"You said that before. What is it you think everyone else is like, Plum? We're all different, but we're all the same, too. What is it you want to be?"

"Average, okay? Conventional. I want to think like most other people, make choices like them. Blend into the crowd, not stand out. I don't want to be a…freak." Ever since Claire threw that word at her, Plum hadn't been able to forget it.

"Average?" Flo brought her fist down on the counter with a loud thump.

Seemingly startled by Flo's banging the counter, Scrappy jumped from the chair on which she'd been settling down for a nap and started to run. After an instant, she seemed to grasp there was no danger. Then, Scrappy leaped onto the counter, head-bumped Plum, and started purring. Plum absently pet her.

"Plum, no one average could have done what you did. You gave the people of this town faith when we'd lost it. You gave us all what we wanted, when none of us could figure out how to make it happen. Honey, you saved Applewood."

"You're exaggerating, Flo. I stupidly took a bag of cash and went to jail."

"And you're minimizing it. You made things work out in a way that nobody else could. You want to trade that in for average? Baby, don't you know how uniquely wonderful you are?"

Now it was Plum's turn to stare at Flo in disbelief. "Not a freak?"

"Plum, you're my hero. You're everything I wish I could be." Flo's voice trembled when she said, "Most of us only get one color. For some, it's awfully bland. But you, you glow in a rainbow of colors. Why would you want to trade that for beige?"

CHAPTER FORTY

Plum stumbled out the door of High Desert Books into the Pony Lane sunlight, her mind reeling.

She'd told Flo that she wanted to go see Brian, to let him know she was back.

"You should give a little thought to what I said, Plum. So you don't blow the best thing to ever happen to you," Flo insisted.

Hey, which of us is the most evolved? Plum had a feeling their continuing role reversals were going to give them both whiplash.

She also found she couldn't *help* but think about what Flo said to her. A rainbow? She had never considered her goofiness in those terms. Once again her personal kaleidoscope changed, and she saw her own life in a new way. From the grab bag of her crazy hopscotch choices she really had pulled out a way to save this town. To hold back the relentless march of progress. Maybe not forever, but long enough for everyone in Applewood to savor their small town charm for a while longer. *She* did it. In a way that no beige person ever could have.

Maybe Plum's take on her hopscotch life had always been wrong. What if everyone just fell somewhere on a spectrum? And while they were probably all trying their best, they all seemed to stumble sometimes. Look at Sunni. If Plum had to pick someone nailing that straight-ahead path in life, it would be Sunni. Yet Sunni struggled in ways that Plum had never suspected. And Brian? The high-flying boy from Venice High—he considered himself his family's outcast. Nobody would classify Flo, or Nora, or DeeDee as highly functional. And forget about Crystal. Was anyone really normal? Maybe everyone was a little bit strange, even if it wasn't obvious to others. Was it possible that Plum's hopscotch simply placed her on the more daring and creative part of life's continuum? She'd never suspected it, but she saw now how that could be true.

Suddenly even more eager to see Brian, she started toward his office. Then a better first stop occurred to her. She remembered the jeweler Brian had recommended she take her engagement ring to, if she truly wanted to sell it. Plum wanted so much to be rid of it now, she ran the three blocks separating her from it.

A man in overalls leaving held open the door for Plum at Nicolas Banks Jewelry. Plum had grown so accustomed to Applewood's Western Americana style that the sight of a more traditional jewelry store—with gold instead of silver, diamonds instead of turquoise—startled her. Now, the gleaming pieces sparkling brightly under the glowing lights over the u-shaped counters told her she'd come to the right place.

There weren't any other customers there when she went in. Just a gaunt, fiftyish man who stood behind one of those counters, whose ashen face closely matched his impeccable pearl gray suit. Without a word, Plum unclipped her necklace and slipped the ring off the chain.

"Ah, you're the young lady who wants to sell her ring," he said in a British accent as crisp as the creases in his pants. "Brian Coburn told me about you. You're named after some kind of fruit, correct? I'm Nicky Banks."

Nicky seemed like too casual a name for the formally-dressed man to Plum. But who was she to talk? "That's right. Fruit. Specifically plums. Uh, Plum." She handed him the ring.

Nicky took a jeweler's loop from the small black velvet pad beside where his hand rested on the counter, and studied her diamond through it. "Not an exceptionally high quality stone by any means, but somewhat valuable for its large size."

Plum supposed there was a metaphor for her relationship with Noah contained in there, but she didn't choose to work it out.

Still, he offered her more than she expected. After a bit of half-hearted dickering, he upped the offer a little more, and Plum accepted. She left Nicolas Banks Jewelry with a check that was going to do a lot more to make her dreams come true than that ring ever had.

On the way to Brian's office, Plum heard music coming from

somewhere. Probably one of the apartments over the street-level storefronts. Something waltzy. She began to sway along with it. Before she knew it, her arms were flying and she had slipped into full dance-mode. She did notice lots of beige pedestrians had stepped off the wooden sidewalks and were walking in the street, but that didn't stop Plum from dancing.

Suddenly, a pair of firm arms circled around her, drawing her to a strong chest. Brian. His lips found hers, his tongue leaving a lingering promise for later. When they came apart, Plum felt like a puddle.

"Plum, promise me you'll never change."

"I don't think I can." She snickered. "Though maybe I should learn to quote adages the way other people do."

"Don't you dare!"

After whispering a few more promises of what he intended to do the instant they were alone, Brian swept her up into his arms and circled her around to the music. When he placed her down, a few strangers clapped for them. Plum scarcely noticed.

"Dinner tonight?" Brian asked, as they walked arm-in-arm toward his office.

"I'm having dinner with..." She almost said, "the parents." Premature, though she hoped not too much. "...with Flo and Jake. My treat. I'd love it if you could join us."

Brian said he would.

"But later, when we're alone..." Plum whispered a few promises of her own. With a sigh, she added, "There's really so much I have to tell you."

"Starting with...?"

"Selling my engagement ring."

Brian stopped and stared into her eyes. Plum saw some of the same anxiety Jake had shown earlier when he seemed unsure whether Flo would retreat from him. *Flo, we both have to avoid wrecking the best things that ever happened to us. I will, if you will.*

"How do you feel about that?" he asked, frown lines now wiping out the joy he'd displayed only moments earlier.

"I can't think of why it took me so long."

Brian pulled Plum to him again, and whispered, "I'm glad."

They came apart again, promising to meet up later for dinner. Brian went into his office, while Plum walked back toward the bookstore.

Along the way, she came across a pair of little girls playing hopscotch on a chalk court drawn across the wooden slats. She stopped to watch them, though apparently, their game was over. The little brunette went off in the other direction, but when the pigtailed blonde came abreast of her, Plum stopped her.

"Can I play on it?" Plum asked, pointing to the hopscotch outline. The kid squinted up at her. Plum suspected no adult had ever asked her that.

"Okay. You're gonna need this." The little girl extended a small beanbag hopscotch token. "But I'll want it back."

Plum shook her head. "I don't need it."

The girl wrinkled her small face. "How can you play without it? How can you win?"

"I think I already have," Plum said.

With a shake of her head, the little girl walked off, muttering under her breath.

Plum approached the chalk outline and began jumping through it, on one foot or two. Forward, back, into this square or that. She had told the girl the truth. She had already won, in every way possible. And the game was just beginning.

Jumping outside the outline, Plum thrust her fists into the air, finally embracing her amazing hopscotch life.

AUTHOR NOTES

The town of Applewood, Arizona does not exist, except in my imagination. Although I kept its location ambiguous, I probably also took liberties with Arizona geography in even my vague placement of it. If, in your travels, you come across someplace like it, please let me know. I'm sure I'd like to spend some time there.

ACKNOWLEDGMENTS

My deepest appreciation goes to:

My husband, Joe Neri, my first reader. As a former bookseller, his knowledge of what makes a good novel is exceptional. Joe, I'm grateful for your excellent advice, and for your unwavering belief in me and this book.

My editor, Lisa Kline, whose guidance and insights helped me to shape this into a better novel than it would have been without her.

And Greg Lilly, publisher of Cherokee McGhee Publishing, for being a supportive publisher for many years. Thank you, Greg, for giving me such a good home.

I'm grateful to all of you.

BOOK CLUB QUESTIONS

1. What do you see as the major turning points of this novel? How about its theme? Is it the need for self-acceptance? Allowing time to heal?

2. Which character did you relate to most strongly? Plum, Sunni, or Flo? Or even Claire? Did your feelings change as the novel progressed?

3. Do you believe that Plum ever truly loved Noah? What event supports your belief? Do you think Noah really loved Plum? What drew him to her? What made him turn to Claire?

4. Why do you think Plum can't be as sensible as Sunni? Why can't Sunni be as free-spirited as Plum? Why is change so hard for so many people? Is change impossible for some people?

5. Why did Plum seem to get stalled in life? What about Flo— why did she seem to have gotten stuck? What do all their self-destructive choices say about the process of healing? Is it significant that, in different ways, both lost a child?

6. Do you understand Plum's belief about the money in the satchel, that it contained what Noah amassed by keeping her mortgage payments and the second mortgage he took out on their house? Would you have taken that bag of money? Or do you believe Plum deserved everything that happened thereafter?

7. Have you ever longed, as Plum does, to live "life on the fly," taking off and starting life over wherever you happened to land? Why is integrating into her new life hard for Plum? Would it be hard for most people?

8. Can you visualize Plum's transformation of High Desert

Books? How might you have designed that space? Have you ever wanted to own a bookstore?

9. Do you understand how Plum's lack of self-confidence causes her to flip-flop on her choices and behave erratically, or do you consider her a flake? Why do some people have trouble sticking to decisions they've made?

10. Is Flo's dysfunction understandable, given the circumstances of Plum's conception? Do you believe Plum's quirkiness is the result of nature or nurture, or some combination of both?

11. Where do you stand on the Budget-Mart divide in this novel, or the advancement of big box stores in real life? Do you understand why Gil and Bonnie welcome this form of progress? Or would you be on the side of Jake and Brian, in trying to retain their town's rustic charm?

12. Were you surprised when Plum was arrested? Did you believe some serious consequence was inevitable for her theft of the satchel? Do you think she deserves punishment?

13. Was Plum right for going directly to Claire to settle her legal woes? Was roping in Hannah justified? Were you surprised by how successfully Plum tricked Claire? Was Plum right to keep Brian away while in jail, to work through things on her own?

14. Is Plum right to want a relationship with Gil and Hannah, her grandparents, in spite of how they treated Flo? Should Plum forgive her grandparents for their treatment of her birth mother? Why are family relationships so complicated?

15. Did Plum's return to cooking surprise you? Will she stick to it? Do you view it as a sign of her healing, or another hopscotch move? Is her epiphany that nobody is truly "normal" well-founded? Do you agree?

KRIS NERI

Kris Neri writes the Tracy Eaton mystery series, *Revenge of the Gypsy Queen*, *Dem Bones' Revenge*, *Revenge for Old Times' Sake*, and *Revenge on Route 66*. The novels in this series have been nominated for such prestigious awards as the Agatha, Anthony, Macavity, Lefty, and the New Mexico-Arizona Book Awards.

Her other books include *Never Say Die*, *Trust No One*, *The Rose in the Snow*, as well as the Lefty Award-nominated Samantha Brennan and Annabelle Haggerty magical mystery series, *High Crimes on the Magical Plane* and *Magical Alienation*. *Magical Alienation* was a New Mexico-Arizona Book Award-winner.

Kris makes her home in Silver City, New Mexico, along with her husband and two pushy terriers.

Readers can follow her through her blogs with the Femmes Fatales: https://femmesfatales.typepad.com. And through her website: http://www.krisneri.com.

CPSIA information can be obtained
at www.ICGtesting.com
Printed in the USA
BVHW030058130320
574872BV00015B/32